"He's an adulterer. And now he's a murderer."

Jessie spoke firmly, and her words struck home to the girl.

"So," Inspector Queen said, "who is he?"

"All right," the girl said. "I'll tell you." She brought the flame of the lighter to the tip of her cigarette. The flame seemed to explode with a sharp crack, and a black hole appeared in the middle of her forehead. Then the hole gushed red, and the lighter fell, and the cigarette fell, and the girl fell.

Inspector Queen's Own Case:
NOVEMBER SONG

by Ellery Queen

BALLANTINE BOOKS • NEW YORK

BALLANTINE BOOKS
A Division of Random House, Inc.
201 East 50th Street, New York, N.Y. 10022
Simultaneously published by
Ballantine Books, Ltd., Toronto, Canada

Inspector Queen's Own Case

1.

AT FIRST
THE INFANT

THE dove-colored Chevrolet was parked fifty feet from the hospital entrance. The car was not new and not old, just a Sunday-hosed-looking family job with a respectable dent here and there in the fenders.

The fat man squeezed behind the wheel went with it like a used tire. He wore a home-pressed dark blue suit with a few food spots on the lapels, a white shirt already damp from the early morning June sun, and a blue tie with a wrinkled knot. A last summer's Macy's felt hat with a sweat-stained band lay on the seat beside him.

The object in point was to look like millions of other New Yorkers. In his business, the fat man liked to say, visibility was the worst policy. The main thing was not to be noticed by some nosy noonan who could lay the finger on you in court afterwards. Luckily, he did not have to worry about impressing his customers. The people he did business with, the fat man often chuckled, would avail themselves of his services if he came to work in a Bikini.

The fat man's name was Finner, A. Burt Finner. He was known to numerous laboring ladies of the nightclubs as Fin, from his hobby of stuffing sharp five-dollar bills into their nylons. He had a drab little office in an old office building on East 49th Street.

Finner cleaned his teeth with the edge of a match packet cover, sucked his cheeks in several times, and settled back to digest his breakfast.

He was early, but in these cases the late bird found himself looking down an empty worm hole. Five times out of ten, Finner sometimes complained, they wanted to change their confused little minds at the last second.

He watched the hospital entrance without excitement. As he watched, his lips began to form a fat O, his wink-less eyes sank deeper into his flesh, the pear-shaped face took on a look of concentration; and before he knew it he was whistling. Finner heard his own music happily. He was that rarity, a happy fat man.

The tune he whistled was *Ah! Sweet Mystery of Life.* My theme song, he called it.

When the girl came out of the hospital the fat man was on the steps to greet her, smiling.

"Good morning!" the fat man said. "All checked out okay?"

"Yes." She had a deep, slightly hoarse voice.

"No complications or anything?"

"No."

"And our little arrival is well and happy, I hope?" Finner started to raise the flap of the blue blanket from the face of the infant the girl was carrying, but she put her shoulder in the way.

"Don't touch him," she said.

"Now, now," the fat man said. "I'll bet he's a regular lover-boy. How could he miss with such a doll for a ma?" He was still trying to get a look at her baby. But she kept fending him off.

"Well, let's go," Finner said curtly.

He took the rubberized bag of diapers and bottles of formula from her and waddled to his car. She dragged after him, clutching the blanketed bundle to her breast.

The fat man had the front door open for her. She shook his hand off and got in. He shrugged.

"Where do you want I should drop you?"

"I don't care. I guess my apartment."

He drove off cautiously. The girl held the blue bundle tight.

She wore a green suède suit and a mannish felt pulled down over one eye. She was striking in a theatrical way, gold hair greenish at the scalp, big hazel eyes, a wide mouth that kept moving around. She had put on no makeup this morning. Her lips were pale and ragged.

She lifted the blanket and looked down at the puckered little face with tremendous intentness.

"Any deformities or birthmarks?" the fat man asked suddenly.

"What?"

He repeated the question.

"No." She began to rock.

"Did you do what I told you about his clothes?"

"Yes."

"You're sure there are no identifying marks on the clothes?" he persisted.

"I told you!" She turned on him in fury. "Can't you shut up? He's sleeping."

"They sleep like drunks. Had an easy time, did you?"

"Easy?" The girl began to laugh. But then she stopped laughing and looked down again.

"Just asking," Finner said, craning to see the baby's face. "Sometimes the instruments——"

"He's perfect merchandise," the girl said.

She began to croon in a sweet and throbbing contralto, rocking the bundle again. The baby blatted, and the girl looked frantic.

"Darlin', darlin', what's the matter? Don't cry . . . Mama's got you . . ."

"Gas," the fat man said. "Just bubble him."

She flung him a look of pure hate. She raised the baby to her shoulder and patted his back nervously. He burped and fell asleep again.

A. Burt Finner drove in delicate silence.

All at once the girl burst out, "I can't, I won't!"

"Sure you can't," Finner said instantly. "Believe me,

I'm no hard-hearted Hannah. I got three of my own. But what about *him*?"

She sat there clutching her baby and looking trapped.

"The important thing in a case like this is to forget yourself. Look," the fat man said earnestly, "every time you catch yourself thinking of just you, stop and think what this means to this fine little fella. Do it right now. What would it mean to him if you goofed off now?"

"Well, what?" she said in a hard voice.

"Being raised in a trunk, is what. With cigar smoke and stinking booze fumes to fill his little lungs instead of God's wonderful fresh air," the fat man said, "that's what. You want to raise a kid that way?"

"I wouldn't do that," the girl said. "I'd never do it like that! I'd get him a good nurse——"

"I can see you been thinking about it," A. Burt Finner nodded approvingly, "even though we got an iron-bound agreement. Okay, you get him a good nurse. So who'd be his mother, you or this nurse? You'd be slaving all day and night to pay her salary, and buy certified milk and all, and it's her he'd love, not you. So what's the percentage?"

The girl closed her eyes.

"So that's out. So there he is, back in the trunk. So who'd baptize him, some hotel clerk in Kansas City? Who'd he play with, some rubberlips trumpet player on the junk? What would he teethe on, beer openers and old cigar butts? And," the fat man said softly, "would he toddle around from table to table calling every visiting Elk from Dayton daddy?"

"You bastard," the girl said.

"Exactly my point," the fat man said.

"I could get married!"

They were on a side street on the West Side, just passing an empty space at one of the curbs. Finner stopped, shifted, and backed the Chevrolet halfway in.

"Congratulations," he said. "Do I know this Mr. Schlemihl who's going to take another guy's wild oat and call him sonny-boy?"

"Let me out, you fat creep!"

4

The fat man smiled. "There's the door."

She backed out, her eyes blazing.

He waited.

Not until her shoulders sagged did he know that he had won. She reached back in and laid the bundle carefully on the seat beside him and just as carefully shut the door.

"Good-by," she whispered to the bundle.

Finner wiped the sweat off his face. He took a bulky unmarked envelope from his inside pocket and reached over the baby.

"Here's the balance of your dough," he said kindly.

She looked up in a blind way. Then she snatched the envelope and hurled it at him. It struck his bald head and burst, showering bills all over the seat and floor.

She turned and ran.

"Nice to have met you," the fat man said. He gathered up the scattered bills and stuffed them in his wallet.

He looked up and down the street. It was empty. He leaned over the baby, undid the blanket, examined it. He found a department-store label on the beribboned lawn nightgown, ripped it off, put the label in his pocket. He found another label on the tiny undershirt and removed that, too. Then he looked the sleeping infant over. Finally, he rewrapped it in the blanket and replaced it beside him.

Then he examined the contents of the rubberized bag. When he was satisfied, he rezipped it.

"Well, bubba, it's off to a long life and a damn dull one," he said to the bundle on the seat. "You'd have had a hell of a lot more fun with her."

He glanced at his wristwatch and drove on toward the West Side Highway.

On the highway, driving at a law-abiding thirty, with an occasional friendly glance at the bundle, A. Burt Finner began to whistle.

Soon his whistle changed to song.

He sang, *"Ahhhhh, sweet mys-tery of life and love I found youuuuuuuuuu . . ."*

5

The seven-passenger Cadillac was parked in a deserted lane just off the Hutchinson River Parkway, between Pelham and New Rochelle. It was old-fashioned, immaculate, and wore Connecticut plates. A chauffeur with a red face and white hair was at the wheel. A buxom woman with a pretty nose sat beside him. She was in her late forties. Under her cloth coat she wore a nurse's nylon uniform.

In the tonneau sat the Humffreys.

Sarah Stiles Humffrey said, "Alton, isn't he *late?*"

Her husband smiled "He'll be here, Sarah."

"I'm nervous as a cat!"

He patted her hand. She had a large hand, beautifully groomed. Mrs. Humffrey was a large woman, with large features over which she regularly toiled and despaired.

Her husband was an angular man in a black suit so dreary it could only have been planned. A Humffrey had made the Mayflower crossing; and from the days of Cole's Hill and Plimoth Plantation Humffreys had deposited their distinguished dust among the stones of New England. His wife's family was very nearly as distinguished.

Alton K. Humffrey withdrew his hand quickly. Tolerant as he could be toward his wife's imperfections, he could not forgive his own. He had been born without the tip of the little finger on his right hand. Usually he concealed the offending member by curling it against his palm. This caused the ring finger to curl, too. When he raised his hand to hail someone the gesture looked Roman, almost papal. It rather pleased him.

"Alton, suppose she changed her mind!" his wife was saying.

"Nonsense, Sarah."

"I wish we could have done it in the usual way," she said restlessly.

His lips compressed. In crucial matters Sarah was a child. "You know why, my dear."

"I really *don't.*"

"Have you forgotten that we're not exactly the ideal age?"

6

"Oh, Alton, you could have managed it." One of Sarah Humffrey's charms was her clinging conviction that her husband could manage anything.

"This way is safest, Sarah."

"Yes." Sarah Humffrey shivered. Alton was so right. He always was. If only people of our class could live like ordinary people, she thought.

"Here he comes," the white-haired chauffeur said.

The Humffreys turned quickly. The dove-colored Chevrolet was pulling up behind them.

The buxom nurse with the pretty nose got out of the Cadillac.

"No, I'll get him, Miss Sherwood!" Alton K. Humffrey said. He sprang from the limousine and hurried over to the Chevrolet. The nurse got into the tonneau.

"Oh, dear," Mrs. Humffrey said.

"Here he is," Finner beamed.

Humffrey stared in at the blue blanket. Then without a word he opened the Chevrolet door.

"Time," Finner said.

"What?"

"There's the little matter of the scratch," the fat man smiled. "Remember, Mr. Humffrey? Balance C.O.D.?"

The millionaire shook his head impatiently. He handed over a bulky unmarked envelope, like the one Finner had offered the girl in the suède suit. Finner opened the envelope and took out the money and counted it.

"He's all yours," Finner said, nodding.

Humffrey lifted the bundle out of the car gingerly. Finner handed out the rubberized bag, and the millionaire took that, too.

"You'll find the formula typed on a plain slip of paper in the bag," the fat man said, "along with enough bottles and diapers to get you started."

Humffrey waited.

"Something wrong, Mr. Humffrey? Did I forget something?"

"The birth certificate and the papers," the millionaire said grimly.

7

"My people aren't magicians," the fat man said, smiling. "I'll mail them to you soon as they're ready. They'll be regular works of art, Mr. Humffrey."

"Register the envelope to me, please."

"Don't worry," the fat man said soothingly.

The tall thin man did not stir until the Chevrolet was gone. Then he walked back to the limousine slowly. The chauffeur was holding the tonneau door open, and Mrs. Humffrey's arms were reaching through.

"Give him to me, Alton!"

Her husband handed her the baby. With trembling hands she lifted the flap of the blanket.

"Miss Sherwood," she gasped, "look!"

"He's a little beauty, Mrs. Humffrey." The nurse had a soft impersonal voice. "May I?"

She took the baby, laid it down on one of the jump-seats, and opened the blanket.

"Nurse, he'll fall off!"

"Not at this age." The nurse smiled. "Mr. Humffrey, may I have that bag, please?"

"Oh, why is he crying?"

"If you were messed, hungry, and only one week old, Mrs. Humffrey," Nurse Sherwood said, "you'd let the world know about it, too. There, baby. We'll have you clean and sweet in no time. Henry, plug the warmer into the dashboard and heat this bottle. Mr. Humffrey, you'd better shut that door while I rediaper Master Humffrey."

"Master Humffrey!" Sarah Humffrey laughed and cried alternately while her husband stared in. He could not seem to take his eyes from the squirming little body. "Alton, we have a son, a *son.*"

"You're actually excited, Sarah." Alton Humffrey was pleased.

"Nurse, let's not use the things from that bag, shall we? All the nice new things we've brought for you, baby!" Mrs. Humffrey zipped open a morocco case. It was full of powders, oils, sterilized cotton, picks. The nurse took a bottle of baby oil and a tin of powder from it silently. "The first thing we'll do is have him examined by that pediatrician in Greenwich . . . *Alton.*"

"Yes, dear?"

"Suppose the doctor finds he's not as . . . not as represented?"

"Now, Sarah. You read the case histories yourself."

"But not knowing who his people are——"

"Must we go back to that, my dear?" her husband said patiently. "I don't want to know who his people are. In a case like this, knowledge is dangerous. This way there's no red tape, no publicity, and no possibility of repercussions. We know the child comes of good Anglo-Saxon stock, and that the stock is certified as having no hereditary disease on either side, no feeble-mindedness, no criminal tendencies. Does the rest matter?"

"I suppose not, Alton." His wife fumbled with her gloves. "Nurse, why doesn't he stop *crying?*"

"You watch," Miss Sherwood said over the baby's furious blats. "Henry, the bottle should be ready." The chauffeur hastily handed it to her. She removed the aluminum cap and shook some of the milk onto the back of her hand. Nodding, she popped the nipple gently into the little mouth. The baby stopped in mid-blat. He seized the nipple with his tiny jaws and began to suck vigorously.

Mrs. Humffrey stared, fascinated.

Alton K. Humffrey said almost gaily, "Henry, drive us back to the Island."

The old man turned over in bed and his naked arms flew up against the light from somewhere. It was the wrong light or the wrong direction. Or wasn't it morning? Something was wrong.

Then he heard the surf and knew where he was and squeezed his eyelids as hard as he could to shut out the room. It was a pleasant room of old random furniture and a salt smell, with rusty shrimp dangling from bleached seaweed on the wallpaper. But the pale blue wavery water lines ran around and around like thoughts, getting nowhere, and they bothered him.

The night air still defended the room coolly, but he could feel the sun ricocheting off the sea and hitting the walls like waves. In two hours it would be a hotbox.

Richard Queen opened his eyes and for a moment looked his arms over. They're like an anatomical sketch of a cadaver, he thought, wornout cables of muscle and bone with corrugated covers where skin used to be. But he could feel the life in them, they could still hold their own, they were useful. He brought his hands down into focus, examined the knurls of joints, the riveleted skin, each pore like a speck of dirt, the wiry debris of gray hairs; but suddenly he closed his eyes again.

It was early, almost as early as when he used to wake in the old days. The alarm would go off to find him already prone on the braided rug doing his fifty pushups —summer or winter, in green spring light or the gray of the autumn dawn. The hot shave and cold shower, with the bathroom door shut so that his son might sleep on undisturbed. The call-in from the lieutenant, while breakfast was on the hod, to report any special developments of the night. The Sergeant waiting outside, the drive downtown. Headed for another working day. Listening to the general police calls on the way down, just in case. Maybe a direct word for him on the radiophone from the top floor of the big gold-domed building on Centre Street. His office . . . "What's new this morning?" . . . orders . . . the important mail . . . the daily teletype report . . . the 9 a.m. lineup, the parade of misfits from the Bullpen . . .

It was all part of a life. Even the corny kidding, and the headaches and heartaches. Good joes sharing the raps and the kudos while administrations came and went, not touching them. Not really touching them, even in shake-ups. Because when the dust settled, the old-timers were still there. Until, that is, they were shoved out to pasture.

It's hard to break the habits of a lifetime, he thought. It's impossible. What do those old horses think about, munching the grass of their retirement? The races they'd won? The races they could still win, given the chance?

The young ones coming up, always coming up. How many of them could do fifty pushups? At half his age? But there they were, getting set, getting citations and commendations if they were good enough, a Department funeral if they stopped a bullet or a switchblade . . .

There they were. And here am I . . .

Becky was stirring carefully in the next room. Richard Queen knew it was Becky, not Abe, because Abe was like a Newfoundland dog, incapable of quiet; and the old man had been visiting in the beach house with its papery walls long enough to have learned some intimate details of the Pearls' lives.

He lay in the bed idly.

Yes, that was Becky creeping down the stairs so as not to wake her husband or their guest. Soon the smell of her coffee, brown and brisk, would come seeping up from the kitchen. Beck Pearl was a small friendly woman with a big chest and fine hands and feet that were always on the move when her husband was around.

On the beach the gulls were squabbling over something.

Inspector Queen tried to think of his own wife. But Ellery's mother had died over thirty years ago. It was like trying to recall the face of a stranger glimpsed for an instant from the other end of a dark corridor.

Here comes the coffee . . .

For a while the old man let the drum and swish of the surf wash over him, as if he were lying on the beach below the house.

As if he were the beach, being rhythmically cleaned and emptied by the sea.

What should he do today?

A few miles from where Richard Queen was lying in the bed swam an island. The island was connected to the Connecticut mainland by a private causeway of handsome concrete. A fieldstone gatehouse with wood trim treated to look like bleached driftwood barred the island end of the causeway. This gatehouse was dressed in creeper ivy and climber roses, and it had a brief skirt of garden hemmed in oyster shells. A driftwood shingle above the door said:

PRIVATE PROPERTY
Restricted
For the Use of
. Residents & Guests
ONLY

Two private policemen in semi-nautical uniforms alternated at the gatehouse in twelve-hour shifts.

Nair Island had six owners, who shared its two hundred-odd acres in roughly equal holdings. In Taugus, the town on the mainland of which the island was an administrative district, their summer retreat was known—in a sort of forelock-tugging derision—as "Million-Nair" Island.

The six millionaires were not clubby. Each estate was partitioned from its neighbors by a high, thick fieldstone wall topped with shells and iron spikes. Each owner had his private yacht basin and fenced-off bathing beach. Each treated the road serving the six estates as if it were his alone. Their annual meetings to transact the trifling business of the community, as required by the bylaws of the Nair Island Association, were brusque affairs, almost hostile. The solder that welded the six owners together was not Christian fellowship but exclusion.

The island was their fortress, and they were mighty people. One was a powerful United States Senator who had gone into politics from high society to protect the American way of life. Another was the octogenarian widow of a railroad magnate. Another was an international banker. A forth was an aging philanthropist who loved the common people in the mass but could not stand them one by one. His neighbor, commanding the seaward spit of the Island, was a retired Admiral who had married the only daughter of the owner of a vast shipping fleet.

The sixth was Alton K. Humffrey.

Inspector Queen came downstairs shaved and dressed for the day in beige slacks, nylon sports shirt, and tan-and-white shoes. He carried his jacket over his arm.

"You're so early, Richard." Beck Pearl was pouring her husband's coffee. She was in a crisp housedress, white and pink. Abe was in his uniform. "And my, all spiffed up. Did you meet a woman on the beach yesterday?"

The old man laughed. "The day a woman messes with me."

"Don't give me that. And don't think Abe isn't worried, leaving me alone in the house every day with an attractive man."

"And don't think I'm not," Abe Pearl growled. "Squattez-vous, Dick. Sleep all right?"

"All right." He sat down opposite his friend and accepted a cup of coffee from Becky. "Aren't you up kind of early yourself this morning, Abe?"

"My summer troubles are starting. There was a brawl during the night—some tanked-up teenagers at a beach party. Want to sit in, Dick, just for ducks?"

The Inspector shook his head.

"Go on, Richard," Beck Pearl urged. "You're bored. Vacations are always that way."

He smiled. "Working people take vacations. Not old discards like me."

"That's fine talk! How do you want your eggs this morning?"

"Just this coffee, Becky. Thanks a lot."

The Pearls glanced at each other as the old man raised the cup. Abe Pearl shook his big head slightly.

"What do you hear from your son, Dick?" he said. "I noticed you got a letter from Rome yesterday."

"Ellery's fine. Thinking of visiting Israel next."

"Why didn't you go with him?" Mrs. Pearl demanded. "Or weren't you invited?" Her two sons were married, and she had definite ideas about what was wrong with the younger generation.

"He begged me to go. But I didn't feel it would be right. He's roaming around Europe looking for story ideas, and I'd only be in his way."

"He wasn't fooled by that poppycock, I hope," Beck Pearl snorted.

"He wanted to cancel his trip," Richard Queen said

quietly. "He only went because you and Abe were kind enough to ask me up here for the summer."

"Well! I should think so."

Abe Pearl rose. "You're sure you won't sit in, Dick?"

"I thought I'd do a little exploring today, Abe. Maybe take your boat out, if you don't mind."

"Mind!" Abe Pearl glared down at him. "What kind of dribble is that?" He kissed his wife fiercely and pounded out, making the dishes on the sideboard jingle.

Through the window Inspector Queen watched his host back the black-and-white coupé with the roof searchlight out of the garage. For a moment the sun sparkled on the big man's cap with the gold shield above the visor. Then, with a wave, Abe Pearl was gone.

With his ability and popularity, the old man thought, he can hold down this Chief's job in Taugus for life. Abe used his head. He got out of the big time when he was still young enough to set up a new career for himself. He isn't much younger than I am, and look at him.

"Feeling sorry for yourself again, Richard?" Beck Pearl's womanly voice said.

He turned, reddening.

"We all have to adjust to something," she went on in her soft way. "After all, it isn't as if you were like Abe's older brother Joe. Joe never had an education, never got married. All he knew was work. He worked all his life on a machine, and when he got too old and sick to work any more he had nothing—no family, no savings, nothing but the few dollars he gets from the government, and the check Abe sends him every month. There's millions like Joe, Richard. You're in good health, you have a successful son, you've led an interesting life, you've got a pension, no worries about the future—who's better off, you or Joe Pearl?"

He grinned. "Let's give Abe something to be jealous about." And he got up and kissed his friend's wife tenderly.

"Richard! You devil." Becky was blushing.

"Old, am I? Bring on those eggs—sunnyside, and don't burn the bacon!"

14

But the lift was feeble. When he left the house and headed for Abe Pearl's second-hand sixteen-foot cruiser, the old man's heart was bitter again. Every man tasted his own brand of misery. You needed more than a successful past and a secure future. Becky had left one thing out, the most important thing.

A man needed the present. Something to do.

The engine coughed its way into the basin and expired just as the sixteen-footer slid alongside the dock. Richard queen tied up to a bollard, frowning, and looked around. The dock was deserted, and there was no one on the beach but a buxom woman in a nurse's nylon uniform reading a magazine on the sand beside a net-covered perambulator.

The old man waved. "Ahoy, there!"

The nurse looked up, startled.

"Could I possibly buy some gas here?" he bellowed.

The woman shook her head vigorously and pointed to the pram. He walked down to the beach end of the dock and made his way across the sand toward her. It was beautiful sand, clean as a laundered tablecloth, and he had the uneasy feeling that he should not be making tracks in it.

"I'm sorry," he said, taking off his hat. "Did I wake the baby?"

The nurse was stooping over the carriage intently. She straightened up, smiling.

"No harm done. He sleeps like a little top."

Richard Queen thought he had never seen a nicer smile. She was big and wholesome-looking; her pretty nose was peeling from sunburn. Close to fifty, he judged, but only because he had had long experience in such matters. To the amateur eye she would pass for forty.

She drew him off from the pram a little way. "Did you say you were out of gas?"

"Forgot to check the tank before I shoved off. It's not my boat," he said apologetically, "and I'm afraid I'm not much of a sailor. I just about made it to your dock when I saw your pump."

"You're a trespasser," she said with her crinkly smile. "This is private property."

"Nair Island," he nodded. "But I'm desperate. Would you allow me to buy some juice for that contraption?"

"You'd have to ask Mr. Humffrey, the owner, but I'm sure it wouldn't do you any good. He'd like as not call the Taugus police."

"Is he home?" The old man grinned at the picture of Abe Pearl running over to Nair Island to arrest him.

"No." She laughed. "They've taken the cabin cruiser down to Larchmont to watch some yacht racing. Mrs. Humffrey hasn't stuck her nose out of the house since the baby came."

"Then if I helped myself nobody would know?"

"I'd know," she retorted.

"Let me take a few gallons. I'll send Mr. Humffrey a check."

"You'll get me in trouble . . ."

"I won't even mention your name," he said solemnly. "By the way, what is it?"

"Sherwood. Jessie Sherwood."

"My name is Richard Queen, Mrs. Sherwood."

"*Miss* Sherwood, Mr. Queen."

"Oh," he said. "Glad to meet you."

"Likewise," Nurse Sherwood murmured.

For some absurd reason they both smiled. The sun on the old man felt good. The blue sky, the sparks flying off the water, the salt breeze, everything felt good.

"I really don't have any place to go, Miss Sherwood," he said. "Why don't we sit down and visit?"

The crinkles went out of her smile. "If it got back to Mr. and Mrs. Humffrey that I'd entertained a strange man on the beach while I was minding the baby they'd discharge me, and they'd be perfectly right. And I've got awfully attached to little Michael. I'm afraid I can't, Mr. Queen."

Nice, he thought. Nice woman.

"Of course," he said. "It's my fault. But I thought . . . You see, I'm an old friend of Chief of Police Pearl's of Taugus. In fact, I'm spending the summer with him and Mrs. Pearl in their shack on the beach."

16

"Well!" she said. "I'm sure Mr. Humffrey wouldn't mind *that*. It's just that they're so nervous about the baby."

"Their first?"

"Well, yes."

"They're smart. Parents can't be too careful about their children, especially if they're rich."

"The Humffreys are multimillionaires."

"Chief Pearl tells me they're all loaded on Nair Island. I remember a snatch case I investigated a few years ago——"

"Case? Are you a police officer, too, Mr. Queen?"

"Was," he said. "In New York. But they retired me."

"Retired you! At your age?"

He looked at her. "How old do you think I am?"

"About fifty-five"

"You're just saying that."

"I never just say things. Why, are you older?"

"I quote Section 434-a dash two one point O of the Administrative Code of the City of New York," he said grimly, "which states as follows: 'No member of the police force in the department except surgeons of police,' etcetera, 'who is or hereafter attains the age of 63 years shall continue to serve as a member of such force but shall be retired and placed on the pension rolls of the department.'" He added after a moment, "You see, I know it by heart."

"Sixty-three." She looked skeptical.

"My last birthday."

"I wouldn't have believed it," she murmured.

From the depths of the pram came a squawk. Nurse Sherwood hurried to its source, and he followed. He could not helping taking in the curve of her hips, the youthful shoulders, the pretty legs and ankles.

It was just a cry in the baby's sleep. "He'll be waking up for his feeding soon," she said softly, fussing with the netting. "Is your wife visiting with Chief and Mrs. Pearl, too?"

Strong hands.

"I've been a widower almost as long as you're old, Miss Sherwood."

"That's impossible!" She laughed. "How old do you think I am?"

"Thirty-nine, forty," he lied.

"Aren't you sweet! I'll be fifty in January. Why, I've been an R.N. for almost twenty-five years."

"Oh, you're a trained nurse. Is this a sick baby?"

"Heavens, no. He's a sturdy little monkey."

He was, too. He had chubby arms and legs, a formidable little chest, and fat cheeks. He was sleeping with his arms defending his head in a curious attitude of defiance and helplessness; his silky brows were bunched in a troubled way. Richard Queen thought, They look so . . . so . . . He could not think of the word. Some feelings there were no words for. He was surprised to find that he still had them.

"It's just that Mrs. Humffrey is so nervous," Jessie Sherwood was saying. "She won't trust an ordinary nursemaid. And I've been a pediatric and maternity nurse practically my entire career. Ordinarily I wouldn't take a case like this—a perfectly healthy baby—I could be taking care of someone who really needs me. But I've rather overdone it the past few years, and Mr. Humffrey's offer was so generous——"

She stopped abruptly. Why was she telling all this to a perfect stranger? She was appalled.

"Never married?" the old man asked casually.

"Beg pardon? Oh, you mean me." Her face changed. "I was engaged once. During the war."

It was her eyes that were crinkled now, but not with laughter.

"He was a doctor," she explained. "He was killed in Normandy."

The old man nodded. They stood over the carriage side by side, looking through the netting at the tiny sleeping face.

What am I thinking of? he thought. A vigorous, attractive woman . . . and what am I but a withering old fool?

He fumbled with the button of his jacket. "I can't tell you how nice it's been talking to you, Miss Sherwood."

She looked up quickly. "You're going?"

"Well, I'd better lift some of Mr. Humffrey's gas and start back. Becky—Mrs. Pearl—will be having fits if I don't show up for lunch. She's been trying to put some meat on my bones."

"I don't see why," Jessie Sherwood said warmly. "I think you're built beautifully for——"

"For a man my age?" He smiled. "I hope we meet again some time."

"Yes," she said in a low voice. "I don't know a soul here. On Thursdays I go crazy. That's my day off——"

But he merely said, "I know what you mean. Well." His smile was fixed. "Good-by, Miss Sherwood. And thanks. I'll mail Mr. Humffrey a check tonight."

"Good-by," Jessie Sherwood said.

He did not even wave to her as he pulled away from the dock.

Independence Day was a Monday, and it developed into the noisiest Fourth Nurse Sherwood could remember. In spite of the ban on their sale, fireworks crackled, hissed, swooshed, and screeched into the skies over Nair Island all day.

The continuous barrage had made little Michael fret and wail, and his displeasure infected the household. Mrs. Humffrey wrung her hands and hovered all day; Mrs. Charbedeau, the cook, overdid the roast and exchanged bickering sarcasms with Mrs. Lenihan, the housekeeper; Mrs. Lenihan snapped the head off Rose Healy, the upstairs maid, and reduced Marie Tompkins, the downstairs maid, to the sullen verge of Notice. Even old Stallings, the gardener, ordinarily the most unaffected of men, threatened wrathfully to bust Henry Cullum in the snoot if the chauffeur ever again backed a car five feet onto his lawn in the poorly planned apron behind the Humffrey garage.

Alton Humffrey was annoyed. The Island's one road was as crowded all day as Front Street in Taugus; the surrounding waters splashed and spluttered well into the evening with hundreds of holiday craft from the main-

19

land; and Cullum had to be delegated to stand guard on the Humffrey beach to chase trespassing picnickers away.

Worst of all, Ronald Frost made a scene. Frost was Humffrey's nephew, the only child of the millionaire's dead sister. He lived on a small income from his mother's estate, spending most of his time as a house guest of his numerous socialite friends, making a partner for an odd girl or teaching someone's cousin to play tennis.

The young man had come up to spend the weekend, along with some relatives of Sarah Humffrey's from Andover, Malden and Cambridge; and whereas the Stiles clan, all elderly people, had sensibly left on Sunday night to get the jump on the northbound traffic, Ronald Frost lingered well into Independence Day. What the attraction was Jessie Sherwood failed at first to see, unless it was his uncle's liquor cabinet; certainly he made no secret of his boredom, and his visits to the cabinet were frequent.

Ron was a younger edition of his mother's brother— tall, thin, shoulderless, with lifeless brown hair and slightly popping eyes. But he had an unpleasant smile, half unction, half contempt; and he treated servants vilely.

Jessie Sherwood heard the row from the nursery that afternoon while she was changing the baby; Alton Humffrey's upstairs study was across the hall. Apparently Ron Frost was mired in a financial slough and expected his uncle to pull him out.

"I'm afraid, Ronald, you'll have to look for relief elsewhere this time," Jessie heard the older man say in his chill, nasal voice.

"What?" Young Frost was astounded.

"This avenue is closed to you."

"You don't mean it!"

"Never more serious in my life."

"But Uncle Alton, I'm in a rotten jam."

"If you must get into jams, it's time you learned to get out of them by your own efforts."

"I don't believe it." Frost was dazed. "Why, you've never turned me down before. And I'm in the damnedest spot just now . . . What's the idea, Uncle? Don't tell me *you're* in a pecuniary pickle."

"I don't get into pecuniary pickles, Ronald." Jessie Sherwood could almost see Alton Humffrey's glacial smile. "I take it this request was the real purpose of your visit, so——"

"Wait a minute." Ron Frost's tone was ugly now. "I want clarification. Is this a peeve of the moment because your precious castle has been fouled up all day by the common people, or is it a permanent freeze-out?"

"Translated into English," his uncle said, "you're apparently inquiring whether this is a whim or a policy. It's a policy, Ronald. I find now that I have a better use for my money than to pay your gambling debts and enlarge the bank accounts of your heartbroken ladyfriends."

"The brat," mumbled Frost.

"I beg your pardon?"

"This mongrel you picked up somewhere——"

"You're drunk," Alton Humffrey said.

"Not so drunk I can't put two and two together! All your wormy talk about the Humffrey blood—the family name—the promises you made my mother——!"

"You have an obligation, too," his uncle snapped. "Principally, to stop following the life cycle of a sponge. By the way, you'll apologize for the disgusting manner in which you've just referred to my son."

"Your son!" shouted frost. "What is he if he isn't a mongrel?"

"Get out."

"Can't stand the truth, hey? You gave me every reason to expect I'd be your heir, not some puking little——"

"So help me God, Ronald," Alton Humffrey's voice said clearly, "if you don't leave at once I'll throw you down the stairs."

There was a silence.

Then Jessie Sherwood heard young Frost say with a nervous laugh, "I'm sorry, Uncle. I guess I am tight. I apologize, of course."

There was another silence.

21

"Very well," Humffrey said. "And now I take it you're about to leave?"

"Right, right," Ron Frost said.

She heard him stagger up the hall. A few minutes later his footsteps returned and stopped in the study doorway.

"Please say good-by and thanks to Aunt Sarah for me, Uncle. Under the circumstances——"

"I understand." The Humffrey voice sounded remote.

"Well . . . so long, Uncle Alton."

"Good-by, Ronald."

"I'll be seeing you and Aunt Sarah soon, I hope." There was no reply.

Young Frost stumbled down the stairs. Shortly after, Jessie heard his Jaguar roar away.

So the day was intolerable, and she sank into bed thankfully that night, punched her pillow, murmured her nightly prayer, and sought sleep.

At two in the morning she was still seeking.

Nair Island had long ago settled down to silence and to darkness. The rustle of surf that soothed her every night was the only sound she could hear, except for an occasional late guest's car leaving the Island; but tonight its rhythm seemed to clash with her pulse rate. Everyone in the house was asleep; the two rooms above the garage, where Stallings and Cullum had their quarters, had been dark for hours. Her bedroom was not even hot; a cool breeze had swept in from sea at eleven, and she had had to get up for a quilt.

Then why couldn't she sleep?

It was a nuisance, because usually she fell asleep at will. She had always had the gift of instant relaxation. It was one of her assets as a nurse.

It certainly wasn't the baby. Jessie had been a little concerned about his behavior during the day, but with bedtime he had become his healthy little self again, and he had finished his bottle, bubbled mightily, and fallen asleep like an angel. When she had checked him before turning in, his tiny face was serene and he was breathing with such untroubled lightness that she had actually stooped over his crib. Nor was it an imminent feeding

22

that was keeping her wakeful; little Michael had broken himself of his 2 A.M. bottle ten days before, and he had slept peacefully through every night since.

It was the whole disagreeable day, Jessie decided— the fireworks, the general confusion, Mrs. Humffrey's flapping about, the tension in the household climaxed by the row between uncle and nephew. And perhaps—she felt her cheeks tingle—perhaps it had something to do with that man Richard Queen.

Jessie had to admit that she had been acting like a moony teenager ever since their meeting on the Humffrey beach. Thinking about a man of sixty-three! Hinting to him about Thursday being her day off . . . The burn in her cheeks smarted. She had even gone over to the public beach in Taugus on her next day off and sat on the sand under a rented beach umbrella all afternoon, hoping against hope and feeling silly at the same time. What if he had shown up? Her figure in a bathing suit wasn't bad for her age, but she could hardly compete with those skinny brown three-quarters-naked young hussies flitting about the beach. So she had left that day relieved, angry at herself, and yet disappointed. He'd seemed so nice, so youthful-looking, and so troubled about his age and his retirement . . . Of course, he had stayed away. He must know plenty about women, having been a police officer all his life. Probably put her down right off as a coy old maid on the prowl for a victim.

Still, it was a pity. They could have found lots to talk about. Some of her more interesting cases, people of note she had nursed. And he must have had hundreds of exciting experiences. And actually she hadn't looked half bad in her bathing suit. She had studied herself in the bathroom mirror very critically before making up her mind to go that day. At least she had some flesh on her bones. And her skin was really remarkably unlined for a woman of forty-nine. How old was Marlene Dietrich . . . ?

Jessie Sherwood heaved over and buried her face in the pillow.

And in the silence that followed the groan of the bed

she heard a sound that drove all other thoughts from her head.

It was the sound of a window being opened in the nursery.

She lay stiffly, listening.

The nursery was at the rear of the house, a corner room with two windows. One overlooked the driveway and gardens at the side, the other faced the sea. At the baby's bedtime she had opened both windows wide, but when the breeze came up and she had had to get a quilt for herself, she had gone into the nursery to tuck an extra satin throw around the baby and shut the seaward window. The temperature had dropped so low that she had even removed the screen and pulled the driveway window most of the way down, leaving it open no more than three or four inches.

It seemed to her the sound had come from the driveway window.

There it was again.

Again!

They were short, soft, scrapy sounds, as if the window were being opened an inch or two at a time, little secretive upward nudges, with listening pauses between.

"Parents can't be too careful about their children, especially if they're rich . . ."

He had said that.

"A snatch case I investigated a few years ago . . ."

A kidnaper!

With a leap Jessie Sherwood was out of bed. She grabbed her robe, flung it over her cotton nightgown, and dashed through the communicating doorway into little Michael's room.

In the faint glow of the baseboard nightlight she saw a man. He had one leg over the sill of the driveway window. The other was apparently braced against the top rung of a ladder. His head was cut off at the neck by the half-raised venetian blind. He was all flat and colorless. It was like seeing a lifesized cutout made of black paper.

24

Nurse Sherwood yelled and sprang to the crib. The figure in the window disappeared.

There was a great deal of confusion after that. Mr. Humffrey ran in buttoning his pajama coat over his gaunt, furry torso; Mrs. Humffrey flew by him, shrieking, to tear the baby from his nurse's arms; Mrs. Lenihan, Mrs. Charbedeau, the two maids thronged the stairway from the third floor, pulling on assorted negligees and gasping questions; and the men's quarters over the garage lit up. The baby wailed louder, Mrs. Humffrey shrieked harder, Mr. Humffrey roared demands for an explanation, and through the bedlam Jessie Sherwood tried to make herself heard. When she was finally able to communicate, and Alton Humffrey thrust his head out the window, the driveway was empty except for old Stallings and Henry Cullum, in pajamas and barefoot, looking up and asking wildly what was the matter.

A long ladder was leaning against the window.

"Search the grounds," Alton Humffrey shouted to the two white-haired men below. "I'll phone the gatehouse."

When he came back he was fuming. "I don't know what we pay those guards for. Either that imbecile Peterson was asleep or he's drunk. Sarah, *stop* that, please. Give Michael to Miss Sherwood. You're frightening him half to death."

"Oh, Alton, suppose it was a *kidnaper*," Sarah Humffrey said hysterically.

"Nonsense. It was some housebreaker, and Miss Sherwood scared him off. Here, let me have him."

"I'll take him, Mr. Humffrey," Jessie Sherwood said. "Mrs. Lenihan, would you get me a bottle of formula from the refrigerator? I think, darlin', we'll make an exception tonight. But first let's change this diaper . . ." She took the baby into the nursery bathroom and firmly shut the door.

When she came out with him, Alton Humffrey was alone in the nursery watching the bottle in the electric warmer.

"Is Michael all right?" he asked abruptly.

"He's fine, Mr. Humffrey."

"You're sure it was a man?"

"Yes, sir."

"Nothing familiar about him?" His tone was odd.

"I really can't say," Jessie said quietly. "I didn't see his face at all, and the rest of him was just a black silhouette against the moonlight. Mr. Humffrey, I don't think it was a housebreaker."

"You don't?" He glanced at her sharply.

"Why should a housebreaker try to enter through an upper window? The windows aren't locked downstairs."

Alton Humffrey did not reply. Jessie took the bottle from the warner, sat down in the rocker, and began to feed the baby.

"Mr. Humffrey?" It was Cullum, from below.

Humffrey strode to the window. "Yes?"

"No sign of a soul," the chauffeur said. Stallings, beside him, nodded.

"You two had better get some clothes on and stay out there for a while." He put the nursery screen with the animal cutouts on it before the window. Jessie noticed how careful he was not to touch the window.

When he turned back his brow was all knots.

"Don't you think you'd better call the police, Mr. Humffrey?" Jessie murmured.

"Yes," he said.

The telephone rang on the other side of the flimsy wall and the old man was instantly awake. He heard Abe Pearl's sleepy growl say, "Yes?" and then, not sleepily at all, "I'll go right over. Have Tinny and Borcher meet me there."

When Chief Pearl let himself out of his bedroom, there was the old man in the hall in his robe, waiting.

"Dick. What are you doing up?"

"I heard the phone, Abe. Trouble?"

"Something funny over on Nair Island," the big man grunted. "Maybe you'd like to sit in on it."

"Nair Island," Richard Queen said. "What kind of trouble?"

26

"Somebody tried to break into one of those million-aires' homes. Kid's nursery. Might be a snatch try."

"It wouldn't be at the Humffreys', would it?"

"That's right." Abe Pearl stared.

"Anybody hurt?"

"No, he was scared off. But how do you know, Dick?"

"I'll be with you in three minutes."

The Humffrey house was lit up. They found one of Abe Pearl's men examining the ladder in the driveway and another in the nursery talking to Humffrey and the nurse. The screen was around the crib now, and Sarah Humffrey was in the rocker, gnawing her lips but quieted down.

The old man and Jessie Sherwood glanced at each other once, then looked away. He remained in the background, listening, looking around. Her color was high, and she drew her robe more closely about her. It would have to be the *cotton* nightgown tonight! she thought. Why didn't I wash out the orlon?

When they had repeated their stories, Chief Pearl went to the window.

"Is that your ladder, Mr. Humffrey?"

"Yes."

"Where is it usually kept?"

"In the tool shed where Stallings, my gardener, keeps his equipment."

"Take a look, Borcher."

The detective went out.

Abe Pearl turned to Jessie. "This man," he said. "Would you know him if you saw him again, Miss Sherwood?"

"I doubt it."

"He didn't say anything? Make any sound?"

"I didn't hear anything but the window being slid up little by little. When I ran in he disappeared."

"Did you hear a car?"

"No. I mean, I don't recall."

"Did you or didn't you?"

Jessie felt herself growing hot. "I tell you I don't know!"

27

"That's all right," Chief Pearl said. "People get excited." He turned his back on her, and Richard Queen blinked. He knew what his friend was thinking: Tag the nurse as a possible question mark. Of course, Abe didn't know her. He was surprised to find himself thinking of her as if he had known her for a long time. "Did you hear a car drive away, Mr. Humffrey?"

"I can't say. There was a great deal of noise here, naturally, after Miss Sherwood screamed."

Abe Pearl nodded. "The chances are, if he came in a car, he parked on the road off your grounds. You didn't find a note of any kind, did you?"

"No."

Sarah Humffrey whispered, *"Note?"*

Her husband said sharply, "Sarah, don't you think you'd better go to bed?"

"No, Alton, no, please. I couldn't sleep now, anyway. I'm all right, dear."

"Sure she is, Mr. Humffrey. Think you can answer a few questions, Mrs. Humffrey?" The chief's tone was deferential.

"Yes. But I can't tell you anything——"

"About your servants, I mean."

"The *servants?*" Sarah Humffrey repeated.

"Just a matter of form, Mrs. Humffrey. You never know in cases like this. How many you got, and how long they been with you?"

"Our housekeeper, Mrs. Lenihan, has been with us since our marriage," Sarah Humffrey said. "Mrs. Charbedeau, the cook, has worked for us almost ten years. Rose Healy and Marie Tompkins, the maids, are Boston girls who have been with us for a number of years."

"How about those two old fellows out there?"

"Stallings, the gardener," Alton Humffrey said, "is a local man, but we've employed him since we purchased this property. He stays on as caretaker during the winters. Henry Cullum, the chauffeur, drove for my father as a young man. I'll vouch for both of them. For that matter, for the women, too. We're very careful about our servants, Mr. Pearl."

28

"How about Miss Sherwood?" Chief Pearl asked casually.

Jessie said, "I resent that!"

"Miss Sherwood has been with us only since a week or so before the baby came. However, she was highly recommended both by Dr. Holliday of Greenwich, our pediatrician, and Dr. Wicks of Taugus, who is our family physician during the summers."

"Check her references, Mr. Humffrey?"

"Very thoroughly indeed."

"I've been a registered nurse for twenty-three years," Jessie Sherwood snapped, "and I've taken an awful lot in my time, but this is the limit. If I'd been in cahoots with some psychopath to kidnap this darling baby, do you think I'd have let out a yell and chased him away?"

Chief Pearl said mildly, "Just getting the picture," and went out.

Inspector Queen said to nobody in particular, "Don't blame the chief. It's his job."

Nurse Sherwood tossed her head.

When Abe Pearl came back he said to Humffrey, "There's dust on the ladder. We might get some prints. Miss Sherwood, I suppose you can't say whether the man you saw was wearing anything on his hands?"

"I can't say," Jessie replied shortly.

"Well, there's nothing else we can do tonight, Mr. Humffrey. Personally, I don't think you've got anything to worry about. But if you want me to leave a man, I'll leave one."

"I wish you would," Alton Humffrey said slowly. "And, Mr. Pearl."

"Yes, sir?"

"I don't want any publicity about this."

"I'll see that the boys over at Headquarters keep quiet about it. Dick?" The chief glanced at his friend.

"One thing." Richard Queen stepped forward. "If you don't mind my asking, Mr. Humffrey—is this your own child?"

Sarah Humffrey started. Alton Humffrey looked at the old man almost for the first time.

"No offense," Inspector Queen went on, "but you told Chief Pearl you have no other children. It struck me you people are a little on in years to be having a first baby."

"Is this one of your men, Chief?" the millionaire demanded.

"Inspector Queen of the New York police department, retired," Abe Pearl said quickly. "He was my lieutenant when I pounded a Manhattan beat, Mr. Humffrey. He's visiting me for the summer."

"The man who sent me a check for a dollar and fifty cents," Alton Humffrey said. "Are you in the habit of helping yourself to other people's gasoline, sir?"

"I explained that in my note."

"Yes. Well, Inspector, I don't see the relevance of your question."

"You haven't answered it," Richard Queen smiled.

"Michael is an adopted child. Why?"

"There might be something in his background to explain this, Mr. Humffrey, that's all."

"I assure you that's quite impossible." The millionaire's tone was frigid. "If there's nothing else, gentlemen, will you excuse Mrs. Humffrey and me?"

Jessie Sherwood wondered if Chief Pearl's friend was going to say anything to her before he left.

But he merely glanced politely in her direction and followed the chief out.

Tuesday evening after dinner, Jessie Sherwood went upstairs, peeped in at the baby, changed into a cool blue summer cotton, tidied her hair, powdered her nose, and slipped out of the house.

Jessie wondered as she sauntered down the driveway what the Humffreys talked about when they were alone. They were on the terrace now, sipping cherry brandy and staring silently to sea. In company they were articulate enough—Mrs. Humffrey was a positive chatterbox, of the corded-neck variety, while her husband had a caustic volubility—but Jessie had come upon them dozens of times alone together, and not once had she interrupted a conversation. They were strange people, she thought.

And jumped. A man had stepped suddenly from behind a tall clump of mountain laurel at the driveway entrance and flashed a light on her face.

"Oh. Sorry, Miss Sherwood."

"It's all right," Jessie said untruthfully, and strolled into the road. He was the second of the three guards hired by Alton Humffrey early that morning from a private detective agency in Bridgeport. They were rock-faced men who turned up and disappeared like alley cats.

When she rounded the curve in the road she began to walk fast. The air was salty sweet from the sea breeze and flowering gardens; and the road lights, great wrought-iron affairs shaped like sailing-ship lanterns, were besieged by platoons of moths and beetles cheerfully banging away. It was all very peaceful and lovely, but Jessie hurried on.

The gate was across the road at the Island end of the causeway.

"Mr. Peterson?"

The big private guard loomed in the gatehouse doorway. "You walking across?" His voice was sulky.

"No, I'm just out for some air. What's the matter, Mr. Peterson? You sound sour on the world."

"You'd think I'd had a picnic this weekend," the guard grumbled, unbending. "You know how many cars came through here last night? And then they want me to remember who went in and out!"

"That's a shame," Jessie said sympathetically. "With all that outbound traffic, I wouldn't have blamed you if you'd simply left the gate open all night."

"That's what I did, Miss Sherwood."

"Even at two in the morning, I suppose."

"Sure. Why not? How was I to know?"

"Well, of course. And by that time you must have been darn tired. Were you sitting in the gatehouse, resting?"

"I'll say!"

"So of course you didn't see the car that drove in some time after midnight and left around 2 A.M."

Peterson scowled. "I saw the back of it."

Jessie drew a long breath in the perfumed moonlight. "I'll bet it was a car you knew, and that's why you didn't stop him."

"Something like that. I didn't see his face, but him and the car looked familiar."

"What kind of car was it, Mr. Peterson?"

"Foreign job. A Jaguar."

"I see." Jessie's heart was beating faster.

"Like the one run by Mr. Humffrey's nephew—what's-his-name—Mr. Frost. Matter of fact," the guard said, "I thought it was Frost. He'd been off and on the Island all weekend."

"Oh, then you're not sure."

The guard said uncomfortably, "I can't swear to it."

"Well." Jessie smiled at him. "Don't you worry about it, Mr. Peterson. I'm sure you do your job as well as anyone could expect."

"You can say that again!"

"Good night."

"Good night, Miss Sherwood," Peterson said warmly.

He went back into the gatehouse, and Jessie began to retrace her steps, frowning.

"Nice going," a man's voice said.

Jessie's heart flopped. But then she saw who it was.

"Mr. Queen," she cried. "What are you doing here?"

He was in the roadway before her, spare and neat in a Palm Beach suit, looking amused.

"Same thing you are, only I beat you to it. Playing detective, Miss Sherwood?" He chuckled and took her arm. "Suppose I walk you back."

Jessie nodded a little stiffly, and they began to stroll alone beside high fieldstone walls clothed in ivy and rambler roses, with the moon like a cheddar cheese overhead and the salty sweet air in their nostrils. How long is it, she wondered, since I last took a moonlight stroll with a man holding my arm? The last one had been Clem, on leave before shipping out . . .

The old man said suddenly, "Did you suspect Ron Frost all along?"

"Why are you so interested?" Jessie murmured.

"Let's say I don't like cases involving nursery windows." He sounded gruff. "And I can lend a hand to Abe Pearl . . ."

Some tireless patriot out at sea sent up a Roman candle. They stopped to watch the burst and drip of fireballs. For a few seconds the Island brightened. Then the darkness closed in again.

She felt his restless movement. It was like a dash of cold sea.

"I'd better be getting back," Jessie said matter-of-factly, and they walked on. "About your question, Mr. Queen. I suppose I shouldn't be saying this while I'm taking the Humffreys' money, but I like threats to babies even less than you do. Ronald Frost quarreled with Mr. Humffrey over Michael yesterday." And she told him what she had overheard from the nursery.

"So Frost expected to be his uncle's heir, and now he figures the baby's queered his act," Richard Queen said thoughtfully. "And Frost was tanked up when he left, you say?"

"Well, he'd had quite a bit to drink."

"He was nursing a beaut of a hangover this morning, and there was an empty bourbon bottle on his bureau. So he must have worked himself up to a real charge by late last night. Could be . . ."

"You saw him?" Jessie exclaimed.

"I dropped over to his place in Old Greenwich. Sort of as a favor to Abe Pearl."

"What did Frost say? Tell me!"

"He said he came straight home last night and went to bed. He lives alone, so no one saw him. In other words, no alibi."

"But did he actually deny having driven back here?"

"Would you expect him to admit it?" She knew he was smiling in the darkness. "Anyway, he's had a good scare—I'll guarantee that. If Frost was the man who tried to climb in through that window, I don't think he'll try it again."

33

"But what could he have been thinking of?" Jessie shivered.

"Drunks don't make much sense."

"You think . . . ransom? He told Mr. Humffrey he was badly in debt."

"I don't think anything," the Inspector said. "Whoever it was wore gloves—there wasn't an unaccounted-for print anywhere in the nursery or shed, and smudges were evident on the ladder. We have nothing on Frost but a questionable identification by Peterson. Even if we had, I doubt if Mr. Humffrey would press a charge, from the way he talked to Abe Pearl on the phone today. The best thing for you to do is forget last night ever happened, young lady."

"Thank you." Jessie felt herself dimpling, and it made her add tartly, "Young lady!"

He seemed surprised. "But you are young. Some people never age. My mother was one of them. You're very much like her—" He stopped. Then he said, "This is it, isn't it? It's so blasted dark——"

"Yes." Jessie hoped fiercely that the guard from the Bridgeport detective agency would have the decency to remain behind his bush and keep his finger off the flashlight button. "You were saying, Mr. Queen?"

"It wasn't anything."

There was a silence.

"Well," Jessie said. "I must say you've relieved my mind, Inspector. And thanks for walking me back."

"It was my pleasure." But from the way he said it, it sounded more like a sadness. "Well, good night, Miss Sherwood."

"Good night," Jessie said emptily.

She was standing there in the dark, listening to his footfalls retreat and wondering if she would ever see him again, when the light suddenly blinded her.

"Who was that with you, Miss Sherwood?" the private detective said.

"Oh, go away, you—you beagle!" Nurse Sherwood said, and she ran up the driveway as if someone were after her.

34

So that seemed the end of a promising friendship. The weeks went by, and although during little Michael's nap times on the Humffrey beach Jessie kept glancing up at passing small craft, or on her Thursdays off found herself scanning the crowds on Front Street or the Taugus public beach, she did not catch even a glimpse of that wiry figure again.

What children men are! she thought angrily.

If not for the baby, she would have given notice and quit Nair Island. She was desperately lonely. But little Michael needed her, she kept telling herself, trying not to feel the old jealous twinge when Mrs. Humffrey took him from her arms and exercised her proprietary rights.

Sometimes Jessie thought she ought to leave for the baby's sake, before he became too attached to her. But she kept putting it off. In the gloom that had suddenly set in, he was the only sunny thing. Besides, she told herself, there was always that disturbing incident of the night of July 4th. Suppose the attempt should be repeated and she weren't there to protect him?

So the weeks passed, and July drew to a close, and nothing happened. On the 31st, almost four weeks to the day from the date of the nursery incident, Alton Humffrey dismissed the three private detectives.

The following Thursday morning Jessie bathed and dressed the baby, fed him his gruel and bottle, and turned him over to Sarah Humffrey.

"You're sure you're up to it?" Jessie asked her anxiously. Mrs. Humffrey was sniffling with a slight summer cold. "I'll gladly forgo my day off. I can make it up some other time."

"Oh, no." Mrs. Humffrey peered at Michael through her white mask. Jessie privately wished she wouldn't insist on wearing a mask at the least provocation; the baby didn't like it. Besides, Jessie held the unprofessional view that the more an infant was shielded from common germ and virus infections in his early months, when he still had certain immunities, the more susceptible he became later. But Mrs. Humffrey went by the book, or rather by the books; she had a shelf full of them over

35

her bed. "It's not the least bit necessary, Miss Sherwood. It's just a little head cold. We'll be fine without Nursery, love, won't we?"

"Maybe I'd better plan on coming back tonight, though," Jessie said, setting herself for squalls. Michael was staring up at the white mask with apprehension, and his little mouth was beginning to droop at the corners.

"I won't hear of it." Mrs. Humffrey took this moment to tickle his abdomen. "Kitchy-kitchy! Come on, darling, *laugh*."

"I really wouldn't mind," Jessie said, choking back a sharp command to stop. Michael solved the problem by throwing up and howling. Mrs. Humffrey guiltily backed off. "It's nothing," Jessie said, taking him. "It's just not a very good idea to tickle an infant, especially on a full stomach." She burped him, cleaned him up, and handed him back.

"Oh, dear," Sarah Humffrey said. "There's so much I have to learn."

"Not so much," Jessie couldn't help saying. "It's really only a matter of common sense, Mrs. Humffrey. I do think I'll come back tonight."

"I absolutely forbid you. I know how you've looked forward to a night in town . . ."

In the end Jessie was persuaded. Driving her sturdy little 1949 Dodge coupe, she told herself all the way to the railroad station that she really must stop being so possessive. It would do Mrs. Humffrey good to have to care for her baby around the clock. Women had no business turning their children over to someone else. But if they were that kind—and it seemed to Jessie that she rarely encountered any other kind—the more responsibility that was forced on them the better off they and the children were.

Still, Jessie was uneasy all day. It rather spoiled the good time she had planned. She met an old friend, Belle Berman, a supervisor of nurses at a New York hospital; and although they shopped at Saks's, had lunch in a winy-smelling restaurant on 45th Street with French travel posters on the walls, and took in a matinée, Jessie found her thoughts going back to Nair Island and the unhappy little face on the bathinette.

They had dinner in Belle Berman's apartment on West 11th Street. All during the meal Jessie kept glancing at her watch.

"What *is* the matter with you?" her friend demanded as she began to collect the dishes. "Anyone would think you'd left a dying patient."

"I'm sorry, Belle, but I'm worried about the baby. Mrs. Humffrey does have a cold, and if she starts moaning and pampering herself . . . Besides, she's so helpless about the simplest things."

"Heavens, Jessie," Belle Berman exclaimed. "Is there anything more indestructible than an infant? Anyway, it will do the woman good. These rich mothers! Now you stop this foolishness—no, *I'll* wash the dishes, and you're going to sit on your fanny and talk to me. By the way, how do you keep your figure? You eat like a horse!"

Belle Berman had a few friends in after dinner, and Jessie tried hard to catch up on hospital gossip and join in the good-natured character assassination of certain doctors and nurses they all knew. But as the evening wore on she grew more and more restless. Finally, she jumped up.

"Belle, I know you're going to think I'm menopausal or something, but would you mind very much if I change our plans and I don't stay overnight after all?"

"Jessie Sherwood."

"Well, I can't bear the thought of my precious lamb being mishandled by that woman," Jessie said fiercely. "Or suppose she got really sick today? Those maids don't know one end of a baby from the other. If I leave now and take a cab, I can catch the 11:05 . . ."

She just made the train. The trip was stifling and miserable. Jessie lolled all the way in a sickish stupor, dozing.

It was a few minutes past midnight when she got off at the Taugus station and unlocked her car. Even here the night was a humid swelter, and the inside of the

Dodge was like an oven. She rolled down the windows, but she did not wait for the car to cool off. She drove off at once, head throbbing.

She thought Charlie Peterson would never come out of the gatehouse. He finally appeared, yawning.

"What a night," he said, slapping at the mosquitoes.

"Yes."

"Hot in town, too, Miss Sherwood?"

"Beastly."

"At least you could go to an air-cooled movie. What makes this job so tough is having to look at this damn water while you're boiling to death——"

"I have such a headache," Jessie murmured. "Would you please let me through, Mr. Peterson?"

"Sorry!" He raised the barrier, offended.

Jessie drove up the Nair Island road, sighing. Now that she was here, it all seemed rather silly. The Humffrey house up ahead was dark. If the baby were sick or wakeful the house would be blazing with lights. Mrs. Humffrey took it for granted that her employees were delighted to share her troubles and got them all out of bed the moment anything went wrong. Well, this was one night when none of them was going to be disturbed. She'd leave the car just inside the grounds and let herself in the front door quietly and tiptoe upstairs and go to bed. The sound of the car going around the driveway to the garage might wake someone up.

Jessie turned off her ignition, locked the car, and groped toward the front of the house. She located the key in her bag by touch, let herself in, shut the door carefully, felt around until she found the newel post, and climbed the stairs, grateful for the heavy carpeting.

Then, at the door of her room, after all her caution, she dropped her purse. In the silence of the dark house it sounded like a bomb going off.

Jessie was feeling around on all fours, trying to locate the purse and keep her head from falling, too, when a whiplash voice a few feet away said, "Don't move."

"Oh, dear," Jessie said with an exasperated laugh. "It's only me, Mr. Humffrey. I'm sorry."

A light flashed on her.

"Miss Sherwood." As her eyes accommodated to the glare she saw his robed figure utterly still, a flashlight in one hand and a gun in the other. "I thought you were spending the night in New York."

Jessie plucked her purse from the floor, feeling like a fool. "I changed my mind. Mr. Humffrey. I developed a headache, and the city was so hot . . ."

Why did he keep the gun pointing at her that way? "Alton! What is it?"

"Oh, dear," Jessie said again. She wished he would lower the gun.

Light flooded the master bedroom doorway. Mrs. Humffrey peered out, clutching one of her exquisite negligees at the bosom. Her face looked pinched and old with fear.

"It's Miss Sherwood, Sarah." Only then did Alton Humffrey drop the gun into the pocket of his robe. "That was foolish of you, Miss Sherwood, stealing in this way, without warning. You might have been shot. Why didn't you phone?"

"I didn't have time. I made my mind up at the last minute." Jessie began to feel angry. Questioning her as if she were a criminal! "I'm terribly sorry my clumsiness woke you up. Is the baby all right, Mrs. Humffrey?"

"He was the last time I looked in." Sarah Humffrey came out into the hall and switched on the lights. Her husband went back to their room without another word. "Have you been in to Michael yet?"

"No. How is your cold?"

"Oh, it's all right. Baby was cross all day, I can't imagine why. I didn't leave him for a moment. And I've been in to him twice since I put him beddy-bye. Do you suppose he could have caught my cold?"

"I'll have a look," Jessie said wearily. "But I'm sure he's all right, Mrs. Humffrey, or this noise would have made him restless. Why don't you go back to bed?"

"I'll look with you"

Jessie shrugged. She opened her door, turned on her bedlamp, and tossed her hat and gloves on the bureau.

"I hope I did all the right things," Mrs. Humffrey

said. "He was so fretful at 10:30, the last time I looked at him before I went to bed, that I put a big pillow between his head and the headboard. I was afraid he'd hurt himself. Their tender little skulls . . ."

Jessie wished her tender little skull would stop aching. She tried to keep the irritation out of her voice. "I've told you, Mrs. Humffrey, that's not a wise thing to do when they're so tiny. The bumpers give him all the protection necessary." She hurried toward the nursery.

"But he's such an active child." Sarah Humffrey stopped in the doorway, a handkerchief pressed hygienically over her mouth and nose.

The nursery was hot and close, although Jessie noticed in the faint glow of the nightlight that the Venetian blind on the window overlooking the driveway was drawn all the way up and the window was wide open. Also, someone had removed the window screen, and the room was full of bugs.

She could have slapped the ineffectual woman in the doorway.

She tiptoed over to the crib.

A vice closed over her heart, and squeezed. The baby had kicked his covers off. He was lying on his back, his fat little legs helter-skelter, and the pillow was over his face and torso.

It seemed to Jessie Sherwood that a million years passed between the constriction of her heart and its violent leap. In that infinite instant all she could do was stare down at the motionless little body, paralyzed.

Then she snatched the pillow away, kicked the side of the crib down, and bent over.

"Put the overhead light on," she said hoarsely.

"What? What's the matter?" quavered Mrs. Humffrey.

"Do as I say. The light!"

Mrs. Humffrey fumbled for the switch on the wall, the other hand still over her mouth and nose.

Jessie Sherwood, R.N., went through the motions as prescribed, her fingers working swiftly, by training and habit as cool as a surgeon's—as if they were, in fact, the fingers of a surgeon, or of anyone not herself. Inside a sick something was forming, a nausea of disbelief.

Two months old. Two months.

And as she worked over the cold little limbs, trying not to see him as he was but only as he had been—in her arms, in his bath, in his pram on the beach—she knew he would never be any older.

"He's dead," Jessie said without stopping, without looking up. "He's suffocated, I'm giving him artifical respiration but it's useless, he's been dead for some time, Mrs. Humffrey. Call your husband, call a doctor—not Dr. Holliday, Greenwich is too far away—call Dr. Wicks, and don't faint till you do, Mrs. Humffrey. Please don't faint till you call them."

Mrs. Humffrey screamed piercingly and fainted.

With some surprise Jessie found herself a long time later wrapping another blanket around Sarah Humffrey in the master bedroom. The spirits of ammonia were on the bed shelf near the books on infant care, with the stopper out, so she knew she had done the right things automatically, or perhaps it was at Dr. Wicks's direction —she could hear his voice from the hall. Mrs. Humffrey was lying across the bed, her head hanging over the side; she was conscious, moaning, and Jessie thought it a pity that her professional training had made her bring the woman out of the blessed land of shock. In fact, Jessie thought, Sarah Humffrey would be better off dead.

Then she remembered, and the memory brought her to her senses.

Dear God, she thought.

She hauled the moaning woman to a comfortable position on the bed and walked out on her.

Now she remembered everything. Where had she been? How long was it? It would have taken some time for Dr. Wicks to dress and drive over. How long had he been here?

The doctor was in the hall talking to Alton Humffrey. The gaunt millionaire was leaning against the wall, shading his eyes as if the light hurt them.

"It's always a question, Mr. Humffrey," Dr. Wicks

41

was saying. "I'm afraid we don't know very much about this sort of thing. In some cases we find a widespread, diffuse infection, probably viral, that simply doesn't show up except on autopsy, and not always then. It could have been that. If you'd consent to an autopsy——"

"No," Alton Humffrey said. "No."

She remembered his running into the nursery at Sarah Humffrey's scream, the look on his face as he caught sight of the body in the crib, the terrible frozen look, like the *risus sardonicus* of tetanus. For fully a minute that look had held possession of him as he watched her trying to restore the function of the dead lungs, trying to coax the flaccid little rib cage into an elasticity it would never have again, trying to revive a tiny heart that had stopped beating long ago.

Then he said, "He's really dead."

And she had said, "Phone Dr. Wicks, *please*."

And he had picked up his wife and carried her out, and a moment later Jessie had heard him phoning Dr. Wicks in a voice as frozen as his look had been.

After a while Jessie had stopped working the cold baby arms, covered the body, and gone to Mrs. Humffrey. Her husband was trying to revive her.

"I'll do it," Jessie had said, and he had gone out with long strides, in a release of stopped-up energy, as if his need for expending himself were overwhelming. As she worked over the unconscious woman she had heard him talking to the servants in a strangely considerate tone, and there were weepy female sounds and a sudden unbelievable shout from him—the patrician who never raised his voice!—a shout of pure rage, and immediately shocked silence. After that he had merely prowled downstairs and up, in the room and out, until Dr. Wicks arrived.

Jessie went up to them and leaned against the wall, too.

"Oh, Miss Sherwood." Dr. Wicks looked relieved. He was a fashionable little man with a sun-blotched scalp. "How is Mrs. Humffrey?"

"She's conscious, Doctor."

"I'd better have a look at her. You're going to have to

42

handle your wife very carefully for a while, Mr. Humffrey."

"Yes," Alton Humffrey said, rousing himself. "Yes."

Dr. Wicks picked up his bag and walked quickly into the master bedroom. The gaunt man unfolded himself and followed. Jessie shuffled after, her feet dragging. A wave of weakness surged over her, and for a moment the hall rocked. But she steadied herself and went into the bedroom.

Sarah Humffrey was weeping now, her bony shoulders jerking like something at the end of a fisherman's line. Dr. Wicks was saying as if to a child, "That's all right, Mrs. Humffrey, don't mind us at all. It's nature's way of relieving tension. A good cry will make you feel better."

"My baby," she sobbed.

"It's terribly unfortunate, a great tragedy. But these things do happen. I've seen babies go like that in the best-regulated nurseries."

"The pillow," she wept. "I put the pillow there to protect him, Doctor. Oh, God, how was I to know?"

"There's no point in dwelling on it, Mrs. Humffrey, is there? What you need now is sleep."

"I shouldn't have let Miss Sherwood go off. She offered to stay. But no, I had to pretend I knew all about taking care of him . . ."

"Mrs. Humffrey, if you're going to carry on like this——"

"I loved him," the woman sobbed.

Dr. Wicks glanced at Jessie as if for professional support. But Jessie was standing there like a stone, stuck fast, wondering how to say it, wondering if it could be true, knowing it was true and loathing the knowledge.

I'm going to be sick any minute, she thought. Sick . . .

"I think," Dr. Wicks said with a show of firmness, "we'll have to give you something."

Jessie heard him with surprise. Did it show that much? But then she saw that he was still talking to Mrs. Humffrey.

"No!" the woman screamed. "No, no, *no!*"

"All right, Mrs. Humffrey," the doctor said hastily. "Just quiet down. Lie back . . ."

"Dr. Wicks," her husband said.

"Yes, Mr. Humffrey."

"I assume you're intending to report this to the County Coroner's office?" The millionaire had sheathed himself like a sword.

"Yes. A formality, of course——"

"I needn't tell you how abhorrent all this is to me. I have some influence in Hartford, Doctor. If you'll be good enough to cooperate——"

"Well, now, I don't know, Mr. Humffrey," Dr. Wicks said cautiously. "I have a sworn duty, you know."

"I understand." Jessie had the feeling that he was holding himself in the scabbard by sheer will. "Still, there are sometimes considerations above a sworn duty, Dr. Wicks. In exceptional cases, let us say. Haven't you found it so in your practice?"

"I can't say I have," the physician replied in a stiffening tone. "Whatever it is you have in mind, Mr. Humffrey, I'm afraid the answer must be no."

The millionaire's mouth tightened. "All I'm asking is that Mrs. Humffrey and I be spared the ordeal of a coroner's inquiry. It will mean newspaper reporters, an inquest, public testimony. It's intolerable to have to face that, Doctor. Certainly my wife can't in her condition. As her physician, surely you know that."

"I'm as unhappy about this misfortune as you are, Mr. Humffrey. But what can I do?"

"It was an accident! Are people to be crucified in public because of an accident?"

Jessie Sherwood thought if they did not stop she would scream.

"I know it was an accident, Mr. Humffrey. But you're placing me——"

She heard herself saying in a very loud voice, "No, it wasn't."

Dr. Wicks turned sharply. "What did you say, Nurse?"

Mrs. Humffrey's body swiveled on the bed as she tried to focus her swollen eyes on Jessie.

44

"I said, Dr. Wicks, it was not an accident."

For a faraway moment Jessie thought Alton Humffrey was going to spring at her throat. But he merely said, "What do you mean, Miss Sherwood?"

"I mean that somebody else entered the nursery after Mrs. Humffrey went to bed."

The tall man looked at her with burning eyes.

Jessie steeled herself and returned his look.

"That baby was murdered, Mr. Humffrey, and if you don't call the police—this minute—I'm going to."

2.

CREEPING
LIKE SNAIL

FACES kept floating about the steamy room. All the weight had bobbed out of Jessie's head. It felt taut and airy, like a balloon. In the nightmare she knew with curious certainty that her alarm would go off any minute. She would wake up in a solid world, jump out of bed, listen for the baby's gurgling, shuffle into the nursery with a bright good morning . . .

"Sit down, Jessie."

"What?"

It was miraculously Richard Queen. He was urging her back into the rocker, putting a glass to her dehydrated lips. He had called her Jessie, so it was still the nightmare. Or perhaps the nightmare was turning into a harmless dream.

"Drink it."

The flow of cold water down her throat awakened her. She saw the room now as it was. The nursery was full of men peering, measuring, talking, weighing, as impersonal as salesmen—state troopers and Taugus policemen and an unshaven man without a tie whom she distantly recalled as having arrived carrying a briefcase.

"Are you feeling better now, Miss Sherwood?" That was Chief Pearl's rumble.

"It's just that I haven't had any sleep," Jessie explained. What had they been talking about when the room began to swim? She couldn't remember. All she could remember was Chief Pearl's bass voice, the enormous mass of him, his drilling eyes.

"All right. You went into the nursery with Mrs. Humffrey, you bent over the crib, you saw the pillow lying on the baby's face, you grabbed it away, you saw that he had suffocated, and you automatically began to give him first aid, artificial respiration, even though you had every reason to believe he was dead.

"Now think back, Miss Sherwood. How long would you say it took you—starting from your first sight of the pillow over the baby's face—to get past the shock and snatch that pillow off him?"

"I don't know," Jessie said. "It seemed like an eternity. But I suppose it wasn't more than a second or two."

"One or two seconds. Then you grabbed the pillow and did what with it?"

Jessie knuckled her eyes. What was the matter with him?

"I tossed it aside."

"Tossed it where?" the Taugus police chief persisted.

"Toward the foot of the crib."

The tieless, unshaven man said, "Would you remember exactly where at the foot of the crib the pillow landed, Miss Sherwood?"

They were all touched by the heat, that was it, Jessie decided. As if where it landed made any difference!

"Of course not," she said acidly. "I don't think I gave it a glance after I threw it aside. My only thought at that time was to try and revive the baby. I didn't really think back to what I'd seen on the pillow until a long time afterward. Then it came back to me with a rush, and I realized what it meant."

"Suppose you tell us once more just what you think you saw on that pillow, Miss Sherwood," the tieless man said again. Had she imagined someone's saying he was from the State's Attorney's office in Bridgeport?

47

"What I think I saw?" Jessie flared. "Are you doubting my word?"

She glanced at Richard Queen in her anger, to see if he was on their side after all. But he merely stood over her rubbing his gray stub of mustache.

"Answer the question, please."

"I *know* I saw a handprint on the pillow."

"An actual, recognizable human handprint?"

"Yes! Someone with a dirty hand had placed it on that pillow."

"What kind of dirt, Miss Sherwood?"

"Kind? How should I know?"

"What color was it? Black? Brown? Gray?"

"I really couldn't say. Maybe grayish. Like dust."

"Well, was it grayish, like dust, or wasn't it?"

"I think it was."

"You *think* it was?"

"I'm not sure about the color," Jessie said tiredly. "How can I be? My impression is that it looked like a dust print. I could be wrong about that, but I don't think I am. That it was dirt of some kind I'm positive."

"You say it was as if someone had placed a dirty hand on the pillow," the tieless man said. "Placed it how, Miss Sherwood? Flat? Doubled up? Partially?"

"Perfectly flat."

"Where on the pillow?"

"Just about in the middle."

"Was it a clear impression? That is, could you tell unmistakably that it was a human handprint?"

"Well, it wasn't really sharp, as I recall it. Sort of blurry—a little smudged. But it couldn't be mistaken for anything but what it was. The print of a hand." Jessie shut her eyes. She could see it with awful clarity. "The print was indented. I mean . . . there had been pressure exerted. Considerable downward pressure." She opened her eyes, and something happened to her voice. "I mean someone with a filthy hand had pressed that pillow hard over the baby's face, and kept pressing till he stopped breathing. That's why I told Mr. and Mrs. Humffrey that Michael had been murdered. At first, as I say, it didn't register. I saw it, and my brain must have

48

tucked it away, but I wasn't conscious of it till later. Then I told them to call the police. Why are you asking me these questions? Why don't you just examine the pillow and see for yourselves?"

"Stand up, Miss Sherwood," Chief Pearl growled. "Can you stand?"

"Oh, I'm all right." Jessie got to her feet impatiently.

"Go over to the crib. Don't touch it. Just take a look at the pillow."

Jessie was convinced now that it was the treacherous kind of dream where you thought you'd waked up but even that thought was part of the dream. Look at the pillow! Couldn't they look at it themselves?

Suddenly she felt a reluctance to go the crib. That was queer, because she had seen death regularly for many years, in a thousand forms. Jessie had feared death only three times in her life, when her parents died and when she received the telegram from the War Department about Clem. So it was love, perhaps, that made the difference . . . because it was she who had tended his unhealed navel . . . because it was on her face that he had kept his bright new eyes fixed with such absolute trust while she fed him.

Let him not be there, she prayed.

"It's all right, Jessie," Richard Queen's voice murmured close to her. "The little boy's been taken away."

He knew, God bless him.

She walked over to the crib blindly. But then she shook her head clear and looked.

The expensive pillow was at the foot of the crib, one corner doubled over where it lay against the footboard.

The lace-edged pillowcase was spotless

Jessie frowned. "It must have flipped over when I tossed it aside."

"Borcher, turn it over for Miss Sherwood," Chief Pearl said.

The Taugus detective took the lace between thumb and forefinger at one corner and turned the pillow carefully over.

The other side was spotless, too.

"But I don't understand," Jessie said. "I saw it with

my own eyes. I couldn't possibly have been mistaken."

"Miss Sherwood." The voice of the man from the State's Attorney's office was unpleasantly polite. "You would have us believe that you had your attention fixed on this pillow for no more than a second or two, in a room illuminated only by a dim baseboard nightlight, and not only saw a handprint on the pillow, but saw it clearly enough to be able to say that it seemed made by a human hand filthy with dust?"

"I can't help what you believe," Jessie said. "That's what I saw."

"It would be a feat of observation even if we found the handprint to back it up," the tieless man said. "But as you see, Miss Sherwood, there's not a mark on either side of the pillow. Isn't it possible, in your shock and excitement—and the feeble light in the room—that it was an optical illusion? Something you imagined you saw that never was there?"

"I've never had an optical illusion in my life. I saw it just as I've described it."

"You stick to that? You don't want to reconsider your recollection?"

"I most certainly do not."

The tieless man seemed displeased. He and Chief Pearl conferred. The old man caught Jessie's eye and smiled.

Then they went to the window overlooking the driveway, where a man was doing something with some bottles and a brush, and the tieless man looked out and down while the chief said something about an aluminum extension ladder.

"Ladder?" Jessie blinked over at Richard Queen.

He came quickly to her. "Just like that night last month, Jessie. The same ladder, in fact. Didn't you notice it standing against the wall when you drove into the driveway?"

"I didn't drive into the driveway. I left my car on the road."

"Oh, that was your car." His face said nothing at all.

"Then that's how that—that monster's hand got all dirty! The dust on the ladder while he was climbing

50

up." Jessie was staring at the pillow. "Why didn't I notice that before?"

"Notice what, Jessie?" He was instantly alert.

"This isn't the same pillow slip!"

"Isn't the same as what?"

"As the one I saw that had the handprint on it. *Inspector Queen, this is a different slip.*"

The old man looked at her. Then he called his friend and the State's Attorney's man over.

"Miss Sherwood says she now notices that this isn't the same pillowcase that had the handprint on it."

"It isn't?" Chief Pearl glanced at the tieless man. "That's an interesting addition to the story, Merrick."

The tieless man said to Jessie, "How can you tell?"

"The edging—Mr. Merrick, is it? The other slip was edged with a different kind of lace. Both slipcases are made of very fine batiste, but the edging of the other one was Honiton lace, while this, I think, is an Irish crochet. Anyway, it's not the same."

"You're sure of this, Miss Sherwood?" Merrick demanded.

"Positive."

"Changed," Richard Queen remarked. "If you accept Miss Sherwood's story, somebody removed the soiled case from the pillow afterward and substituted this clean one. It's a break, Abe."

The big policeman grunted, looking around the nursery. He pointed to what looked like a drawer in the wall near the door. "Is that a laundry chute, Miss Sherwood?"

"Yes."

He went over to the wall and opened the chute door, trying to peer down. "Where does this lead to?"

"To the laundry in the basement."

"Who does the laundry here?"

"Mrs. Smith, Mrs. Sadie Smith."

"Sadie Smith." Abe Pearl's heavy brows bunched. "Who's she? There's nobody of that name in the house."

"She's an outside laundress from Norwalk. She comes in twice a week to do the hand laundry and ironing for the better things. The . . . baby's diapers I've been doing myself." Jessie closed her eyes. Friday was one of

Mrs. Smith's days. Tomorrow—today—she would show up, and she would wash and iron those exquisite little garments of Michael's . . .

"Tinny, Borcher." Chief Pearl's two detectives came over. "Take a couple of men and split up. Look for a pillowcase with a lace edging, a case with a dirty handprint on it. Cover the laundry basement, hampers, linen closets, fireplaces, garbage—the likely ones first. If you don't find it, tear the place apart."

People with watery outlines and sounds that mixed and jangled endlessly kept floating in and out of Jessie's awareness. She knew she had to sit there and hold on to herself in this strange world outside time, or horrible things would happen. Through it all she strained to hear little Michael's voice, more than ever convinced by the unsubstantial quality of things that it had all happened in a dream, or a film. Sooner or later there would be a snap, the film would break, and the world would be restored to sanity and rightness.

Occasionally she felt Richard Queen's touch on her shoulder. Once he put his palm to her forehead. His hand felt dry and cool, and Jessie looked up at him. "Please keep it there. It feels good." But he took it away after a moment, embarrassed.

One of the fragments involved Sarah Humffrey and their attempts to question her. Jessie heard the commotion going on in the master bedroom without much interest. The frantic woman kept screaming that it was all her fault, that she had killed her baby, her blessed baby, she deserved to die, she was a monster, a criminal, let her die, oh her poor innocent baby. The men's voices came up and through and around her self-accusing aria in discordant counterpoint, her husband's by turns soothing, mortified, pleading, like a violin twanging the gamut; Dr. Wicks's snappish and brittle—he's the oboe, Jessie thought, pleased with her fancy; the insinuating trombone of Merrick, the Bridgeport man, sliding in and out of the conversation; Chief Pearl's bass horn underscoring the whole crazy fugue. Finally the men came out, the chief and the State's Attorney's man bleak with anger at Dr. Wicks, Alton Humffrey almost female in his distress and irritation.

"She's not a well woman," the millionaire kept exclaiming in a high excited voice, oddly unlike the voice Jessie knew. "You've got to understand that, gentlemen . . . my wife has never been strong emotionally . . . hypersensitive . . . this shocking experience . . ."

Dr. Wicks snapped, "Mrs. Humffrey is in a dangerous state of emotional agitation. As a matter of fact, her distress is so severe that I doubt whether her judgment can be relied on. I'm speaking as her physician, gentlemen. If you insist on keeping this up, you'll have to assume the responsibility."

"I can't allow it, Mr. Pearl," Alton Humffrey said, waving his long arms. "I can't and I won't, do you hear?"

Abe Pearl glanced at Merrick, and Merrick shrugged.

"I know when I'm licked, I guess," the chief growled. "All right, Doctor, put her under"; and Dr. Wicks disappeared.

Jessie heard his voice going in the other room, on and on like a go-to-sleep record for insomnia, and the clash of bedsprings as Sarah Humffrey threw herself about. Finally the sobs and shrieks stopped.

Later Jessie became aware of a shift in focus. They were back at her again. The house had been ransacked from basement to attic, it seemed, and the searchers had failed to turn up a pillowslip such as she had described, a lace-edged case with a dirty handprint on it.

Yes, the nightlight in the nursery had been quite dim. But no, she had not been mistaken. There was enough light to see the handprint by.

No, she didn't wear glasses. Yes, she had 20/20 vision.

No, it couldn't have been a trick of lighting, a conformation of shadows that just looked like a handprint. It *was* a handprint. Of a right hand.

"How do you know it was a *right* hand?"

"Because the thumb part of the print was on the left side."

Someone laughed, a masculine sound halfway between a chuckle and a snort. Jessie found herself not caring at all.

"Either she was seeing things, or it's been burned or cut to pieces and flushed down a toilet."

"What do they have on the Island, septic tanks?"

"No, regular city sewage installations. Emptying into the Sound, like in Taugus."

"Then we'll never know."

"Looks like it."

They were just voices. But the next one had that precious quality of nearness. Strange how every time he made a sound, even an ordinary sound, she felt safer.

"It's the big point, Abe," Richard Queen was saying mildly. "If you don't mind my horning in——"

"Don't be a jackass, Dick."

"It's the difference between murder and accident. I wouldn't give up on that pillowcase if I were you."

"We aren't even sure it exists!"

"Miss Sherwood is."

"Hell, Dick, she could be——"

"I don't think so, Abe."

The voices drifted off and became a mumble. Jessie was tickled. He's defending me, she thought gleefully. How kind of him. No one's ever done that before. Or not for a long, long time. Then she thought: How silly can you get. He knows I'm telling the truth and he's merely sticking to his point.

The joy went out of Jessie's thoughts and she sat blankly, dozing.

The voices swept up suddenly, startling her. Chief Pearl sounded harassed.

"Well, what about the ladder, Dick!"

"It confirms the murder theory."

"It does not. Mr. Humffrey put it there himself. Mr. Humffrey, would you mind telling Inspector Queen how the ladder came to be there?"

The millionaire's exhausted voice said, "I heard a banging sound from the nursery about ten o'clock. A wind had come up from sea and pulled one of the shutters loose outside the driveway window. I was afraid the noise would wake the baby. I removed the screen, tried to secure the shutter from the nursery, and found I couldn't reach it. Stallings and Cullum were out—they have Thursday evenings off—so I had no choice but to get the ladder out of the shed, climb up, and fix it myself. Then the baby did wake up, my wife became very nervous, and by the time we got him back to sleep I'd completely forgotten about the ladder. I can't see that any of this has any relevance."

"Mr. Humffrey's right, Dick. The ladder doesn't mean a thing."

"It certainly doesn't disprove murder, Abe. If this was murder, the killer simply came along and used the ladder he found standing here. And Miss Sherwood is so positive about that pillowslip——"

"Dick, for God's sake, what do you want me to do?"

"Keep looking for the slip till you find it."

"Mr. Humffrey, did you see a pillowslip with a handprint on it?"

"No."

"Did you, Dr. Wicks?"

The doctor's voice said shortly, "I'd have reported it if I had."

"And about the only thing Mrs. Humffrey said that made sense was that she didn't see it, either. And she was in the same room, Dick."

"She was in the doorway," the familiar voice said. "The footboard of the crib might have limited her range of vision. How about the servants, Abe?"

The big man made a disgusted sound. "The gardener and the chauffeur didn't pull in till almost 1 A.M. The women know from nothing."

"Jessie Sherwood against everybody."

And that was her own voice. What a funny thing to have said. Jessie heard herself laugh, a shrill hoppy sort of laugh that wasn't like her laugh at all.

Immediately the noises swooped away, leaving silence.

The next thing she knew was she was lying on something softly embracing, and Dr. Wicks was forcing her to swallow the bitter contents of a spoon.

After that everything stopped.

Inspector Queen was wandering along the water's edge when Cheif Pearl came tramping down to the Humffrey beach. The sky over the sea was all pearl shell and salmon belly as the dawn turned to day.

"I've looked all over for you," the Taugus policeman bellowed. "What the hell are you doing?"

The old man looked up. "Nothing much, Abe. Just checking to see if a boat mightn't have beached here last night."

Abe Pearl stared. "Why a boat?"

"Because he'd have been a fool to try his luck twice at getting past that gatehouse in a car."

"You mean Frost?" the chief said in an odd tone.

"Who else? But there's nothing. Tide's almost all the way in. I should have thought of it when we got here." He glanced at his friend. "All through at the house?"

"Yeah."

They went up through the belt of trees side by side in silence, the big man and the small one, an invisible something between them. As they crossed the perfect lawns Chief Pearl spoke to several of his men, who were still searching the grounds.

"Keep looking till I call you off," he ordered. "Tell the boys in the house ditto."

They got into the black-and white police car, and the big man turned on his ignition.

"Talk to that gatemen, Peterson?" the old man asked.

"The state troopers talked to him. He didn't see anything." Abe Pearl grunted. "Dumb as they come, sure. But on the other hand, Dick, a man can't see what isn't there."

The old men did not reply.

At the gatehouse Chief Pearl crooked his finger at Peterson. Inspector Queen listened quietly.

"All right, Peterson, let's have it all over again," Abe Pearl said.

The guard pushed his fleshy lips forward. "I'll give it to you just once, Chief, then I'm getting the hell off this Island and so help me I'll never come back! The last car that went through this gate last night before the Humffrey kid was found dead, like I told the troopers,

56

was that Dodge coop belongs to the nurse up there, that Miss Sherwood, who came in around 12:30 A.M. Before Miss Sherwood, there was an incoming car about an hour earlier, some of old Mrs. Dandridge's servants coming back from the Taugus movies. Before that, around 11 P.M., the Senator's chauffeur——"

"Did a car drive through at any time since you came on duty, going in or out," the chief interrupted, "that you didn't recognize? Had to check?"

"No."

Richard Queen's voice startled Peterson. "Did anyone walk through?"

"Huh?"

"Somebody on foot? Going either way?"

"Nope."

"But somebody could have come through on foot without your seeing him. Isn't that so?"

"Listen, friend," Peterson snarled, "this gatehouse is a joke. I got to sit down sometimes. I got to step into the bushes once in a while. I got to feed my face. There's a hundred ways a guy can get onto this Island without being seen. Go look for your patsy some place else. I'm taking no fall but for nobody."

"You know, Abe, Peterson's right," the old man murmured as they crossed the causeway. "Nair Island is accessible to anyone who wants to go to a little trouble. A rowboat to one of the private beaches at night . . . a sneak past the gate . . . a young fellow like Ron Frost could even have swum over from one of the Taugus beaches and got back the same way."

His friend glanced at him. "You're dead set that this is murder, Dick, aren't you? And that the Frost kid pulled it?"

"I'm not dead set on anything. It's just that I believe Jessie Sherwood saw something on that pillowslip. *If* it was a handprint she saw, murder is indicated. And *if* it was murder, young Frost is your hottest suspect."

"Not any more he isn't. The report came in while you were nosing around the beach for rowboat tracks. Frost can't possibly have been on Nair Island last night."

"Why not?"

"The baby died on the Island between 10:30 P.M. and around half-past midnight. In that two-hour period Ronald Frost was in Stamford, unconscious."

"Unconscious?"

"He was rushed to Stamford Hospital in an ambulance from a friend's house on Long Ridge Road about 9 P.M. He was operated on for an emergency appendectomy at 10:07 P.M., and he didn't come out of the anesthetic till three o'clock this morning." Abe Pearl grinned as he swung his car into the street of little beach houses. "What do you think of your Nurse Sherwood's pillow-slip yarn now?"

Richard Queen blinked.

His friend pulled up, turned off the motor, and clapped him on the back. "Cheer up, Dick! Do you have to see a murder to make time with the Sherwood number? Take her out like a man!" He sniffed mightily. "I can smell Becky's bacon from here. Come on, Dick—hot breakfast—few hours' shuteye——"

"I'm not hungry, Abe," the old man said. "You go on in. I'll sit here for a while."

He sat there for a long time.

Jessie Sherwood braked up to the barrier and honked impatiently for Monty Burns, the day guard, to come out of the gatehouse and pass her through. It was a week after the tragedy, seven days that had dragged like years. The weekend had brought with it the first hurricane of the season; some Nair Island cellars were flooded, and fifteen-foot breakers had weakened the causeway—it was still under repair.

But it would have taken more than a hurricane to keep Nurse Sherwood on the Island that Thursday. The week had been hellish. A dozen times she had regretted giving in to Alton Humffrey's stiffish request that she stay on to nurse his wife. The big house was too full of the dead baby, and Sarah Humffrey's antics had Jessie's nerves at the shrieking point. But what else could I have done? she thought. That Mrs. Humffrey was on the verge of a nervous breakdown Jessie's professional eye told her quite with the necessity of Dr. Wicks's warnings. *Mea culpa* . . . The inquest and funeral by themselves would have unnerved a healthy woman, let alone a guilt-ridden hysteric.

Her chief recollection of the inquest was of sweaty bodies, goggling eyes, and her own humiliation and anger. They had treated her as if she were some malicious trouble-maker, or a psychopath. By contrast Sarah Humffrey had got off lightly. Alton Humffrey, Jessie thought grimly, had seen to that.

The verdict had been death by inadvertence, an accident. Accident!

And the funeral . . .

The coffin had been white and woefully tiny. They had tried to keep the time and place secret, but of course there had been a leak, and the pushing, craning crowds . . . the shouting reporters . . . that hideous scene in the Taugus cemetery when Sarah Humffrey screamed like an animal and tried to jump into the grave after the little flower-covered coffin . . .

Jessie shuddered and leaned on the horn. Monty Burns came out of the gatehouse, hastily buttoning his tunic.

She got over the workman-cluttered causeway at last, and she was about to kick the gas pedal when a familiar gray-mustached figure stepped out from under a maple tree into the road, holding up his hand and smiling.

"Morning!"

"What are you doing here?" Jessie asked confusedly.

"Remembered it was your day off, and decided to walk off Beck Pearl's breakfast in your direction. I've been waiting for you. Going anywhere in particular?"

"No."

"How about going there together?"

"I'd love it."

He's got something on his mind, Jessie thought as he got in. She drove slowly north, conscious of the intentness under his smile.

Signs of hurricane damage were everywhere. Between Norwalk and Westport the shore road was still under water in places. Jessie had to detour.

"A sailboat would have been more practical!" Jessie

59

said. "What have you been doing with yourself, Inspector Queen?"

"This and that. You know," he said suddenly, "when you let your face relax, Jessie, you get pretty as a picture."

"Do I, now," Jessie laughed. She was laughing! She scaled her black straw behind her and threw her head back. "Isn't this breeze scrumptious?"

"Lovely," he agreed, looking at her.

"It's making a mess of my hair, but I don't care."

"You have beautiful hair, Jessie. I'm glad you keep it long."

"You like it that way?" Jessie said, pleased.

"My mother's hair reached to her knees. Of course, in those days no women bobbed their hair but suffragettes and prostitutes. I guess I'm old-fashioned. I still prefer long hair in a woman."

"I'm glad," Jessie murmured. She was beginning to feel glad about everything today.

"How about lunch? I'm getting hungry."

"So am I!" Jessie cried. "Where shall we go?"

They found an artfully bleached seafood place overlooking an inlet of the Sound. They sat behind glass and watched the spray from the still-agitated water trying to get up at them, hurtling from the pilings and dashing against the big storm window almost in their faces. They dipped steamed clams into hot butter, mounds of them, and did noble archeological work on broiled lobster, and Jessie was happy.

But with the mugs of black coffee he said abruptly, "You know, Jessie, I spent a whole day this week in Stamford. Part of it at the Stamford Hospital."

"Oh," Jessie sighed. "You saw Ronald Frost?"

"Also his hospital admission card, and the doctor who operated on him. Even talked to the people he was visiting when he got the appendix attack. I wanted to check Frost's alibi for myself."

"It stands up, of course."

"Yes. It was a legitimate emergency appendectomy, and from the times involved, Frost couldn't physically have been on Nair Island when the baby died."

"Lucky emergency." Jessie frowned out the window. "For him, I mean."

"Very," Richard Queen said dryly. "Because he *was* the one who made that first attempt on the night of July 4th."

"He admitted it?" Jessie cried.

"Not in so many words—why should he?—but I'm convinced from what he said and how he said it that he was the man that night, all right. God knows what he thought he was trying to do—I don't think he knew, or knows, himself. He was drunk as a lord. Anyway, Jessie, that's that. As far as the murder is concerned, Frost is out."

Jessie picked up her coffee mug, set it down again. "Are you trying to tell me you don't think it was murder after all, Inspector Queen?"

He stirred his coffee carefully. "How about dropping this Inspector Queen stuff, Jessie? If you and I are going to see a lot of each other——"

"I didn't know we were," Jessie murmured. I'll really have to go into the ladies' room and fix my hair, she thought. I must look like the Wild Woman of Borneo. "But of course, if you'd like . . . Richard . . ."

"Make it Dick." He beamed. "That's what my friends call me."

"Oh, but I like Richard ever so much better."

His beam died. "I guess Dick sounds pretty young at that."

"I didn't mean *that*. It has nothing to do with age. Goodness!" Jessie prodded her hair. "And don't change the subject. Was it or wasn't it murder? And don't tell me the coroner's jury called it an accident!"

"Well, look at it from their viewpoint," he said mildly. "Your testimony about that dim nightlight, for instance. Those couple of seconds you'd mentioned as being the maximum period you had the handprint in view, for another. And on top of that, Jessie, your detailed description of the print. You'll have to admit, with the pillowslip not produced, it takes a bit of believing."

Jessie felt tired suddenly.

61

"I could only testify to what I saw. What *happened* to that pillowslip?"

"Probably destroyed. Or disposed of in some way."

"But by whom?"

"By somebody in the house."

"But that's ridiculous!" Jessie was appalled.

"If you start from the existence of the handprint, it's the logical conclusion."

"But who in the Humffrey house would do a thing like that, Richard?"

He shrugged. "Your guess is as good as mine."

Jessie said, "You do believe me, don't you? Somebody has to . . ."

"Of course I believe you, Jessie," he said gently. "And that's where I'm jumping off from."

"What do you mean?"

"I had a talk with Abe Pearl last night. Abe's the salt of the earth, and he was a good big-city cop, but maybe he isn't as good a judge of character as I am." He grinned. "Your character, anyway."

But Jessie did not smile back. "In other words, Chief Pearl has made up his mind not to believe my story, either."

"Abe's not prepared to kick up a fuss about a murder when there's nothing concrete to back it up. And then, of course, the inquest jury did bring in a verdict of accidental death. Put that together with Frost's alibi for last Thursday night, and you see the spot Abe's in."

"What you're trying to tell me," Jessie said bitterly, "is that he's dropping the case."

"Yes." Richard Queen rubbed his jaw. "That's why I informed the Pearls last night that they'd soon be losing their star boarder."

"You're going to leave?" And suddenly the spray on the window made an empty sound, and the lobster began to weigh heavily. "Where are you going?"

"Back to New York."

"Oh." Jessie was silent. "But I thought you said——"

He nodded wryly. "I've been doing a lot of thinking about the case and I've decided New York is the place to start an investigation. Abe can't, the Humffreys won't

—who else is there but me? I have nothing to do with myself, anyway."

Tears sprang into Jessie's eyes. "I'm so glad. So glad, Richard."

"In fact . . ." He was looking at her across the table with the oddest expression. "I was hoping you'd go with me."

"Me?"

"You could help in lots of ways," he said awkwardly. He fumbled with his cup.

Jessie's heart beat faster. Now don't be foolish, she kept saying to herself. He's just being kind. Or . . . after all, what do I really know about him? Maybe . . .

"I think I'd have to know in what ways, Richard," she said slowly. "For one thing, I've promised to stay on at Nair Island for a while to keep an eye on Mrs. Humffrey——"

"Let Humffrey get another nurse."

"No, I gave my word."

"But how long——?"

"Let's talk about it in the car," Jessie said abruptly. "If I'm getting into something, I want to know just what it is. Do you mind?"

He leaned forward suddenly and took her hand. "You're quite a woman, Jessie. Did anyone ever tell you that?"

"And none of your blarney!" Jessie laughed as she withdrew her hand and rose. "I'll meet you in the car."

Richard Queen watched her make her way among the empty tables toward the rest rooms. She walks like a young girl, he thought. A young girl . . .

He signaled the waitress and caught himself staring at his hand.

He pulled it quickly down and out of sight.

In the end, it was Alton Humffrey's wife who made up Jessie's mind. The following Tuesday—it was the 16th of August—Sarah Humffrey slipped out of her bedroom while Jessie was in the kitchen fixing a tray, ran down to the Humffrey beach in her nightgown, waded out into the Sound, and tried to drown herself.

63

She might have succeeded if Henry Cullum had not been on the dock tinkering with the engine of the Humffrey cruiser. The white-haired chauffeur jumped in and pulled the hysterical woman out. She was screaming that she wanted to die.

Dr. Wicks put her under deep sedation and spoke to her husband grimly.

"I'm afraid you're going to have to face it, Mr. Humffrey. Your wife is a damned sick woman, and I'm not the doctor for her. She needs specialized help. This obsession of hers that she killed the baby, these hysterical feelings of guilt about the pillow, now an attempt at suicide—I'm over my depth."

Alton Humffrey seemed all loosened, as if the binder that held him together was crumbling away. Jessie had never seen him so pale and depressed.

"Your wife is on the edge of a mental collapse," Dr. Wicks went on, blotting the freckles on his bald spot. "In her unstable condition, in view of what happened here, this house is the last place in the world she ought to be. If you'll take my advice——"

"What you're trying to tell me, I believe, is that I ought to put Mrs. Humffrey in a sanitarium?"

"Er, yes. I know a very good one up in Massachusetts. In Great Barrington. The psychiatrist in charge has an excellent reputation——"

"And can he keep his mouth shut?" the millionaire said. "This running down into the water business . . . if the newspapers should get wind of it——"

Dr. Wicks's lips flattened. "I wouldn't recommend him otherwise, Mr. Humffrey. I know how you feel about publicity."

"A psychiatrist, you say?"

"One of the soundest."

"I'll have to think about it." And Humffrey rose with an imperious gesture of dismissal.

The physician was red-faced when he came into the adjoining bedroom for a final look at his patient. He snapped some instructions to Jessie and left.

It was Dr. Wicks's last visit to Sarah Humffrey.

On Wednesday afternoon Jessie heard the door open

and looked up from her patient's bedside to see Alton Humffrey crooking a bony forefinger at her.

"Can you leave her for a few minutes, Miss Sherwood?"

"I've just had to give her another hypo."

"Come into my study, please."

She followed him across the hall to the study. He indicated an armchair, and Jessie sat down. He went to the picture window and stood there, his back to her.

"Miss Sherwood, I'm closing this house."

"Oh?" Jessie said.

"I've been considering the move for some time. Stallings will stay on as caretaker. Henry and Mrs. Lenihan will go along with me to the New York apartment. I'm sending Mrs. Charbedeau and the maids back to the Concord house. The best part of the summer is gone, anyway."

"You're intending to spend most of your time in New York?"

"All winter, I should think."

"The change ought to be good for Mrs. Humffrey."

"Mrs. Humffrey is not coming with me." His voice was nasally casual. "I'm sending her to a sanitarium."

"I'm glad," Jessie said. "She needs sanitarium care badly. I heard Dr. Wicks telling you yesterday about a place in Great Barrington——"

"Wicks." The narrow shoulders twitched. "In matters as important as this, Miss Sherwood, one doesn't rely on the Wickses of this world. No, she's not going to Great Barrington."

It's the psychiatry that's scared you off, Jessie thought. "May I ask which sanitarium you've picked out, Mr. Humffrey?" She tried to keep her voice as casual as his.

She thought his long body gathered itself in. But then she decided she had been mistaken. When he turned he was smiling faintly.

"It's a convalescent home, really—that's all nonsense about her need for psychiatric treatment. Mrs. Humffrey is in a highly nervous state, that's all. What she requires is complete rest and privacy in secluded surroundings, and I'm told there's no better place in the East for that than the Duane Sanitarium in New Haven."

Jessie nodded. She knew several nurses who had worked there—one, Elizabeth Currie, had been on Dr. Samuel Duane's nursing staff for eight years. The sanitarium was an elaborate closet for distinguished skeletons, restricted to a rigidly classified clientele at exclusive rates. It was surrounded by a tall brick wall topped with four-foot pickets ending in lance points, and it was patrolled by a private police force.

Exactly the sort of place Alton Humffrey would choose! Jessie thought. Once Sarah Humffrey was safely inside Dr. Duane's luxurious prison, her husband could relax. Dr. Duane's guards could smell a reporter miles away.

"When is Mrs. Humffrey leaving?" Jessie asked.

"This evening. Dr. Duane is calling for her personally in a sanitarium limousine, with a nurse in attendance."

"Has Mrs. Humffrey been told?" At the millionaire's frown, Jessie added hastily, "The reason I ask, Mr. Humffrey, is that I've got to know just how to handle preparing her to go away——"

"I haven't told her, no. Dr. Duane prefers that I break the news when he's present."

"You'll be going out with her?"

"I don't know. That will depend entirely on Duane." His wedge of face lengthened. "You'll keep all this confidential, of course, Miss Sherwood."

"Of course."

He went over to his desk, sat down, and began to write a check. She watched his long white fingers at their deliberate work, the little finger curled in hiding, as secretive as the rest of him.

"I suppose this means," Jessie said, "that you want me to leave as soon as possible."

"Oh, nothing like that. You're entirely welcome to stay on for a few days. The staff isn't leaving until next week some time."

"I'm a restless sort, Mr. Humffrey. It's kind of you, but I think I'll go tomorrow morning."

66

"As you wish."

He blotted the check carefully and reached over to lay it on the desk near her.

"Oh, but Mr. Humffrey," Jessie protested. "This is far too much. You're paid up through last week——"

"I see no reason why you should be penalized by my sudden decision about Mrs. Humffrey," he said, smiling. "So I've paid you for a full week, and I've added a little something in appreciation of all you've done for Mrs. Humffrey and Michael."

"A little something." Jessie shook her head. The bonus was five hundred dollars. "You're awfully kind, Mr. Humffrey, but I really can't accept this."

"Heavens, Miss Sherwood. Why not?" He seemed genuinely surprised.

"Well . . ." Her hands felt clammy. But she looked straight at him. "Frankly, Mr. Humffrey, I'd rather not be under obligation to you."

"I don't understand." Now his tone was icy.

"If I felt differently about little Michael, I could take this. As it is, I'd rather not."

He made it easy for her. "You mean if you felt differently about the cause of his death?"

"Yes, Mr. Humffrey."

The four whole fingers drummed on the desk, their maimed companion curled tightly. Then he leaned back in his leather chair.

"You still don't agree it was an accident, Miss Sherwood."

"It was murder," Jessie said. "That baby was deliberately and wickedly smothered to death with the pillow in the pillowcase that's disappeared."

"But no pillowcase has disappeared."

"Oh, yes, it has. They just haven't found it."

"My dear Miss Sherwood." His tone was patient. "The coroner's jury are satisfied it was an accident. So are the police. So am I. How can you set yourself up as the sole dissenting judge?"

"I saw the pillow with the handprint, Mr. Humffrey," Jessie said quietly. "No one else did."

"Obviously you were mistaken."

"I was not mistaken."

"There's not a scintilla of evidence—I believe that's the approved phrase—to back your opinion up."

"It's not an opinion, Mr. Humffrey. It's a fact. I know what I saw."

"Show me one competent person who agrees with you——"

"Richard Queen."

Humffrey arched his sparse brows. "Who?"

"Chief Pearl's friend. He used to be an inspector in the New York police department. He believes me."

The millionaire shrugged. "These old fellows have nothing to do but poke their noses into other people's affairs. He was probably retired for senility."

"He's only sixty-three, and he's in complete possession of his faculties, I assure you!" Jessie bit her lip; Humffrey was regarding her with amusement. "Anyway, Inspector Queen agrees with me it was murder, and we're going to——"

Jessie stopped.

"Yes?" Alton Humffrey no longer looked amused. "You and this man are going to what, Miss Sherwood?"

"Nothing." Jessie jumped up nervously. "I'll have to be getting back to Mrs. Humffrey——"

"Miss Sherwood." He had his hands flat on the desk. For a moment Jessie had the queerest feeling that he was going to spring at her. She remembered having had the same feeling about him once before. "Do you suppose for an instant that if I thought the child was murdered I'd let the case drop?"

"I'm sure I can't answer that, Mr. Humffrey." She was actually backing away. When she realized it, she stopped herself. "Please, I must go to Mrs. Humffrey. But I do wish you'd tear up this check and make out another simply for the amount you owe me."

But his eyes kept bulging and burning. "Don't you know what that baby meant to me, Miss Sherwood?"

"I'm sure he meant everything to you," Jessie said desperately. "But . . . you force me to say this . . . now that little Michael's dead you want the whole thing buried, along with his remains. You'd rather see the case written off as an accidental death than involve your family name in a murder case. I don't understand people like you, Mr. Humffrey. There are some things in this world a lot worse than getting your name bandied about by the common people. Letting a baby killer get off scot free is one of them."

"Are you finished?" Alton Humffrey said.

"Yes," Jessie whispered.

"No, wait, Miss Sherwood. Before you go."

Jessie turned at the door, praying for escape.

"You know my wife's condition." The nasal tones dripped venom. "I don't know what it is you and this man Queen are up to, but if through any act of yours my wife gets worse or my name is exposed to further public humiliation, you will account to me. To *me*. Do you understand?"

"Perfectly." Jessie's throat was dry. "May I go now, Mr. Humffrey?"

"By all means."

She fled those unwinking pop-eyes, fixed on her like something in a museum.

Ten minutes later Jessie was on the phone, crying. "Richard, please ask Mrs. Pearl if I can come over tonight. I don't care where I stay. I'll sleep in my car or bed down on the floor. Anywhere! But I won't stay in this house another night."

Inspector Queen was waiting for her on the other side of the causeway in Beck Pearl's Plymouth. He got out, waving wildly, as Jessie pulled up.

"Jessie! You all right?"

"Oh, Richard, I'm so glad to see you."

"But what happened?"

"Nothing, really. Mr. Humffrey's sent his wife to a sanitarium and discharged me, and I'm afraid I let on that you and I weren't going to let the case drop, and he sort of threatened me——"

"He did, did he?" the old man said grimly.

"I don't know what you're thinking of me. I've never

69

acted this way before in my life. Mrs. Pearl must be having visions of some hysterical female throwing fits all over her rug——"

"You don't know Beck Pearl."

"I'd go back home—I have a little house in Rowayton—but I rented it to some summer people till after Labor Day. I'm so ashamed, Richard. I'll go to a motel or some place for the night——"

"Becky says if I don't bring you right over I don't have to come back myself. You follow me, Jessie!" . . .

In the plain sanity of the Pearls' little beach cottage Jessie felt safe for the first time in weeks. Mrs. Pearl looked into her eyes and smiled approvingly at Richard Queen, and Chief Pearl blundered about making her feel as if she were an honored guest.

"You're not really an ogre after all, Mr. Pearl," Jessie told him. "Do you know I was afraid of you?"

The big man glanced guiltily at his wife.

"Did he bully you?" Beck Pearl looked at her husband.

"I'll get your bag out of your car, Miss Sherwood." Abe Pearl went out hurriedly.

"Put it up in Richard's room, Abe!"

"Mrs. Pearl, I won't hear of it——"

"You'll have Richard's room, Abe and Richard will sleep in our room, and I'll take the daybed down here. It's the most comfortable bed in the house."

"Oh, no——"

"That's the way it's going to be," Mrs. Pearl said firmly. "Now I'm going to fix you and Richard some supper. Then Abe and I are going to the movies . . ."

When the Pearls were gone, Jessie said softly, "You're lucky to have such friends, Richard."

"You like them."

"They're absolute darlings."

"I'm glad," he said simply. "Now you tackle this casserole, or Becky will feel terrible. Abe says she can do more things with clams than a Siwash Indian."

Afterward, Jessie washed the dishes in Beck Pearl's tiny kitchen and Richard Queen dried them and put them away, while he told her about his summer with the

Pearls and never once referred to what had brought her flying to him. Jessie listened mistily. I mustn't feel so happy about this, she kept thinking. I'll just build myself up to another letdown, the way I did with Clem . . . It was hard to keep from comparing them, hard and unfair. It had been so many years ago. Clem had been so much younger—tall and self-sufficient, with quick surgeon's fingers and his eyes always tired-looking. Thinking about him even now, when he had been dead such a long time, Jessie felt her pulse quicken . . . This, this was so different. Working over a kitchen sink and drainboard side by side. She couldn't visualize herself doing that with Clem. Clem had meant excitement, a life of high spots and crises, and long stretches of loneliness. This quiet man, with his fine-boned face and gray brush of mustache, his reserve of strength and knowledge about ordinary people—it was hard to think of anything they couldn't do together, the everyday little things that made up a life. And she could be very proud of him, she knew that instinctively. Proud and complete . . . I *mustn't* let myself run on this way! Jessie thought despairingly.

"You're tired," Richard Queen said, looking at her. "I think, Jessie, I'm going to send you to bed."

"Oh, no," Jessie cried. "I'm enjoying this so much. I want to tell you everything that's happened in the past few days, Richard. Please."

"All right. But just for a few minutes. Then up you go."

He put the dish towel over the towel bar to dry, and they went into the little living room. He sat her down in the most comfortable chair, lit her cigaret for her, and listened noncommittally while she told him about Sarah Humffrey's suicide attempt and the substance of her conversation with Alton Humffrey. He made no comment beyond, "He's a queer duck, all right," and then he said, "Time's up, Miss Sherwood."

"But aren't we going to talk about your plans?"

"Not tonight."

"Then how about mine?"

He laughed. "I've made six-foot police sergeants

shake in my time, but I guess I'll never learn how to handle a woman. All right, Jessie, shoot."

"I'm coming with you."

"I know that."

"You don't!" Jessie said, piqued.

"I'm not flattered," he said dryly. "I didn't do it. It's Alton Humffrey who's made up your mind."

"Well, it's true I don't like to be threatened," Jessie said, pinching her skirt down, "but that's not the only reason."

"The baby."

"*And* other reasons."

The old man looked at her searchingly. "It might not be a picnic, Jessie." He got up suddenly and began to walk about. "In fact, I'm wondering if I haven't let you in for something risky out of plain selfishness. This is a very peculiar case. *Why* was the baby murdered? While Frost was a suspect, with his inheritance motive, it made some sort of crazy sense. With Frost eliminated, the Humffrey fortune doesn't seem to be involved. So the motive must lie in a different direction. Do you see a lead, Jessie?"

"I've thought about it, too," Jessie said quietly. "The only thing I can think of is that it must be connected with Michael's adoption."

"Ah," the Inspector said, and he sat down again, eagerly. "You saw that. Where does it take you, Jessie?"

"It may have something to do with the real parents. You know, Richard, neither side knows who the other side is. The whole adoption was handled by a lawyer acting for *both* sides."

He nodded. "A lawyer named A. Burt Finner. That was his name, wasn't it?"

"Yes. Do you know him?"

"I know of him. He's a clever shyster who specializes in black-marketing babies for people who either can't swing a legitimate adoption or for some reason would rather handle it under the counter. If Humffrey's had dealings with him, it's probably because Finner guarantees no trouble and no publicity. The important thing,

Jessie, is that Finner knows the real parentage of that baby. So that's where we start."

"With Finner?"

"With Finner."

"But if the real parents don't know who got Michael——"

"One step at a time," Richard Queen said. "We'll go into the city in the morning. Meanwhile, you're going to bed."

He got up and took her hand.

Jessie giggled. "You make me feel like a little girl. Don't I have any say about things like where I'm going to stay?"

"Not a word," he said firmly. "You're staying at my apartment in town."

"*Inspector* Queen," Jessie murmured. "I'm going to do no such thing."

Even his neck reddened. "I mean I'll go to the Y or some place. Ellery isn't due back from abroad for a long time yet——"

"Silly. I'm hardly at the age when I'm worried about my reputation." Jessie giggled again, enjoying his embarrassment. "But I wouldn't dream of putting you out of your own home."

"I'd come up every morning and have breakfast with you——"

"No, Richard," Jessie said softly. "I have loads of friends in New York, nurses who live alone in little apartments and don't particularly like it. But . . . thank you. So much."

He looked so forlorn that Jessie impulsively squeezed his hand. Then she ran upstairs.

For some reason he felt very good suddenly. He walked about the cottage with long strides, smiling at his thoughts and occasionally glancing at the ceiling, until the Pearls came home.

Jessie spent nearly an hour Thursday morning on the telephone, running up New York City toll calls.

"I'm in luck," she told Richard Queen. "Belle Berman, she's a supervisor I know, wants me to move right in with her. And Gloria Sardella, a nurse I took my training with, is leaving tomorrow on her vacation. She's going on a six-week cruise, and she's offered me her apartment."

"Where are the two places?"

"Belle's down in the Village—West 11th Street. Gloria's place is on 71st Street off Broadway, in a remodeled walkup."

"The Sardella apartment," he said promptly.

"That's my thought, because I'll get Gloria to sublet it to me for whatever her rent is, whereas Belle wouldn't hear of my sharing expenses." Jessie looked at him. "What's your reason, Richard?"

"Geography," he said sheepishly. "I'm on West 87th. We'd be less than a mile apart."

"You want to watch this man, Jessie," Beck Pearl said. "He's a regular wolf."

"Don't I know it!"

He mumbled something about having to pack, and beat a retreat.

Jessie phoned her friend again to arrange for her stay in the West 71st Street apartment, paid for the calls over Mrs. Pearl's protests, and at last they were off in Jessie's car, Beck Pearl waving from her doorway like a happy relative.

"She's such a lamb," Jessie said, turning into the Taugus road that led to the Merritt Parkway. "And so is Abe Pearl. Do you know what he said to me this morning before he left?"

"What?"

"He said you were a changed man since—well, since the Fourth of July. He seemed tickled to death, Richard. The Pearls have been very worried about you."

He seemed flustered and pleased. "A man needs an interest in life."

"Yes. This case——"

"Who's talking about the case?"

"You know, I do believe you are a wolf!"

They chattered happily all the way into New York.

74

Jessie had decided to take her coupé into the city because Richard Queen had no car, and his son's car was in summer storage. "What good is an assistant without a car?" she had said. "It isn't as if you still had a police driver at your disposal, Richard. My jalopy may come in handy."

"All right, if you'll let me pay the garage bills."

"Richard Queen. Nobody pays my bills but me!"

They stopped at the old brownstone on West 87th Street to drop his bags. Jessie got one whiff of the Queen apartment and threw the windows wide. She aired the beds, inspected the kitchen with horror, and began opening closets.

"What are you looking for?" he asked feebly.

"Fresh linen, a vacuum cleaner. You have to sleep here tonight! Who takes care of your apartment, anyway?"

"A Mrs. Fabrikant. She's supposed to have come in once a week——"

"She hasn't stuck her nose in this place for two months. You go on—make your phone calls, or whatever you have to do. I'll make your bed and straighten up a bit. First chance I get I'll do a thorough housecleaning. Imagine your son coming home to this!"

He retreated to Ellery's study with a warm feeling. He did not even think about the blank space on his bedroom wall, where his direct line to Headquarters used to be.

When he went back to the bedroom he found Jessie moaning. "It's hopeless. Take *hours* to do just this room properly."

"Why, it looks as clean as a hospital room," he exclaimed. "How'd you do it so fast?"

"Well, you'll be able to sleep here without getting cholera, but that's about all," Jessie grumbled. "Fast? A nurse does everything fast. Did you get that man Finner?"

"Finally, after about a dozen calls. He'll be in all afternoon, he said. I didn't fix a time, Jessie, because I don't know how long you'll take getting settled."

75

"Forget about me. I can't get into Gloria's place until 4:30 or a quarter of five, anyway. She's on an eight-to-four case."

"But she's going away tomorrow!" he said, astonished.

"Nurses don't live like people. Let me wash some of this grime off, and I'll be right with you to tackle Mr. Finner."

"You're going to tackle some lunch at the Biltmore first. *With* cocktails."

"Oh, wonderful. I'm hungry as a wolf."

"I thought I was the wolf," he said gaily.

"There are she-wolves, aren't there?"

He found himself whistling like a boy to the homey sound of splashing from the bathroom.

The building was on East 49th Street, an old-timer six stories high with a clanky self-service elevator. His name was on the directory in the narrow lobby: *Finner, A. Burt 622.*

"Jessie, let me do most of the talking."

"As if I'd know what to say!" Then Jessie thought of something. "I wonder, Richard . . ."

"What about?" he asked quickly.

"When we drove out to that rendezvous near Pelham the morning we picked up the baby, Finner drove right up behind where we were parked. I'd gone along to take charge of the baby. Finner may recognize me."

"Not likely, but I'm glad you remembered to tell me." He looked thoughtful. "All right, we'll use it just on the chance. And, Jessie."

"Yes?" Her heart was beginning to thump.

"It's going to cut some corners for us if Finner thinks I'm still with the Department. Don't act surprised if I make like a police officer."

"Yes, sir," Jessie said meekly.

Six-twenty-two was on the top floor at the other end of the corridor from the elevator. The corridor had dirty tan walls, and there was a smell of old floor polish and must.

The old man smiled at her, then suddenly opened the door.

A. Burt Finner half rose behind the desk in the small office, scowling.

"Come in, Miss Sherwood," Richard Queen snapped. "It's all right, he won't bite you. He's an old dog at this game, aren't you, Finner?"

Jessie stepped into the office gingerly. She did not have to act scared. She was.

The fat man crashed back in his swivel chair. As far as Jessie could recall, he was wearing the same wrinkled blue suit and sweaty white shirt he had driven up in that morning near Pelham. The dingy office was stale with his odor. There was nothing in the room but a burn-scarred metal desk, a sad-looking imitation leather chair, a costumer leaning to one side with a dirty felt hat hanging from it, an old four-unit filing cabinet with a lock, and the swivel chair creaking under Finner's weight. No rug, nothing on the walls but a large calendar put out by a baby foods company showing a healthy-looking infant in a diaper. The blind on the single window was limp and streaked. The walls were the same grubby tan shade as the corridor, only dirtier.

Richard Queen shut the door, took Jessie by the arm, and steered her over to the unoccupied chair.

"Have a seat, miss," he said. He looked coldly at the fat man. "Now."

"Wait a minute." A. Burt Finner's little pale-blue eyes went from Jessie to the old man and back to Jessie. He seemed puzzled. My face looks familiar to him, Jessie thought, but he can't place it. She wondered why she was so nervous. He was just a fat man, not at all danger-ous-looking. Maybe it's his professional relations with women, she thought. He doesn't leer; he's seen it all. "What is this? Who are you people?"

"I phoned you two-three hours ago," the old man said. "Remember the $64,000 word I dropped, Finner?"

"What word?"

"Humffrey."

The moon face widened. "Oh, yes. And I told you I didn't know what you were talking about."

"But to drop in, anyway, you'd be here all afternoon." Richard Queen stared at him with contempt. "Well, here we are, Finner. You're up to your fat face in real jam this time, aren't you?"

"Who are you?" Finner asked slowly.

"The name is Queen." He brought out a small flat leather case and flipped it open. A gold shield glittered for a moment in the sunshine struggling through the dusty window.

Finner blinked.

The old man put the case back in his pocket.

"Inspector's shield," Finner said. "Well, well, this is a real pleasure, Inspector. And this lady is——?"

The pale eyes turned on Jessie again. Jessie tried not to fumble with her skirt.

"Don't you recognize her, Finner?"

"No." The fat man was worried. He immediately broke into a smile. "Should I, Inspector?"

"I'd say so," Inspector Queen remarked dryly, "seeing that she's the baby nurse who was in the Humffrey car that day."

"What car, what day, what baby?" Finner asked amiably. "And that about somebody named Humffrey. I don't know anybody named Humffrey."

"Counselor, you and I will get along a lot chummier if you cut out the mullarkey and start recollecting your sins. Miss Sherwood, is this the man you saw pull up behind the Humffrey limousine on a deserted back road near Pelham on Friday morning, June 3rd, behind the wheel of a Chevvy and hand over to Mr. Alton K. Humffrey of Nair Island, Connecticut, a blue blanket wrapped around a week-old baby?"

"That's the man, Inspector Queen!" Jessie said shakily. She wondered if she ought to point at the fat lawyer, the way they did in movie courtrooms, but she decided against it.

"The lady is mistaken." Finner beamed, and cleared his throat. "She never saw me in any such place at any such time doing any such thing."

"How can you lie like that?" Jessie cried indignantly.

78

"I saw you with my own two eyes, and you're not exactly an ordinary-looking man!"

"I've built a whole career, miss," the fat man remarked, "on being just that. However, my memory could be failing. Got anything else to give it a jab, Inspector? Like, say, a corroborating witness?"

"Three, Finner," Inspector Queen said, as if he were enjoying himself. "Mr. and Mrs. Humffrey are two, and their chauffeur—white-haired party with rosy cheeks—he's the third."

"The chauffeur driving the Humffrey car that morning, you mean?" Finner said reflectively.

"That's right."

"But how do you know he'd corroborate this lady's identification, Inspector? I don't see him here."

"Well, we can soon find out. Mind if I use your phone?"

Finner said, "Skip it." He sucked his rubbery lower lip, frowning, then swiveled to clasp his hands behind his overlapping folds of neck and stare out the window. "Supposing I was weak-skulled enough to admit having been there that day," he asked the window, "then what, Inspector?"

Jessie glanced at Richard Queen. But he shook his head.

"You mean, Finner, what do I have?"

"Put it any way you want."

"Well, it's like this. You work deals with an angle. You specialize in unmarried mothers. You shop around for a buyer, you arrange for the girl to give birth in a hospital under a false name, with a phony background, you pay the girl—with the buyer's money—and you take possession of the baby when the mother is discharged from the hospital. Then you turn the baby over to your buyer, collect the balance of your fee, probably furnish a forged birth certificate, and you're ready for the next client. It's a sweet racket, Finner, and the sweetest part of it is that everybody involved has a vested interest in protecting you. You see, I've been looking you up."

"I haven't heard a thing," Finner said, still to the window, "and I'm listening with both pink ears."

"I'm not passing judgment on the dirty way you earn those fins you scatter around the night spots, Finner," Richard Queen said. "Some day the boys are going to prove it on you. But if it's the black-market baby rap you're worrying about, right now I'm not interested in you at all. I'm after other game."

"What do you mean?" Finner spun about so suddenly the spring under his chair squealed.

"You're going to tell me who the Humffrey baby's real parents are."

Finner stared at him. "Are you kidding?"

"Tell me, Finner," the old man said.

Jessie held her breath.

The fat man laughed. "Even supposing this junkie jive you been popping around the premises were the McCoy, Inspector—and I'm not admitting a goddam thing—why should I tell? An operator in a racket like that—I'm told—works on a confidential basis. Run off at the tonsils and you're out of business. You know that."

"I know you're in this up to your top chin, Finner," Richard Queen smiled. "Of course you know the baby's dead."

"Dead, uh?" Finner squinted along the top of his desk and hunched down to blow some dust off. With fascination, Jessie watched his fat lips working. "Seem to recall reading about some baby named Humffrey up in Connecticut being found suffocated in his crib. Was that the same baby you're trying to hook me up to, Inspector?"

"That's the one."

"Tough. I got a soft spot for kids. Got three of my own. But so what? It was an accident, wasn't it?"

"It was a murder, Finner."

Finner's bulk came up like a whale surfacing. "The hell you say. I read the papers, too. Coroner's jury brought in a verdict of accidental death. The case is closed. What you trying to pull on me, Inspector?"

"It was a murder, Finner."

Finner swallowed. He picked up a steel letter-knife

from his desk, made as if to clean his fingernails, put the knife down again.

"New evidence?"

Richard Queen said nothing. He merely kept looking at the fat man's fat hands.

Finner's hands vanished below the level of the desk. "Look, Inspector," he said rapidly. "You got me on something of a spot here. Without incriminating myself in any degree, you understand, maybe I can get some information for you. About the kid's real parents, I mean. One of my contacts might . . ."

"I don't care what you call yourself, Counselor. I want those names."

"Tell you what. What's today?—Thursday. Maybe I can do even better for you, Inspector. I'm not promising, see, but maybe."

"Maybe what?"

"Maybe my contact can get them right here in my office for you."

The old man's lips drew back. "That would be just dandy, Finner. When?"

"Say this Saturday. That's the 20th. Four P.M. okay with you?"

"When the building's empty, eh? Nothing like a deserted office building for a little get-together, I always say."

"With me murder is strictly sucker." Finner was breathing noisily. "If I pull this off for you, Inspector, no cross-up? I got your word?"

"No deals, Finner. But co-operation never hurt anybody." Richard Queen looked down at Jessie Sherwood. "That's it, Miss Sherwood. Thanks for the make."

"The make?" Jessie said, bewildered.

"The identification." He poked her to her feet. "You come through for me Saturday afternoon, Finner."

Finner nodded sadly.

Jessie phoned Richard Queen Friday morning from Gloria Sardella's apartment to say that she would be busy all day getting her friend off on the cruise and herself settled. When he pressed her to meet him for dinner

Jessie hesitated, then asked him to phone her later in the day. He called promptly at five o'clock and she said she was so fagged she would be poor company. She was going to make a sandwich and go to bed. Did he mind very much?

"Seems to me I haven't seen you for years," he complained.

Jessie laughed uncertainly.

"It's been a long day, and it's going to be a longer evening," he said. "At least let me take you to breakfast tomorrow morning."

"Make it lunch," Jessie said, "and it's a date . . . I admit I'm a little nervous about tomorrow, Richard. Maybe having to shake the hand that pressed the pillow over Michael's little face . . ."

"Not much chance of that."

"What do you mean? Finner said——"

"I know what Finner said," he retorted. "That guff about getting them down to his office Saturday was a stall. Finner wants time to put the screws on them, see what information he can squeeze out of them."

"But if he doesn't produce them tomorrow——"

"He'll either produce them or he'll produce their names. In the end, A. Burt Finner will protect A. Burt Finner. What time tomorrow, Jessie?"

"Make it one-ish."

"That late?" He sounded dismayed.

"Why, your appointment isn't until four o'clock. How many hours do you usually take for lunch?"

He hung up, feeling deserted. He had spent most of the day down at Centre Street, wandering into the Squad Room, leafing through recent copies of *General Orders* to see who had been cited, commended, promoted—gabbing with old cronies in the Central Office bureaus and squads in the Annex at the corner of Broome Street. They had been glad to see him, but he had come away miserable. Friday was the working officer's busiest day of the week, and he had had the sickening feeling that he was in the way.

The Queen apartment was no sanctuary. It seemed to him dull and empty.

What did men on the shelf *do* with their days and nights? the old man wondered. How many newspapers could you read? How many movies could you see? How many hours could you spend on a Central Park bench watching cooing humans and pigeons? How long could you hang around men you'd worked with who were still active, before you got into their hair and they began to show it?

Richard Queen went to bed Friday night at a quarter past nine, wishing fiercely it was four o'clock Saturday afternoon.

He muttered: "Now I don't know what I'm going to run into. You remember what I told you."

"But *why* can't I go in with you, Richard?" Jessie whispered.

"We're tangling with a lot of unknowns. The chances are Finner's in there all alone, but a detective's life is full of surprises."

"I'm some assistant," she said disconsolately.

"You listen to me, Jessie. I'll go in and you'll wait here at the end of the hall. Keep the cage slide open so the elevator can't get away from you, just in case. If I think it's all right, I'll signal you from the doorway. Otherwise stay out of sight. If you hear anything that sounds like trouble, get out quick."

"You just watch me!"

"You hear me, Jessie?"

"You'd better go."

"You won't forget?" He looked up the corridor. "If you got hurt, Jessie, I'd never forgive myself."

"Funny," Jessie said with a shaky laugh. "I was just thinking the same thing."

He stared at her. Then he grinned, pressed her hand, and walked quickly up the hall.

She saw him stop before 622, put his ear to the door. After a moment he straightened and knocked. He immediately tried the door. It gave, and he went in.

The door did not close at once.

But then, suddenly, it did.

The office building made a pocket of silence in the noisy world.

The door stayed closed.

Now don't be a goop, Jessie told herself. This is the kind of thing he's done all his life. He couldn't have become a veteran police officer without learning how to handle violence. Anyway, there's nothing to be afraid of. The fat man is certainly harmless; he'd run like a rabbit rather than risk his skin. The other . . . the others, whoever they are . . . they're probably more scared right now than I am.

But her heart kept galloping.

He'd been so awkwardly high-spirited when he called for her at Gloria's, and over lunch. Like a boy on a heavy date. And looking so spruce. He'd pressed his suit and his tan-and-white shoes gleamed. And he'd shown up with a corsage of mignonette for her.

"The florist thought I was crazy," he had said, embarrassed. "Seems nobody buys mignonette for corsages any more. But I remember how my wife used to love it . . ."

She had not had the heart to tell him that the greenish mignonette was just the wrong thing for the green linen suit she was wearing. Or that a woman wasn't necessarily thrilled by being given flowers loved by a dead wife, even one dead thirty years. She had exclaimed over the corsage while pinning it on, and then she had gone into Gloria's bedroom and changed her hat, with which the mignonette clashed, too.

The trouble is, Jessie thought, it isn't really me. It's just that he's rediscovered the world of women.

In the solitude of Gloria Sardella's two disordered rooms yesterday, the dismal thought had come to her like a headache. Any woman could have done it. Any woman could still do it. Any other woman . . .

What was going on in there?

Jessie strained, but she could hear nothing except the tumult of the 49th Street traffic.

She had spent a miserable day and night examining herself. How could she have maneuvered herself into a sublet apartment in New York . . . New York, which

84

she loathed! . . . into an adventure with a man she hardly knew? And that call from Belle Berman— "What's this I hear about you and some *man,* Jessie?" Gloria, of course, who had met him Thursday after the visit to Finner's office. And Gloria's probing afterward . . . Endlessly Jessie had debated phoning him to say it was all a mistake, they were both too old for this sort of thing, let's part good friends and I'll go back to my bedpans and catheters and you to sunning yourself on a beach . . .

Oh, I oughtn't to be here! Jessie told herself. I ought to be coming onto a maternity case, checking the chart, being oh so cheery to Mrs. Jones, wondering if my feet will hold out till the midnight relief while she yakketyyaks about her nine hours of labor and how she'll make that husband of hers pay through the nose for what she's been through . . .

He was in the hall.

Jessie started. She hadn't even heard the door of 622 open.

He was standing in the hall and he was beckoning to her.

Jessie hurried to him.

He was all tightened up, careful. His eyes had a tight careful look, too. He had the door open no more than an inch, his hand on the knob holding it that way.

"Yes, Richard?" Jessie whispered breathlessly. "It's all right for me to go in?"

"That depends on *you,* Jessie." Even his voice was on the alert. "On how much you can take."

"What? Isn't Finner in there?"

"He's in there, all right. He's dead."

3.

AND THEN
THE LOVER

THE fat man looked different dead. He looked like a jumbo balloon with the air leaking out. He was wedged in the swivel chair, head flopped over, flippers dangling. The chair was half turned from the desk, as if he had been struggling to get up. His whole left side was soaked with blood.

The metal handle of a knife stuck out of his chest. Jessie recognized it as the handle of the steel letter-knife she had seen on his desk Thursday.

"Stay where you are, Jessie," Inspector Queen said. He had shut the door. "And hold your purse with both hands. That'll keep them out of trouble. You don't have to look at him."

"I've seen a homicide case or two in my time," Jessie said. She was holding on to her purse for dear life.

"Good girl."

He went around the desk, looked under it, rose, looked out the window.

"It's a cinch nobody saw anything." The vista from the window was a tall blank wall, the rear of a photo-electric plant on the next street.

86

"Key-ring on the floor behind the desk. Torn from loop on his pants. Key still in the lock of the filing cabinet. Somebody was in a hurry, Jessie. But careful, careful."

"Maybe we ought to——"

"Don't move from that spot."

Forty-eight hours ago that fat man had been sitting in that same chair, wearing the same suit and a shirt just as gray with damp, and now it was half-dyed with his heart's blood and he looked like nothing so much as a Macy's Thanksgiving Day balloon with the paint running and a knife stuck in it. So there would be no more under-the-counter arrangements for babies, and the unmarried mothers would have to seek elsewhere. And how many satisfied customers would read about the fat man and look at their wives or husbands and clutch their purchases tight? And would Mrs. A. Burt Finner erect a headstone saying HUSBAND AND FATHER and weep for the vanished provider? And how many nightclub girls would shed a blackened tear over the baby-made five-dollar bills that would invade their nylons no more?

Jessie stifled an impulse to laugh.

The Inspector wrapped a handkerchief around his right hand and went to the swivel chair again and leaned over Finner. When he drew up straight there was a wallet in his swathed hand. He flicked it open.

"Crammed with bills, Jessie."

He put the wallet back as carefully as he had taken it out.

"Not robbery," Jessie's voice was as tight as his had been.

"No."

He looked over the top of the desk. There was an afternoon newspaper folded back to the sports section, a well-pen, a telephone with a memorandum pad clipped to it, a pack of filter cigarets almost empty, a pocket lighter, and a cheap glass ash tray with chipped corners. The ash tray was filled with half-smoked butts and ashes. The old man squatted to desk level and squinted along the surface of the memo pad. Then he turned some of the butts in the tray over with one fingernail.

"Nothing written on a torn-off sheet of pad. No lipstick on any of the butts. And the basket under the desk is empty except for an empty cigaret pack, same brand as this one. All Finner's. This was a cool operator, Jessie. Clue-conscious."

"How about the desk drawers?" Jessie wet her lips.

He grinned. "I'll leave those to Homicide. Finner wouldn't have kept anything in this desk. No locks on the drawers." He glanced at her. "Just at a guess, Jessie —seeing that you're in the respectable branch of this business—how long would you say he's been dead?"

"That's very hard to say."

"Say it anyway."

"It's a hot day. The window is shut . . . At the least, I'd have to touch him."

"Without touching him."

"I've handled dead bodies, Richard. I'll do it."

"Without touching him."

"Not long." Jessie considered. "From the appearance of the blood maybe an hour. I don't know. I could be way off."

He placed the back of his left hand lightly against the dead man's cheek, nodded. Then he went over to the filing cabinet and tugged at the handle of the top drawer. The drawer slid out with a rasp that made Jessie's teeth ache.

The drawer contained file envelopes with identifying plastic tab holders containing white slips of cardboard on which names had been hand-printed in red ink. The first envelope in the drawer was marked ABRAMSON, the last DUFFY. He shut the top drawer and opened the drawer below it. The file envelopes were separated slightly about two-thirds of the way in. The tab on the exposed envelope said HYAMS. The tab on the envelope immediately preceding it said HUGHES.

There was no envelope in between.

"No Humffrey," Richard Queen said softly.

"Maybe the names on the tabs are of the mother," Jessie mumbled. "Not the adopter."

He looked at her. "You're a smart woman, Jessie."

He checked a file at random, using his swathed hand. "However, you're wrong. The names are of the adopters."

He replaced the file and ran his eye over all the tabs on the envelopes. He shut the drawer and checked the tabs of the third drawer, then of the bottom one.

He shut the bottom drawer and rose.

"No doubt about it, Jessie. Finner's kill is tied in with the Connecticut case. Finner used our Thursday visit to try to screw some inside information about Michael's death out of one or both of he real parents. So they've shut his mouth about the parentage and walked off with the whole file on the case. Finner probably was the only outsider who knew at least who the mother was, the hospital Michael was born in, and every other fact that might have led to an identification."

"The same one who murdered the baby," Jessie said slowly. "That means we're on the right track."

"We're stranded on a siding in Podunk," Richard Queen said grimly. "With the contents of that envelope destroyed we're at another dead end. The question is, where do we go from here?"

He gave A. Burt Finner a glum look. But Finner wasn't talking.

"I think, Jessie——"

The telephone rang.

Jessie's heart landed in her mouth with a bump.

He moved nearer the desk, eying the telephone thoughtfully.

"You're not going to answer it?" Jessie said in terror. "Richard, for heaven's sake!"

"Shh."

His right hand was still bound round with the handkerchief. He used it to lift the phone from its cradle.

He said hoarsely, "Yes?" in a fair approximation of Finner's voice.

Jessie shut her eyes. She heard a phone operator's unmistakable cadence. The old man said, "Yes?" again in the same hoarse voice and the operator said something back and then there was silence.

"New Haven calling," he told her.

"New Haven?" Jessie opened her eyes wide.

"Always play a hunch. This may foul me up with my old friends, but I'm here and they aren't.—Yes?"

The man's voice was clipped, successful-sounding. "This is Dr. Samuel Duane calling. Is Mr. Alton K. Humffrey there?"

"Humffrey?" Richard Queen said in the Finner voice. "What do you want him for?"

"It's confidential." The doctor's tone had an urgent, almost a harried, vibrato. "I must speak to Mr. Humffrey."

"You'll have to tell me what it's about, Dr. Duane." He glanced over at Jessie, winking.

"I'm Mrs. Humffrey's physician. She's . . . worse, and I must find her husband. Do you know——?"

"How bad is she?"

"See here, is Mr. Humffrey there, or isn't he?"

"Well, no, Doctor, but maybe I can find him for you. Did you call his summer place in Connecticut?"

"Good lord, man, do you think I'm an idiot? His housekeeper tells me he left Nair Island yesterday driving the small car and saying he wouldn't be back till tonight or tomorrow. Is——?"

"Didn't he say where he was going?"

"No! She gave me the phone numbers of all the places he might be—clubs, Park Avenue apartment, his home in Concord, even Mrs. Humffrey's relatives in Massachusetts. But I haven't been able to trace him. Have you any idea where he might have gone? I understand you've done some confidential legal work for him."

"Who told you that?"

"The chauffeur, I think, suggested your name. What difference does it make?" Dr. Duane sounded at the point of explosion. "Will you give me something definite or won't you? I tell you this is urgent!"

"I guess I can't help you at that, Doctor. But if I should hear from him . . ."

Dr. Duane slammed his receiver.

Richard Queen looked at Jessie as he hung up. "Queer . . ."

"What did he *say*, Richard?"

He told her.

"But I don't see anything queer about it. Except the coincidence of calling here just when . . ."

He was shaking his head, frowning, staring at Finner. Finally he said, "Jessie, I want you to go home."

"Without you?"

"I've got to notify the police. A homicide has to be reported as soon as it's discovered."

"Then why didn't you pick up the phone and call the minute you walked in here?" Jessie retorted.

"You're a hard woman, Jessie," he murmured. "All right, maybe I've come to feel that this is my case. Mine and yours . . . You and I know the two homicides are connected, but with the Humffrey envelope gone, there's no reason for them to link Finner's murder up with a Connecticut baby-smothering case that's been written off as an accidental death. Not right away, anyway. Meanwhile, we'll have some room to stretch in."

"Wouldn't it be better to ask for reinstatement, Richard?" Jessie asked quietly. "If they knew you'd been in on this from the start, maybe they'd give you a special assignment to take charge of the case."

He smiled faintly. "It doesn't work that way. The New York police department has two thousand detectives working out of precincts and Headquarters, not to mention some twenty or so thousand men and women in other police jobs. They don't need old man Queen. Come on, Jessie, I'll see you out of the building. I don't want some night man to spot you."

Jessie looked back just before he shut the door.

The fat man was still sitting there like an abandoned balloon.

It was after eleven that night when the phone rang.

"Jessie?"

"Richard, why haven't you called before? Where are you?" Jessie exclaimed. "Is everything all right?"

"Fine," he said. "I'm down at Headquarters chewing the fat with the boys. Going to bed?"

91

She understood that he couldn't talk freely and wouldn't be able to come over

"You can't see me tonight, is that it?"

"Right. I'll ring you in the morning."

"Good night, Richard."

Jessie hung up and surveyed the table she had set. She had bought minute steaks, frozen French frieds, and some salad vegetables in a delicatessen on 72nd Street, thinking to treat him to a home meal when he came. So that's what policemen's wives' lives were like . . .

What am I thinking of! Jessie thought guiltily, and she went to bed.

She was still in curlers and an old wrapper Sunday morning when the doorbell rang. She opened the door to the width of the latch chain, wondering who it could be.

"Richard!"

"Thought I'd surprise you," he grinned. "I've got the Sunday papers, frozen juice, fresh rolls, eggs—got any ham? I forgot the ham. Jessie? Where are you?"

"You mustn't *do* things like this," Jessie moaned, flat against the door. "Don't you know how a woman looks first thing in the morning? I'll undo the chain, but don't you dare walk in till you finish counting ten!"

"All right," he said, stricken.

When she came out of the tiny bedroom, he was sitting on the edge of a chair with the paper sack in his lap.

"Richard Queen, I could strangle you. Is anything more hideous than a woman in curlers? Don't just sit there. Let me have that bag."

"I'm sorry." He looked so deflated that Jessie laughed. "Anyway, I thought you looked fine. It's a long time since I saw a woman in curlers."

"I suppose it is at that," Jessie said. She took the bag to the kitchen alcove and got busy.

"Did I say something wrong, Jessie?" he asked anxiously.

"Heavens, no. Make yourself useful. I don't have any ham, but you'll find a couple of minute steaks in the fridge and a box of French frieds in the freezer drawer. How does that sound?"

"Oh, boy!"

It was not until she was pouring his second cup of coffee that Jessie asked, "Well, what happened yesterday?"

"Nothing much," he said in a careless tone. "The first men there were a patrolman and sergeant, radio patrol car, 17th Precinct—I know both of them pretty well. Then a couple of detectives from the 17th I know very well, and after that a lot of old buddies of mine—Deputy Chief Inspector Tom Mackey in charge of Manhattan East, Chief of Detectives Brynie Phelan, the Homicide boys—it was like Old Home Week."

"And when they asked their old buddy how he happened to stumble over a corpse," Jessie said, "what did their old buddy say?"

He set his cup down, shrugging. "All right, I lied. The going was rough for a while, but I think I pulled it off." He sounded ashamed. "I suppose an honorable lifetime in and out of uniform counts for something, especially when the men you're lying to are friends of yours."

"What was your story, Richard?" Jessie asked quietly. "I have to know, in case they get to me."

He glanced at her with admiration. Then he stared at the floor. "I said I'd been going crazy doing nothing, began thinking about some rats I'd known in harness whom we'd never been able to collar, and remembered Finner and his vicious racket. I said I thought it would be nice to get something on him—he doesn't even have a yellow sheet down at the B.C.I., no record at all. So I dropped in on Finner Thursday, I said, and let him think I was still on active duty and that we'd come up with something on him at last . . . on the theory that if you rattle a rat, he'll panic. I said Finner hinted at a payoff to keep the boys off his back, and I said I pretended to play along and made a date to visit his office again Saturday afternoon, and I said when I got there I found him dead. That's what I said, Jessie, and may the Lord have mercy on my soul."

"But that wasn't really a lie," Jessie said quickly. "It's not so far from the truth."

"Only about a million miles," he snarled. "It's the

worst kind of lie there is. It doesn't tell them a single thing I know that could help them. Jessie, I think I'll have another cup of coffee."

She emptied the pot into his cup in silence.

"So they're off to the races," he said, swishing the coffee around. "They figure the killer's somebody who wanted to get at Finner's files for blackmail purposes but was maybe scared off. They don't discount the possibility that the answer may lie in one of the night spots Finner patronized. So they're checking all the babes he's fooled around with, some of them linked with some pretty tough characters. They've got every angle covered except the right one." He nudged the Sunday papers, which were lying on the floor, with his toe. "Read all about it."

"Don't feel so bad, Richard." Jessie leaned across the table to put her hand on his.

He gripped it and held on.

After a moment, pink-cheeked, she withdrew it and began to collect the dishes.

"What do we do now?"

He got up and began to help her. "Well, the problem is still to find out who the baby's parents are."

"I don't see how we possibly can, now."

"There's a way."

"There is?" Jessie stared. "How?"

"Isn't every child born in a hospital handprinted for identification purposes?"

"Or footprinted." Jessie nodded. "Most hospitals take footprints these days."

"Knowing Finner's methods, it's likely he had the mother give birth in a hospital. What we've got to do is get hold of Michael's prints. It means an exhumation, of course——"

Jessie said, without turning from the sink, "What would you say, Inspector, if I told you I have his footprints?"

"What!"

"Mrs. Humffrey'd bought one of those baby books put out by the Chicago Lying-In hospital—you know, where you keep a record of feeding, teeth growth, and so on. There's a place in them for recording the footprints. I pressed his feet on that page myself."

"And you have it?" he asked incredulously.

"Yes. After the funeral I asked Mrs. Humffrey where she wanted me to put the book. She got hysterical and told me to take it away, she never wanted to see it again. So I appropriated it," Jessie said defiantly. "He was a lot more my baby than hers . . . Wait, I'll get it for you. It's in one of my bags."

She hurried into the bedroom and came out with an oversized book with a baby-blue cover.

"Of course, we couldn't fill in the birth data except for the date of birth——" Jessie gasped. "The date of birth!"

"This is going to be a cinch," he chortled. "With these footprints and the birth date, it's only a question of locating the hospital. Finner brought the baby to that Pelham meeting in the morning, so the odds are he picked him up in a New York hospital. I'll have these prints photostated first thing tomorrow, and . . . Jessie, what's the matter?"

She was staring blearily down at the tiny black feet impressions. "Nothing, Richard." She fumbled for a handkerchief, turning away.

He started to touch her, withdrew his hand awkwardly. "It's a brutal business, Jessie . . ."

"He was so little," Jessie sobbed. "That perfect body . . . his feet . . . I used to kiss his toes one at a time reciting Piggy, and he'd gleep . . ." She blew her nose angrily. "I'm sorry. I don't know what's happened to me lately."

"You're a woman," he muttered. "Maybe you haven't had time to find that out before, Jessie."

She kept her face averted. "What do I do, Richard?"

"The first thing you do is recognize the spot you're in."

"The spot *I'm* in?" She swung about at that.

"If I'd known about your having this baby book, I'd never have let you get into this. It's a dangerous thing for you to have. Finner was murdered because he was a link in the chain leading to little Mike's mother. This book, with his footprints, is another such link. Who knows you've got it?"

Jessie sank into a chair, staring at him. "Only Sarah Humffrey, I suppose. For all I know, maybe even she doesn't know. She may have assumed I destroyed it."

He scowled. "Maybe the killer's assumed the same thing. Or doesn't know it exists. All the same, Jessie, you're going to have to watch your step. In fact, the more I think of it the less I cotton to the idea of your living in this apartment alone. I wish——"

"Yes?" Jessie said.

"Well, I can be your bodyguard in the daytime, anyway." He smiled down at her. "What would you like to do today?"

Before they set out Monday afternoon with the photostats, Richard Queen said, "It's going to be a long pull, Jessie. There must be seventy-five or eighty hospitals in Manhattan and the Bronx alone, not to mention Brooklyn, Queens, Staten Island, Westchester, Long Island, and nearby Jersey."

"Why not start off with the maternity hospitals?" Jessie suggested. "Those would be the logical places."

"Which is why Finner would have avoided them. And he'd certainly not use places like the New York Foundling Hospital or the Shelter for Unmarried Mothers. No, I think he'd figure a big general hospital would give his brood mares a better chance of getting lost in the shuffle. Let's start with those."

"All right, suppose we make a list and split it up. That would halve the time."

"I'm not letting you out of my sight," he said firmly. "Besides, I doubt if you could get access to hospital files, even in the places where they know you. I've got a natural in with this shield."

On Wednesday afternoon, the third day of their hunt, they were leaving a hospital in the East 80s when Jessie said, "What's wrong, Richard? You've acted strange all day. You said yourself it's going to be a long search."

He steered her across the street to her coupé. "I didn't think it showed," he said dryly.

"You can't fool me. When you're worried about something you get all tight and quiet. What is it?"

"Watch. In the rear-view mirror."

He started the Dodge and moved out into traffic, heading north. Jessie slid over close to him and kept her eyes on the mirror. As they passed a corner, a black Chrysler sedan badly in need of a washing moved out from the side street and turned in after them. For a moment it was just behind them and Jessie caught a glimpse of the driver's face. It was all jaw and cheekbone in sharp angles, hard and gray. The man was alone.

Then the Chrysler fell back, other cars intervened, and Jessie lost sight of it. But when the Inspector turned west a few blocks north of the hospital, Jessie saw the gray-faced man turn west, too.

"We're being followed." Her mouth felt sticky.

"He's been on our tail all day."

"A city detective?"

"City detectives general work in pairs."

"Then who is he?"

"A small-time private detective named George Weirhauser. Fleabag office near Times Square. Mostly divorce evidence jobs. He rates pretty low downtown—he's pulled plenty of shady stuff—but he's always managed to steer clear of open violations. Enough to hold on to his license, anyway."

"But what's he doing watching us?"

"I don't know." Richard Queen looked grim. "Well, there's no point trying to shake him with what he's seen today already. A tail can work two ways—he keeps an eye on us, we keep an eye on him. Maybe we'll find a use for him."

"He looks awfully hard."

"That's Weirhauser's stock-in-trade," he said contemptuously. "It's all front, Jessie. Don't worry about him."

Weirhauser tailed them until after ten o'clock, when they put Jessie's car away for the night in the garage on 70th Street where she had arranged for a month's parking. When they walked over to 71st and stopped before

Gloria Sardella's walkup, the Chrysler drove past, picked up speed, and did not come back.

"Thank goodness," Jessie said. "He makes me nervous. Won't you come up, Richard? I'll make some coffee."

"No, you're going to bed, Jessie."

"I am a little weary," Jessie confessed. "And you're a dear to have seen it.—*Richard*." She clutched his arm. "Yes?"

"There's another one!"

"Another what, Jessie?" He seemed calm.

"Another man following us! I noticed him lounging around near the garage when we drove in. And now he's across the street in a doorway!"

"You certainly missed your calling," he said.

"Richard, what are you doing——?"

He was guiding her by the elbow across the street toward the offending doorway. The man who had been watching them retreated into the dimness of the vestibule. To Jessie's consternation, Richard Queen marched her right in after him.

"Shame on you, Wes," he said, chuckling. "Jessie, this is Wes Polonsky, ex-detective first grade, Automobile, Forgery, and Pickpocket Squad, retired."

"Good heavens," Jessie said. "How do you do, Mr. Polonsky."

"Glad to meet you, Miss Sherwood," the man said sheepishly. "Or maybe not so glad. I'm sure rusty." He was a massive old man with a mashed nose and white hair and innocent blue eyes. He looked as if he had once been powerful, but his chest was sunken and Jessie noticed his puffy hands trembling as he lit a cigaret. "You going to take me off, Inspector? This is the first kicks I've had in eight years."

"Don't be silly. This woman has eyes in the back of her head." Richard Queen sounded proud. "Wes, we were tailed today."

"I noticed a black Chrysler sedan ambling after you just now," Polonsky said, "but I couldn't get a good look at the driver."

"He wasn't around here last night, was he?"

"No. At least not in that car."

"It's George Weirhauser."

"That crum." Polonsky made a disgusted sound. "Want me to run him off if he shows again?"

"Let him be. Just don't let him get near Miss Sherwood."

"Okay, Inspector."

"But what is all this?" Jessie demanded. "I don't understand, Richard!"

"Now don't get mad, Jessie," he said placatively. "I ran into Wes Sunday night while I was walking home from your place—he lives in this neighborhood—and, well, Wes was saying how sick he was of being idle——"

"I'd get me a job," Polonsky said apologetically, "but it's impossible for a man my age to find anything."

"So," Richard Queen said, "one thing led to another, and before I knew it Wes was begging me to declare him in."

"And that's how Mr. Polonsky came to be my guardian angel, is it?"

"Since Sunday night," the ex-detective said, beaming.

"It's only for the night trick, Jessie. The times when I'm not with you."

"It's very sweet of you, Mr. Polonsky," Jessie said in a low voice.

The second old man said, "It's my pleasure, miss." Jessie slept soundly that night.

They struck the trail in the seventh day of their search.

It was at one of the big general hospitals on the West Side, in midtown. The old man was going through a file of baby footprints when Jessie felt him stiffen. He turned a pocket magnifying glass from the hospital record he was examining to the photostat and back again several times.

"We've found it, Jessie," he muttered.

"I don't believe it! Are you sure?"

"Positive."

The name identifying the set of footprints was "Baby Exeter."

"Let's see what they have on the mother."

He came back with some scribbled notes, and they sat down on a sofa in the waiting room.

"Mother's name Mrs. Willis P. Exeter, maiden name Lois Ann Edwards. Phonies, of course. Address . . . this house number on East 55th is misleading, Jessie. It's actually a small residential hotel. My guess is Finner maintained a room there under the name of Willis P. Exeter—probably had a number of such rooms around town under different aliases—and simply assigned one of them with a 'Mrs.' attached to every girl he did business with, for purposes of hospital registration."

According to his notes "Mrs. Willis P. Exeter" was twenty-four years old, white, with blond hair and hazel eyes. She had been admitted to the hospital on May 26th at 9:18 A.M., the baby had been born on May 27th at 3:56 P.M., and mother and baby had been discharged on June 3rd as of 10:15 A.M. The woman had occupied a semi-private room in the Maternity wing.

"I wonder if the doctor was in on it," Jessie said balefully. "What's his name?"

The old man shook his head. "Finner worked through legitimate doctors who never knew he existed. He simply sent the girl during her pregnancy to this doctor under the name of Mrs. Willis P. Exeter, armed with a phony background, and the doctor took care of her in good faith. All Finner had to do was use a different doctor for each girl, and he was all right. No, this tells us nothing." He squinted at Jessie. "Ever work this hospital?"

"Yes."

"Then you'd probably know the floor nurses in Maternity."

"Some of them."

"Why don't you go up and scout around? Maybe you'll run into one who remembers this girl. It's only three months back."

"What excuse do I give?"

"You're helping to trace Mrs. Exeter for a lawyer. She's come into an inheritance and the lawyer can't locate her." He grinned. "That one never fails."

When Jessie came back her eyes were sparkling. "Genevieve Fuller. She'll meet us in the Coffee Shop in ten minutes."

"I certainly do remember Mrs. Exeter, Mr. Queen," Nurse Fuller said. Jessie's friend was a small lively woman with gray hair and inquisitive eyes. "She was so sad all the time. Hardly said a word. The other patient in her room thought she was a drip, but I knew there was something special about her. Pretty girl in a kind of hard way. She had the sweetest baby. A little boy."

Jessie took a gulp of coffee.

"Did she ever tell you anything about herself, Miss Fuller?" Richard Queen asked.

"No, and I didn't press her. I knew she'd had some tragedy in her life. Do you know her husband never showed up once?"

"Really?"

"Some men! I'd drop in on her when she was in heavy labor, and she'd grab my hand and cry, she was so glad to see a sympathetic face. *No* one showed up. No parents, no sister, no brother, no friends—what kind of family she comes from I can't imagine. They must be animals."

"Didn't she ever say anything that might give us a clue to her present whereabouts, Miss Fuller?"

"No." The nurse looked around the Coffee Shop, lowering her voice. "But I am practically a hundred per cent sure Exeter wasn't her real name!"

"Is that so?" Inspector Queen said. "Well, now, that may account for it. Why did you think that?"

"Because from the second I laid eyes on her I knew I'd seen her somewhere before. Only I couldn't place her. Then one morning she gave herself away."

"How?" Jessie exclaimed.

"Oh, I didn't let on that it meant anything to me. Just made an offhand remark about what a nice voice she had. *You* know."

"But I don't, Gen! What's her voice got to do with it?"

"One morning," Genevieve Fuller looked around

again "—it was the day before she was discharged—I was passing her room when I heard somebody singing in a low, sweet, sexy voice. It really gave me a turn. I looked in, and darned if it wasn't this Exeter girl. The screen was around her bed and they'd brought her the baby for a feeding—that's another thing I liked about her, a girl in her line insisting on nursing her own baby, not like some of the parasite sluts we get around here who sit around Schrafft's all day in their minks while strangers prepare their children's formulas. They seem to think God gave them breasts for just ornaments——"

"In her line, Miss Fuller?" Richard Queen prompted.

"I started to tell you. She was nursing her baby and *singing* to him. Well, you can't fool me about voices. You know, Jessie, what a bug I am on pop singers. Well, I'd have recognized that voice anywhere. You can have your Rosemary Clooneys and Dinah Shores and Jo Staffords and Patty Pages and Doris Days—oh, they're very good, of course, and they're a thousand times better known than this girl, she's only made a few recordings, but she'll hit the top one of these days, you mark my words, she'll be the biggest seller of them all instead of just somebody a few people rave about."

"And her real name is——?"

"I'm not sure it's her *real* name, Mr. Queen. Her professional name is Connie Coy." And Nurse Fuller leaned back, narrowing her eyes to get the full effect of her revelation. She seemed disappointed. "Anyway, I figured she was incognito, and I wouldn't have let on for the world. Besides, as I say, I knew she was in some kind of trouble. But I'll swear on a stack of Bibles that was Connie Coy, the nightclub singer. And you say she's come into money! I think that's wonderful. God bless her. Too many people with real talent wither away on the desert air unseen. When you find her, Mr. Queen, will you tell her I'm her absolute number one fan? And what a darling baby she has! . . ."

When Genevieve Fuller had left, the old man said, "Connie Coy. Ever hear of her, Jessie?"

Jessie said, "I haven't been inside a nightclub since December 18, 1943. No, Richard."

But he ignored her sally. "If it wasn't Sunday, I could get her address in any one of a dozen ways. As it is, we'll have to hold it over till tomorrow."

"I know a thirteenth way," Jessie murmured.

"What's that?"

"Look in the phone book."

He stared at her. "Sometimes, Jessie," he said solemnly, "I wonder what I ever did without you. Excuse me!"

When he came back he was waving a slip of paper.

"It's up on 88th near West End Avenue," he said exultantly. "After you, Commissioner!"

"Still no sign of Mr. Weirhauser," Jessie remarked as Inspector Queen started the car. They had not caught a glimpse of the black Chrysler all day.

"Funny," he muttered.

"Maybe he doesn't work Sundays. Or he's been called off the job."

The old man said nothing. But he kept stealing glances in his rear-view mirror all the way uptown.

The apartment house was turn-of-the-century, a fancy production of stone scrollwork and false balconies, cracked and weatherstained, with bleached awnings that had once been striped, scabby iron-grilled doors, and a sidewalk chalked over with hopscotch squares. The whole building cowered as if it were ashamed.

They entered a lobby powerful with food odors. At a wall switchboard, doubled up on a three-legged stool under a 25-watt light, sat a skinny pimpled youth in a uniform too large for him, reading a comic book.

"Who you want?" The boy did not look up.

"Miss Connie Coy."

"She ain't in."

"When do you expect her?"

"I dunno."

Jessie suggested, "There's a door there says Superintendent."

The old man grunted. They went over to the door and he rang the bell.

A heavy-set man in a collarless shirt, with a green

paper napkin stuck in the neckband, opened the door. "Yeah?"

"I'm looking for some information about one of your tenants, Miss Connie Coy."

"I can't give out information about my tenants." The man began to shut the door, but it refused to shut. He glanced down coldly. "Guys can get their feet knocked off that way. You want I should call a cop?"

The gold shield flashed in Inspector Queen's palm. "That's a hot one," the man grinned. "Come on in."

"We can talk here. By the way, what's your name?"

"McKeown. Joseph N."

"Do you know where Miss Coy is, McKeown?"

"Out of town. She left three weeks ago Friday. She was supposed to be gone only a week, but she didn't come back so I guess they held her over."

"Oh, a professional engagement?"

"Yeah, she's a club singer. You know, a shantoose." McKeown glanced sidewise at Jessie.

"Then she might be back any day?"

"I'd say so."

"She live here long?"

"Seven-eight months."

"Where's she singing?"

"Chicago." McKeown peered over at the switchboard boy and lowered his voice. "Wha'd she do, Cap?"

"Nothing. She may have to be a witness in a case."

"Glad to hear it," the superintendent said. "Nice quiet gal. Too bad about her husband."

"Oh," the old man said. "She's got a husband?"

"A GI. He's in Korea. And he never even got to see his kid. He's still over there." McKeown looked sad. "Hard lines getting your wife pregnant and having to ship out, then she has the kid all alone and loses it in childbirth in the bargain. Came back from the hospital all broke up."

"I see," Richard Queen said. "What hospital was she at, do you know?"

"Some Army hospital over in Jersey, she said. She was just beginning to show when she moved in here. Tough."

"It certainly is," Jessie murmured.

"Does she use her married name here in the building?"

"Yeah. Mrs. Arthur Dimmesdale."

"How do you spell that, McKeown?" He took out a ballpoint pen and a wrinkled envelope with an Italian postmark. McKeown spelled the name, and the Inspector wrote it down on the back of the envelope.

Arthur Dimmesdale . . . Jessie thought, Where have I heard that name?

"Then I take it, McKeown, since Miss Coy—Mrs. Dimmesdale—didn't move in here till after her husband shipped out to Korea, that you've never seen him?"

"Never laid eyes on him."

"Any idea of his branch of service? Rank?"

"I think she said he's a second looey in the Army."

The old man made a note. "Couple more questions, McKeown, and I'll let you get back to your Sunday dinner. What's Miss Coy's apartment number?"

"5-C. That's on the top floor."

"Apartment C, fifth floor. She live alone?"

"All by her lonely, Cap."

"She ever have anybody sleep over?"

McKeown grinned. "This ain't the Barbizon, my friend. We don't keep a check. She don't run no brawls, and that's good enough for me."

"Don't mention this to Miss Coy when she gets back, McKeown."

"I get you, Cap."

As they walked toward Broadway, Jessie said, "But where are we going, Richard? Why didn't we get into the car?"

"You've got to have your dinner, Jessie. There's a nice restaurant on Broadway and 87th——"

"That's not the reason. What is it?"

"I can't keep anything from you, can I? We were wrong about Weirhauser. I just spotted him in a parked car as we came out of the apartment house. He was trying to hide behind a newspaper, but I got a look at him."

"I don't understand it," Jessie exclaimed. "I've kept on the lookout for his Chrysler all day."

"So have I. That's why we didn't see him. Don't turn around, Jessie. He's about to go into the apartment house." Richard Queen steered her around the corner into Broadway. "He pulled a fast one today. Ditched the old Chrysler and tailed us in a new Ford."

"How clever of him," Jessie tried to keep her tone amused. "Then he's finding out right now that we've been asking for Connie Coy. If McKeown doesn't tell him, that pimply boy will."

"More important, he knows we've found her. And by tonight, who ever's paying him to tail us will know it, too." He was preoccupied as they entered the restaurant.

"What are we going to do, Richard?"

He squeezed her arm. "Have dinner."

He took a table commanding a view of the door. But the private detective did not appear.

Over the chicken noodle soup Jessie said, "Do you think she's really married?"

He shrugged.

"Maybe that's why she had her baby under the name of Exeter, Richard. And told the super she'd given birth in a New Jersey hospital when she actually had the baby in New York. If she's married and her husband wasn't the baby's father . . ."

"She'd use a phony name at the hospital if she wasn't married, too. I'll check Washington first thing in the morning on a Lieutenant Arthur Dimmesdale." He stopped talking until the waiter removed the soup plates. "Either way we slice this, Jessie, it comes out the same. If Connie's married, Dimmesdale isn't the father. If she's an unmarried mother, and invented Dimmesdale to make life simpler for herself at the apartment house, we've stilll got to look for the man who got her pregnant."

"And for the other man," Jessie said grimly.

"Which other man?"

"The man who's hired that private detective to shadow us."

He buttered a roll and remarked, "They might be the same man."

Jessie looked surprised. "That's so, isn't it? Or . . . Richard! Do you suppose Weirhauser's client could be Arthur Dimmesdale?"

"From Korea?"

"Don't smile. Suppose the husband does exist. Suppose Dimmesdale knew he hadn't left his wife pregnant. Then some snoopy 'friend' writes to Korea that Connie's having, or had, a baby. He's furious. He goes AWOL, or wangles a leave or something—anyway, gets back to the States. First he traces the baby to the Humffreys and murders him——"

"That would make him a psycho, Jessie. And what about Finner's murder?"

"When Michael was murdered, Finner might have figured the husband did it, pussyfooted around, and decided he was right. If Finner then tried to blackmail Dimmesdale——"

But the Inspector was shaking his head. "I'm pretty sure, from the way Finner reacted, that he'd had no idea the baby was murdered. Hold it. —Fine, waiter. Yes, just the way I like it. Jessie, dig into this roast beef."

There was no sign of George Weirhauser when they left the restaurant. They walked back up to 88th Street, where they had parked Jessie's coupé, and Richard Queen rubbed his jaw.

"He's gone."

"There was no sign of Weirhauser's new Ford, either."

"Well!" Jessie said. "That's a relief."

"Is it?" he said oddly. "It probably means that instead of his client knowing tonight that we've located Connie Coy, he's learning it right now."

When he came downstairs from Jessie's apartment that night he strolled up the street a way and then suddenly pulled open the door of a blue Studebaker parked at the curb and climbed in.

"Evening, Inspector," Polonsky said.

"See anything of a gray-and-salmon Ford this evening, Wes?"

The retired officer looked concerned. "I thought Weirhauser was driving a black Chrysler."

"He switched on us today."

107

Polonsky swore. "Somebody's been teaching that punk his trade. I couldn't say I didn't, Inspector. I wasn't watching out for Fords."

"Neither was I." The Inspector began gnawing on his mustache. "Wes, what ever happened to Pete Whatzis? You know, the Pete you used to team up with."

"Pete Angelo? Pete's wife died two years after he retired. His married daughter's husband got transferred to Cincinnati, the younger daughter is away at college, and his son's a Navy career man. Pete worked for a protection agency a few years and then quit." Polonsky sighed. "At least he tells everybody he quit. He was fired on account of his age. Age! Pete Angelo could still wade into a gang of street corner hoodlums and stack 'em like cordwood."

"Ever see Angelo?"

"All the time. He lives here on the West Side. We meet in the cafeteria, have four cups of coffee apiece, and tell each other how good we used to be."

"Then Angelo's not doing anything?"

"Just going nuts, like the rest of us."

"Do you suppose I could get Pete to handle a plant for me?"

"Inspector, he'd throw his arms around your neck and kiss every hair on your mustache."

"Can you think of any other retired cop who'd be willing to team with Angelo? I'd need them both right away."

The ex-detective pondered. Then he smacked the wheel. "Murph! I ran into him this past week. You remember Sergeant Al Murphy, Inspector—he used to be on radio car patrol in the 16th. Murph was retired this past June, and he told me he's still undecided what to do with himself. Never saw a guy so itchy."

"Anybody else you can think of, Wes? I'd like two teams, one for the night trick, one for daytimes."

"I'll bet Pete or Murph'll come up with a couple. When do you want them for?"

"If possible, starting tonight."

Polonsky climbed out of his Studebaker. "You take this stakeout for a while, Inspector. I'll be right back."

When he slipped behind the wheel again Polonsky was grinning. "Pete Angelo and Al Murphy'll meet you in the cafeteria on 72nd in fifteen minutes. Pete says not to worry, he can get you ten teams. Your problem, he says, is going to be to fight off the ones you can't use."

Richard Queen sat there in silence. Then he pressed Polonsky's arm and got out. The old man in the car watched the old man on the sidewalk stride toward Broadway like a very young man indeed.

On Monday morning Richard Queen phoned to tell Jessie he had started the ball rolling on Lieutenant Dimmesdale with a connection of his at the Pentagon, and that he would have to stick close to his phone all day.

"What are your plans, Jessie?" he asked anxiously. "I haven't got you covered daytimes."

"Oh, I'll be all right. I have some laundry and a few other things to do, and then I thought I'd hop a cab and give that bachelor's sty of yours the thorough house-cleaning I promised. If you wouldn't mind my coming, I mean."

"Mind," he said in a fervent tone. "And here I was all gloomed up. But be careful on the way, Jessie!"

Jessie arrived a little past noon. At her ring he bellowed that the door was off the latch, and she went in to find him on the phone in Ellery's study, waving at her through the study doorway.

"Richard Queen, why didn't you tell me your Mrs. Fabrikant had been here? Or is this your work?"

He grinned and went on talking.

"Not that it still doesn't need doing," Jessie sniffed. She hung her taffeta coat and her hat in the foyer, prepared to take her handbag into the bathroom, change into a housedress, and sail in. But when she got further into the living room, there was the gateleg table set for two with winking silver and fancy paper napkins. He had decorated a big platter artistically with assorted cold cuts, deviled eggs, potato salad, parsley, and tomato slices, and the aroma from the kichen told her the coffee was perking.

Jessie turned the gas down under the coffeepot with the strangest thrill of proprietorship.

So they lunched tête-à-tête, and he told her that he had just finished arranging for an around-the-clock watch on Connie Coy's apartment.

"But who's watching?" Jessie asked, astonished.

"Four retired members of the Force," he grinned. "Al Murphy and Pete Angelo signed up last night. Pete got Hughie Giffin for me this morning, and that was ex-Lieutenant of Homicide Johnny Kripps just now trying to climb through the phone. Murphy and Angelo for daytime duty, Giffin and Kripps for dark-to-dawn. And four better officers who couldn't find between here and the west forty."

"Connie Coy is back, then?"

"No. That's one of the reasons I want the building covered. This way I'll know the minute she gets home."

When Jessie came out of the bathroom after lunch, in a housedress and with her hair bound in a scarf, she found him washing the lunch dishes.

"Here, Richard, I'll do those."

"You go on about your business. I'm a pearl diver from way back."

But afterward he trailed her around the apartment in a pleased way, making a nuisance of himself.

"Haven't you anything to do?" She was washing the living-room windows, and she suspected she had a dirt smudge on her nose. "Goodness!"

"I'll go call Abe Pearl," he said hastily. "Been meaning to do it all day."

"Are you going to tell him about Finner's death and how it ties in with the baby?"

"I called Abe on that early last week."

"You never told me. What did he say?"

"I couldn't repeat it."

"Then Chief Pearl's not so sure about my optical illusions," Jessie couldn't help saying.

"I'm afraid Abe's not sure about anything any more."

He went into the study and called Taugus police headquarters.

"Abe? Dick Queen."

"Dick!" Abe Pearl roared. "Wait a minute." Richard

110

Queen heard him say, "Borcher, shut that door, will you?" and the slam of a door. "Okay, Dick——"

"I thought you were going to call me back last week."

"Call you back? I've called that damn number of yours two dozen times. Don't you ever stay home? What's going on, Dick? Honeymoon—or something—with the Sherwood number?"

"Don't be funny," the old man said huffily.

"All right, all right. But you've tied my hands, I don't dare buzz Centre Street for information—I'm sitting out here like a bump on a log. Come on, Dick, give!"

He told Abe Pearl about their success in tracking down the mother of the dead baby.

"I'm waiting now for the girl to get back to town, Abe. Meanwhile, I'm trying to get a line on this alleged husband of hers, Dimmesdale. What did you find out about the Humffreys? How is Mrs. Humffrey?"

"I can't get to first base on that. This Duane is closer-mouthed than the FBI. I even got a friend of mine, a New Haven doctor who's sent patients to the Duane sanitarium and knows Duane well, to make some wild heaves from left field, but all Jerry could learn was that they'd called in some big specialist for her."

"How about Alton Humffrey, Abe? When did he get back from that mysterious fadeout weekend before last?"

"A week ago Sunday night, late. The help must have told him about Dr. Duane's trying frantically to get hold of him, because my information is Humffrey turned right around and drove up to New Haven. He was back Monday morning."

"That was Monday a week ago? The 22nd?"

"Yeah. The next day—last Tuesday—he closed up the Nair Island house and went into New York for good. The only one left is the gardener, Stallings."

"Richard Queen was silent. Then he said, "Abe, were you able to find out where Humffrey was during his two-day disappearance?"

"Nope. What the devil is this all about, Dick? It's a lot of fog to me."

"Move over," the old man chuckled.

But he looked worried as he hung up.

At 4:12 P.M. the phone rang. It was the operator with a call from Washington.

"This is it, Jessie," Richard Queen shouted. "Hello?"

Two minutes later he hung up.

"The Pentagon says that no such person as Arthur Dimmesdale—either as officer, enlisted man, draftee, or even civilian employe—is carried on the rolls of the United States Army, in Korea or anywhere else."

"So she did make him up," Jessie said slowly. "Poor girl."

"I wish your poor girl would show," he snapped. "I wish something would show!"

Something did. At 4:25 he answered the doorbell to find himself staring into the hard blue eyes of his old friend, Deputy Chief Inspector Thomas F. Mackey in charge of Manhattan East.

If Inspector Mackey's eyes were not affable, the rest of him was. He remarked how long it had been since his last visit to 87th Street, asked after Ellery, complimented his old friend on his taste in cleaning women (Jessie, hurriedly taking her mops into the study at a glance from her confederate, felt a shiver wiggle up her spine), and did not get down to business until he was offered a drink.

"Thanks, Dick, but I'm on duty," Inspector Mackey said awkwardly.

The old man grinned. "I'll go quietly, Tom."

"Don't be a jerk. Look, Dick, you and I can talk frankly. We're up a tree on the Finner homicide. Just a big nothing. We've run down hundreds of leads, mostly from those files of his. His night-spot romances have pretty much washed out. There's something wrong. Not a whisper of anything has come in from the stools. Wherever we turn—in a case that should have been cracked in forty-eight hours—we run up against a blank wall. Dick, are you sure you told us the whole story a week ago Saturday?"

The Queen face got red. "That's a funny question to ask me, Tom."

His friend's face got red, too. "I know. I've been debating with myself all week should I come up here. The damn thing is, I got the queerest feeling that day that you were holding something back." He was miserable, but his glance did not waver. "Were you, Dick?"

"I'm not going to answer that, Tom!"

They stared at each other. For a moment the old man thought his equivocation had been unsuccessful. But Chief Deputy Inspector Mackey misread the emotion in his friend's voice.

"I don't blame you. It was a rotten question to ask a man who's given the best part of his life to the City of New York. Forget I ever asked it, Dick. And now, before I shove off, I think I'll take that hooker!"

When Inspector Mackey had left, Jessie came out of the study. She went over to Richard Queen, slumped in his big armchair, and put her hand on his shoulder.

"You couldn't do anything else, Richard."

"Jessie, I feel like a skunk." His hand crept up and tightened over hers. "And yet I can't turn this over to the Department. The minute I do I'm through with the case. It's our case, Jessie, yours and mine. Nobody else wanted it . . ."

"Yes, Richard," Jessie murmured.

They had had dinner and were in the living room watching television when the phone rang again. Jessie snapped off the set and glanced at her watch as the old man hurried into the study. It was almost 8:30.

"Inspector? Johnny Kripps."

"Johnny. Did Giffin turn up to help you take over from Angelo and Murphy?"

"Hughie's watching the front right now. I'm phoning from a drugstore on Broadway. She's back, Inspector."

"Ah," the old man said. "You're sure she's our gal, Johnny?"

"She pulled up in a cab full of luggage about ten minutes ago, alone. Her bags have the name Connie Coy on them. And Giffin overheard the night man in the lobby call her Mrs. Dimmesdale. What do we do?"

Richard Queen said quietly, "Keep your eyes open and stay under cover. I'm on my way."

They walked over; it was only a few blocks. The night was hot and humid, but Inspector Queen set a quick pace. There was no sign of George Weirhauser.

"I wonder why," Jessie panted. Her girdle was killing her, but she would have died rather than ask him to slow down.

"Either his job is done or our staying in all day's fooled him." He shrugged. "It doesn't matter."

The curbs on both sides of 88th Street were packed with cars. How he knew Jessie could not imagine, but he stopped suddenly near one of the parked cars to light a cigaret, and a man's voice from inside the car said, "Okay, Inspector."

"Where's Giffin staked out, Johnny?"

"Up there on the floor somewhere. If you don't want the lobby man to see you, there's a side service entrance. This side of the building. Delivery elevator is self-service."

"You're clairvoyant, Johnny."

Kripps laughed. Jessie wondered what he looked like.

The Inspector strolled her slowly toward a shadowed area near the service entrance. The entrance had a weak caged bulb over it. He stopped her in the shadow. A car was cruising by, and a portly man in a Hawaiian shirt was trudging toward them from West End Avenue followed by a woman who was walking as if her feet hurt. The woman was jabbering a steady stream; the man kept wading on, deaf. He turned into the apartment house entrance and the woman went in after him.

"Now, Jessie."

Jessie found herself stumbling down three steps into a sort of tunnel. Ahead was darkness. He took her hand and led the way, trailing his other hand along the inner wall.

"Here's the door."

They entered a cluttered, sour-smelling basement, dimly lit. There was a trash can in the elevator.

The elevator went up creaking and groaning. It seemed to Jessie it was making enough noise to be heard over on Broadway. But the old man merely watched the floors move by.

114

"Why are we sneaking in this way, Richard?"

"We're not exactly in a position to operate openly. What the lobby man can't see won't hurt us." He sounded grim.

The elevator stopped, swaying. He opened the door and they stepped into a dingy rear hall. He shut the elevator door noiselessly.

There were four apartment doors, lettered A, B, C and D. He went over to the fire stairway to look down into the well. Then he moved over to the stairs leading up, and peered. They were on the top floor. This flight undoubtedly led to the roof exit, but the whole upper part of the staircase was in darkness.

"Giffin?"

"Yeah, Inspector." The ex-detective's voice sounded a little surprised. "I thought with Kripps covering the street, I'd cover the back stairs."

"Okay."

He went to the door lettered C and put his forefinger on the bell button. C was one of the two rear apartments.

Jessie held her breath. Little Michael's mother at last . . .

A latch chain rattled. The door opened a couple of inches.

"Who is it?"

She had a deep, slightly hoarse voice. Jessie caught a glint of gold hair, a slash of lipstick.

"Miss Connie Coy?"

"Yes?"

Richard Queen held his shield-case up for her inspection. "May we come in?"

"Police?"

Just the merest tremble of fear, Jessie thought, in that sugared voice. One large hazel eye, heavily mascaraed, shot a glance in Jessie's direction.

"What do you want with me?" She made no move to open the door.

"Let us in, please, Miss Coy," he said quietly. "I don't think you want the neighbors in on this."

115

She undid the latch chain then, stepping back with the door fast.

Connie Coy was clutching a green terry cloth housecoat about her, glancing from Richard Queen to Jessie and back again. Jessie saw now that her gold hair had greenish roots and that the makeup did not entirely conceal tired, biting lines. She was wearing dark green sandals. Her toenails were painted gold.

The old man shut the door and hooked the chain back.

"Sorry to barge in on you this way, Miss Coy, but it couldn't be helped. I'm Inspector Queen, this is Miss Sherwood. Where can we talk?"

"But what's this all about?" She was openly frightened now.

"Is that your living room in there?"

He went swiftly through the neat little kitchen into a big studio room.

"Don't be afraid, Miss Coy," Jessie said in her soft voice.

The girl gave her a puzzled look. Then she laughed and poked at her hair. "I've never had a visit from the police before," she said. "Are you a policewoman?"

"I'm a trained nurse."

She seemed rooted to the floor. But then she said, "Won't you come in?" and stepped aside.

They went into the studio room. Richard Queen was in the bedroom, looking into the bathroom. Open suitcases were strewn about the bed and the floor. Evening gowns lay everywhere.

"What are you looking for, Inspector?" the girl asked nervously.

"Just making sure we're alone." He came back, frowning.

It was a gay room in a theatrical way. The furniture was nondescript modern, but the upholstery was brightly colored and there was a striking batik throw over the back of the sofa. An ivory-and-gilt Steinway stood to one side of a big studio window. She had thrown the window wide open to the humid night, and through it Jessie could see the starlit roofline of an apartment

116

building on the other side of a narrow inner court, no more than twenty feet away. The window hangings were of dramatic red velvet. The walls were covered with inscribed theatrical photographs, mostly of jazz musicians, but there were several Degas reproductions of ballet dancers, an airy Dufy, and two small Japanese prints of subtle coloring that looked old. From an Egyptian copper vase on the mantelpiece over the false fireplace drooped some dead red roses. Half of one wall held floor-to-ceiling shelves crammed with books and recordings. There was a hi-fi player, a television set, a tiny bar.

"I'd offer you folks a drink," Connie Coy said with a strained smile, "but I'm out of everything and I only just got back tonight from out of town. Please sit down."

Jessie seated herself on the sofa near an iron-and-glass end table. A book lay open on the table. She wondered what it was.

The girl sat down in a wing chair, stiffly.

"Well?" she said. "I'm ready."

Inspector Queen went over to the fireplace, fingered a dry rose petal that lay on the brass knob of the andiron, suddenly whirled.

"Miss Coy, when did you see your baby last?"

The brutality of his question struck Jessie like a blow. She gave him an angry glance, but he was looking at the blonde girl. Jessie looked at her, too.

She was pale, but under control. She's been expecting it, Jessie thought. She took it better than I did.

"Baby? I don't know what you're talking about."

"Miss Coy." His voice was perfectly flat. "Seven or eight months ago you leased this apartment under the name of Mrs. Arthur Dimmesdale. There is no Arthur Dimmesdale. Some time between then and May of this year you were approached by a lawyer named Finner. You were pregnant, and he offered to see you through in safety to yourself providing you turned the baby over to him. He was in the adoption business, he told you, and he would see to it that your child was placed in a very good home with foster-parents who couldn't have children of their own and wanted to adopt one. All expenses would be paid; you would receive a large sum of

117

money; Finner would take care of all the 'legal' details. You were desperate, and you agreed. Finner sent you to a reputable gynecologist who knew you only as 'Mrs. Willis P. Exeter,' a name Finner provided, and when your time came you entered the hospital Finner designated under that name. The date was May 26th. On May 27th you gave birth to a male child. He weighed six pounds thirteen ounces, was nineteen centimeters long, had blue eyes and blond hair. On June 3rd you and your baby were discharged from the hospital and you turned him over to Finner. He paid you the promised fee and took the baby away. Are you ready to answer my questions now?"

"I threw the money in his fat face!"

The girl was trembling violently. She buried her face in her hands and began to cry.

Jessie made an instinctive move toward her. But the Inspector shook his head emphatically, and she sank back.

"I'm sorry." The Coy girl stopped crying as suddenly as she had begun. "Yes, I was desperate, all right. That slug Finner hung around a club I was singing at. I don't know how he knew I was pregnant. I suppose one of the girls suspected and sold him the information. What do you want to know?"

"Was that morning—June 3rd—the last time you saw your baby?"

"Yes."

She was twisting her hands in her lap, biting her lip.

"Now tell me this. Where were you on the afternoon of August 20th? That would be Saturday a week ago."

"I was in Chicago," she said dully. "That's where I just got back from. I did a three-week singing engagement at the Club Intime."

"Do you remember what you were doing that Saturday afternoon?"

"Sure. I was working a TV show. The club press agent arranged it."

"You were in a TV studio in Chicago all afternoon?"

"All day. We went on the air at 4:30."

For the first time his face softened. "That's an alibi nobody can improve on. I'm glad for your sake."

118

The girl was staring at him. "What do you mean, Inspector? Alibi for what?"

"On Saturday mid-afternoon, August 20th, A. Burt Finner was murdered in his office on East 49th Street in New York."

"Finner . . . murdered?"

"Didn't you know that, Miss Coy?"

"No! Finner murdered . . . Who did it?"

"That," the old man said gently, "is why we're here."

"I see," she said. "You thought I murdered him . . . I hope you never get the one who did! She ought to get a medal. Maybe you didn't know Finner the way I got to. He was the lowest thing that crawled. He was a creep, a fat creep. This baby racket wasn't just business with him. He got kicks out of it. The filthy bastard."

He let the bitter voice run on. His silence finally stopped her.

"You're keeping something from me," she said slowly. "Does Finner's murder have something to do with my baby?"

"Miss Coy." He stopped. Then he said, "Miss Coy, don't you know about the baby, either?"

"Know? About my baby?" The girl clutched the arms of her chair. "Know what, Inspector?"

"Don't you know who bought your baby from Finner?"

"No. That was part of the deal. I had to sign all kinds of papers Finner pushed in front of me. Promise never to try to find out who the adopters were. Promise never to look for him." She jumped up. "You know who they are! Who are they? Tell me! Please?"

"A millionaire Massachusetts couple with a summer home in Connecticut and an apartment in New York. Mr. and Mrs. Alton K. Humffrey."

Her mascara had run, and she kept blinking at him, blinking as if she could not stop. Suddenly she went over to the end table and snatched a cigaret from an open box. Her gesture pushed the book lying there into Jessie's lap. The girl turned away, thumbing a table lighter savagely.

"Tell me more," she said. "These Humffreys. They bought my baby from Finner, and what happened? Because something happened, I know it. What was it, Inspector?"

He glanced at Jessie.

"Well, Miss Coy, I'll tell you——"

"I'll tell her, Richard." Jessie got up, holding the book, and went close to the girl. "Take a good drag, Miss Coy. This is going to be very hard. I was your baby's nurse in the Humffrey household. He's dead."

She touched the girl's shoulder.

Connie Coy turned around. Her lips were apart and the smoldering cigaret was dangling from her lower lip. Jessie took it from her mouth and put it in an ash tray.

"You may as well hear the rest of it," Richard Queen muttered. "Your baby was murdered."

"Murdered . . . ?"

Jessie lunged, and he bounced forward. But the girl pushed their arms blindly aside, went over to the wing chair, sat down on the edge with her hands clasped between her knees, staring.

Jessie hurried into the kitchen. She came back with a glass of water.

"Drink this."

Connie Coy sipped mechanically, still staring.

"No, that's enough. Murdered. When did it happen?"

"August 4th, a Thursday night," the old man said. "Over three weeks ago. Didn't you read about the death of a child named Michael Stiles Humffrey up on Nair Island, in Connecticut? It was in all the papers."

"So that's the name they gave him. Michael. I always called him just Baby. In my thoughts, I mean. Michael . . ." She shook her head, as if the name meant nothing to her. "Papers? No, I guess I didn't. Thursday night, August 4th . . . I left for Chicago on the 5th. I was busy packing, I didn't get a paper that Friday. I didn't see a New York paper all the time I was away." She shook her head again, violently this time. "It's so confusing. You know? Getting hit this way . . . Murdered . . . All this time I've kept kidding myself it was for his good, the advantages he'd have, and never knowing he was illegitimate. How he'd grow up tall and happy and well adjusted, and . . . And he's murdered. At two months old." She laughed. "It's crazy, man, crazy."

She threw her head back and laughed and laughed. Jessie let her laugh it through. After a while the girl stopped laughing and said, "Can I have a cigaret?"

"I wish I had a good stiff drink to give you," Jessie said. She lit a cigaret and put it between the girl's lips. "How about some coffee?"

"No, thanks. I'm all right." She seemed completely composed, as if the laughter, the enormous hazel stare, had never happened. "Let's get this straight. A rich couple named Humffrey bought my baby from Finner. The baby was murdered. A couple of weeks later Finner was murdered. I don't see the connection."

"We don't know yet why the little tyke was murdered, Connie." The Inspector dragged a chair over to her and sat down eagerly. "But the way we see it, Finner got it because he was the only outsider who knew the baby's real parentage. A while ago you said you didn't know how Finner found out you were pregnant—you supposed one of the girls at the club you were singing in suspected and sold him the information. Did you have any real reason for believing that?"

"No," she said slowly. "I never let on to anybody, and it certainly didn't show at that time. But it's the only way I can imagine Finner got to know it."

"It isn't likely. But there's one way Finner could have found out that is likely. Connie, tell me: Did the man who got you pregnant know it?"

Her eyes flickered.

"Yes," she said. "I told him. He wanted me to go to some dirty abortionist. But I was afraid. So then he bowed out." She shrugged. "I didn't blame him. It was my own fault. I thought I loved him and found out I didn't when it was too late. I knew all the time he was married." Then she said, "Pardon me for going into my memoirs. You were saying?"

"Three people knew it," Richard Queen said. "You,

the man, Finner. You didn't tell Finner. Then how did Finner find out? *The man must have told him*."

"That's real touching," Connie Coy murmured. She got up and ground the cigaret out in the ash tray on the end table. She ground it hard. "Keep going, Inspector."

"So Finner knew the identity of both parents. If he was killed because he knew—" the old man rose, too— "then you're in danger, Connie."

"Me?" She swung about to face him, expressionless. "How do you figure that?"

The only ones with reason to shut Finner's mouth for good about the child's parentage are the parents themselves. You're one of them, but you have a solid alibi for the day of Finner's murder. That leaves the other parent. It's my belief, Connie, that Finner was murdered by the baby's real father, and if that's so he may well come after you, too. With Finner dead, you're the only one left who can expose him. That's why I want you to tell us who the father is."

The blonde girl walked over to her grand piano. She ran her left hand soundlessly over the keys.

"Certainly you can't have any sentiment left about him." The Inspector spoke softly from the center of the room, above Jessie's head. "You say he's married. Am I right in supposing he's also somebody prominent—someone who might be ruined if a story like this came out? A certain type of man will run amok under a fear like that. Your protection is to share your information, Connie. The more people know who he is, the safer you are. He can't kill us all. Who is he? Tell us."

There was another cigaret box on the piano, and the girl took a cigaret from it and put it to her mouth. She looked around. He picked up the lighter from the end table and walked over to her.

"Tell us," he said again. He held the lighter up, but he did not finger the flint lever. She took the lighter from him and worked the lever herself.

"Arthur Dimmesdale," Jessie said from the sofa.

The flame remained an inch from the cigaret.

"What, Jessie?" Richard Queen said, puzzled.

The open book from the end table was still in Jessie's

hand. She tapped it. "I thought it sounded familiar, Richard. Arthur Dimmesdale is the name of Hester Prynne's lover in Hawthorne's *Scarlet Letter*."

"Oh, that." Connie Coy laughed. "I picked the book up one day in a secondhand shop. I'd always meant to read it. And I'd just found out I was pregnant. *A for Adultery* . . . Hester's lover's name seemed like just the thing when I had to invent a husband. My mother always warned me my romantic streak would get me into trouble."

"Only a person who's married can commit adultery, Connie," Jessie said. "You're not the adulterer. He is. And now it seems he's a murderer, too. That's the thing to remember, isn't it?"

"So," Inspector Queen repeated, "who is he?"

"All right," the blonde girl said suddenly. "I'll tell you."

She brought the flame of the lighter to the tip of the cigaret.

The flame seemed to explode with a sharp crack, and a black hole appeared in the middle of her forehead.

Then the hole gushed red, and the lighter fell, and the cigaret fell, and the girl fell.

She fell sidewise, glancing off the piano keys. She crashed to the floor before the brilliant clang of the keys stopped.

"Get down, Jessie!"

Jessie found herself in a crouch on the floor, with the sofa between her and the studio window. The old man was skittering like a crab toward the wall switch. Jessie heard two more explosions. Something shattered behind her.

The room plummeted into darkness.

He was pounding through the kitchen now. Undoing the latch chain.

The service door opened and closed. The sounds were definite but not loud. Before the door closed she heard the voice of the ex-detective, Giffin. And soft running steps.

Then silence.

Jessie Sherwood sat up in the dark, rested her head against the sofa seat. Her ears were ringing and it bothered her.

She shut her eyes.

But even her eyes shut she could see him.

He had shot a gun off from the roof of the house twenty feet on the other side of the court, through the open window. The flame of the lighter had made Connie Coy's blonde head a perfect target. A blurry-black figure against the glow of the city sky. As the girl fell. With a glinting something held in front of him. A figure vaguely male. Then she had tumbled off the sofa.

Amazing how quiet everything was.

Not really quiet. Just normal-quiet. As if there had been no man on the roof, no sharp crack, no hole in a human head. It wasn't quiet. TV sets were going all over the place. The court was full of them. Auto sounds from the streets. Buses going by on Broadway. Not the kind of sounds they would make if they knew a girl had been shot. Not the rasp of windows, cries, questions, doors, running.

Girl shot.

Jessie came alive.

The girl . . .

She crawled toward the window, reached up, got hold of the short end of the drape pull, and yanked. Before she climbed to her feet she felt for the drapes to make sure they were drawn.

She located the lamp on the piano, felt for the button, found it. The lamp remained dark. Why didn't it turn on? The wall switch. It controlled all the lights in the room.

She groped toward where Richard Queen had scuttled at the first shot. After a while she located the switch.

Connie Coy was lying between the Steinway and the pulled-out piano bench, on her back. Her robe had twisted open in her fall. She was wearing nothing underneath.

The blonde girl was staring intently at the ceiling, as if something were written there that she could not understand.

4.

EVEN IN THE
CANNON'S MOUTH

"DON'T touch anything, Jessie."

Jessie had not heard him come in. He was just inside the doorway from the kitchen, breathing in heaves, getting his breath. Perspiration was streaming down his cheeks.

"She's dead, Richard."

"I know."

He had a handkerchief on his right hand again. He went into Connie Coy's bedroom, wiped the knob of the bathroom door. He came back and went to the piano and picked up the fallen lighter and wiped it clean and put it back on the end table. He wiped the chair he had used. He glanced at the glass of water Jessie had brought the girl from the kitchen, then at Jessie's hands.

"You're still wearing your gloves. That's good." He went over to the sofa, picked up Jessie's purse, looked around the living room. "You've pulled the drapes." He did not sound angry. He said it like a man taking inventory. He came over to her and led her to the kitchen doorway. "Stay right here." He went to the wall switch and rubbed it with the handkerchief.

Then he flipped the switch.

The room got dark again.

She heard him making his way to the window. The drapes hissed open again.

"Let's go, Jessie." He was back by her side.

"No," Jessie said.

"What?" He sounded surprised, grabbed her arm.

"Just one more minute." She began to pull away.

He held on, pulling gently the other way. "You can't do anything for her, Jessie. Don't you understand that we've got to get out of here? Come on, now."

"I won't leave her exposed like that," Jessie said stubbornly. "It isn't fair. All I want to do is close her robe, Richard. Let me go."

But he did not. "We mustn't touch anything."

"All those men looking at her! A woman's nakedness is her own. It isn't fair."

"She's dead, Jessie."

The street was just the same. No, not quite. Kripps's car was gone. Where Richard Queen had paused to light a cigaret and talk to the retired policeman in the car there was space, signifying flight or chase.

Jessie walked stiff-legged, letting him lead her.

They walked over to Broadway, waited for the light, crossed to the east side, headed downtown.

Jessie kept moving one stiff leg after the other. Once in a while it would come to her that she was somebody named Jessie Sherwood, a registered nurse, and that behind her a blonde girl with her robe open to the navel lay under a grand piano and that none of it should be that way.

The old man did not speak to her. He was busy strolling along, her right arm tucked beneath his left, stopping for signals at corners, nudging her ahead, glancing into shop windows, pausing to light a cigaret, wipe his face, let the cigaret go out, pause to light it again. He lit a great many cigarets.

At 72nd Street he suddenly stepped up their tempo. He hurried her across the intersection, steered her briskly into a cafeteria. The cafeteria was crowded. He picked up a tray, two spoons, two paper napkins. He made her stand on line with him behind the railing. He put two cups of coffee on the tray. He had their tickets punched, paused to look around as if for a table. Then he took her over to where a pair of elderly men were sitting over cups of coffee, too. One had a scar on his face, the other wore heavy glasses. The other two chairs at the table were unoccupied; they were tilted against the third and fourth sides as if they were reserved.

Richard Queen set the tray down, pulled out one of the tilted chairs for her, seated himself in the other.

Only then did he say, "Giffin. Kripps. What happened?"

"We lost him, Inspector."

"You first, Giffin."

The elderly man with the scar stirred some sugar into his coffee, talking to the coffee as if it had ears. "I ducked out onto the roof and shot a flash across the court to the other side. Nobody. I beat it down the stairs into the basement and got over to the other street through the back court. Lots of people walking, kids horsing, plenty of traffic moving in both directions. Nobody running, nobody pulling away from the curb, nobody acting like anything had happened. And as far as I could see, not an empty parking space. I talked to the kids, but they hadn't noticed anybody come out of the house. I knew it was a waste of time, but I checked the stairs, elevators, basement, and roof over there. The roof is absolutely clean. The way I figure it, he cut across the roofs of several buildings and came out near the corner of West End—maybe had a getaway parked there. Anyway, it was a bust."

"You, Johnny?" Inspector Queen said.

The other elderly man looked like a teacher or a librarian, Jessie thought, with his black-rimmed glasses and distinguished white hair. "I drove around to 89th when you ran outside with the news, Inspector. By the time I got there it was either too early or too late, I didn't know which. I hung around for a few minutes with nothing to latch onto. Then a car pulled away from the curb fast, and I tailed it. It turned out to be some college kid late for a date."

"It's the legs," Giffin said gloomily to his coffee. "Let's face it, we're not as spry as we used to be."

"We needed more men is all." Johnny Kripps breathed on his glasses. "Hell, I'm not even packing a gun."

"Who was it?" Jessie thought. To her surprise, the thought was audible.

The men glanced at her curiously.

"Take it easy, Jessie," the old man said. "As a matter of fact, boys, I'm not getting you in any deeper." He sipped some coffee and looked at them. "I want you to go home and forget it."

They laughed. Giffin said, "We haven't met the lady, Inspector."

"I beg your pardon. Miss Sherwood, John Kripps, Hugh Giffin."

"How do you do," Jessie said. "He shot her between the eyes as if she were something in a shooting gallery. Then he fired two more shots. It couldn't have been at her, she was flat on the floor. He shot at us, Richard."

"I know, Jessie," he said gently. His hand came to her under the table. "I want you boys to go home, and one of you phone Pete Angelo and Al Murphy and tell them to forget it, too."

"How about a little something to go with that coffee, Miss Sherwood?" Hugh Giffin asked.

"Maybe a nice cheese Danish?" Johnny Kripps said. "They're tops in here."

"About this deal," the Inspector said insistently. "I appreciate your attitude, boys. But this is murder. I can't let you endanger your pensions, maybe wind up in jail. Jessie and I," his hand tightened, "we're in so far now we couldn't get out if we wanted to. But you——"

"You're wasting your breath," Kripps said. "I'm talking for Pete and Murph, too. Who takes care of the call-in?"

"I will!" the old man said.

"The hell you will," Giffin said hotly. "Your voice is too well known, Inspector. Johnny or I'll do it."

"Call-in?" Jessie said.

"Notifying the police, Miss Sherwood," the ex-homi-

128

cide man explained. He *did* look like a scholar. "We can't let her lie on that floor till the super's nose brings him up there."

"An anonymous call?" Jessie said.

The three men flushed and picked up their cups.

Jessie picked up her cup, too. She remembered now that she hadn't touched it.

He took the key from her cold fingers. He unlocked the apartment door and shoved it open and reached for the switch and ducked all in one movement. Then he stood there looking. After a moment he went into Jessie's bedroom.

He came back.

"All right."

He shut the apartment door and latched it.

"Why am I so cold?" Jessie shivered. "Did the temperature drop?"

He felt her forehead, her hand.

"It's the nervous reaction," Richard Queen said. "I used to break out in a sweat afterward, even in the dead of winter. You're going to bed, young woman."

"I'm not a young woman," Jessie said, standing there trying to keep her teeth from clacking. "I'm an old woman and I'm scared."

"I could kick myself for letting you in for this." He took her purse and gloves, clumsily removed her hat. "I'd send you back to Connecticut tomorrow—"

"I won't go."

"—only I want you where I can keep an eye on you. For all he knows, she told us his name."

"He shot at us," Jessie said. "A bullet hit something behind me and broke it. He doesn't take chances, does he?"

"He's taking all kinds of chances," the old man said gently. "But we'll talk about it tomorrow. You go in there and get undressed. Do you have any phenobarb?"

"What are you going to do, Richard?" Now her teeth *were* clacking.

"Stay over."

She knew she should protest, send him home, or at least make up the daybed for him in the living room.

But the connection between her larynx and her will seemed broken. On the edge of things lay the body of Connie Coy with the spattery hole in her forehead and the greenish roots of her gold hair slowly dyeing red. But the core of herself felt a great warmth. As long as he was here nothing like that hole and that bloody dye could happen to *her*. All she had to do was drift . . . let go . . . Goodness, Jessie thought dreamily, I'm getting to be a female woman.

"Can you make it by yourself all right?" he asked anxiously.

"Why do you ask?" Jessie giggled at the consternation that flooded his face. He was so easy to tease . . .

Later, when she was in bed, he knocked and she said, "Come in," and he came in with a cup of warm milk and a sleeping tablet.

"Take this."

"Yes, sir," Jessie said obediently.

It was hard lifting her head from the pillow. He hesitated, then slipped his arm around her shoulders and sat her up. The coverlet dropped away and Jessie thought, Now, Jessie! But she really didn't have the strength to pull it back up . . . And me in my most décolleté nightgown. How shameless can you get? He'll think I purposely . . .

Jessie drank the milk very slowly.

"It's hot."

"I'm sorry. Take your time." His voice sounded funny. When she sank back he removed his arm as if it hurt.

"Thank you, Richard." Is this really *me?* Jessie thought.

"Feeling better?" He was addressing the badly reproduced Van Gogh still-life over Gloria Sardella's bed.

"Worlds."

But it's so nice . . . Jessie slipped under the covers, giggling again.

He went over to the window and looked out. The fire escape seemed to disturb him. He pulled the window down and locked it, lowered the Venetian blind, closed the vanes. Then he went into the bathroom.

One second her forehead was smooth and white, the next it had a hole in it, a real hole, black and then red . . .

"I've opened the bathroom window, Jessie. I'll leave the door to the living room open for circulation. Unless light bothers you?"

"Just don't go away." She began to shiver again.

"I won't. Remember, I'll be in the next room. At anything—for any reason—sing out."

"Yes . . . The linen's in that closet next to the kitchenette. Richard, she's dead."

"Go to sleep now, Jessie."

"I don't know what's the matter with me. I don't seem to have any strength at all."

"It's been a rough night. If you're not better in the morning I'll call a doctor."

"Oh, no . . ."

"Oh, yes."

The light snapped off, but she could not hear him move.

"Good night," Jessie said drowsily.

"Sleep well, Jessie."

He went out then, in a sort of stumble.

He didn't look at me as if I were just any woman. He looked at me as if . . .

The last thing Jessie heard as she fell asleep was the scream of police sirens heading uptown.

The voice of Abe Pearl at the other end of the wire was so loud the old man glanced over at the bedroom doorway.

"Stop bellowing, Abe," he grumbled. "I'm not deaf yet."

"Where in the name of God have you been?" Chief Pearl demanded angrily. "I've been trying to reach you all night. Where you calling from?"

"Jessie Sherwood's place in New York."

"Look, Dick, if you want to shack up, shack up, but the least you can do is leave me her phone number so I can contact you. I didn't start this, you did!"

"You cut that out, Abe," Richard Queen growled. "I'm not shacked up with anybody——"

"Okay, so she's playing hard to get—Becky, will you shut up! . . . Can you give me five minutes?"

"Go ahead," he said shortly.

"I got a call tonight from New Haven, from this Dr. Duane. He's been phoning all over creation trying to reach Humffrey again. He finally contacted me out of desperation, wanted me to run over to Nair Island and see if maybe Humffrey hadn't gone back there—he'd tried to reach Stallings, but there was no answer. I've found out that Stallings had gone to a movie; anyway, he hadn't seen or heard from Humffrey. The point is, Mrs. Humffrey is bad again, and it sounded to me like Duane's got hold of a hot knish and would like to let go. You don't know where Humffrey is, Dick, do you? I thought I'd check with you before calling Duane back."

"I haven't seen Humffrey, no," Richard Queen said slowly. "Abe."

"Yes?"

"What time did Humffrey leave his Park Avenue apartment today? Did Duane talk to Mrs. Lenihan?"

"She told him he'd left early this morning and didn't say where he was going. At the time Duane called me, which was about nine tonight, Humffrey still hadn't got back."

"Did Cullum chauffeur him? Or did Humffrey leave alone?"

"I don't know." Abe Pearl paused. "Dick, what's happened? Something happened tonight."

"Connie Coy's been knocked off."

"The *mother*?"

When Abe Pearl heard the story, he said, "One minute, Dick. Just hang on." The silence was prolonged. "I'm trying to piece this together——"

"It's complicated," Richard Queen said dryly.

"Dick. Why did you ask me what time Humffrey left his New York apartment today?" He said, "Dick? You there?"

"I'm here." The old man said rapidly, "Abe, doesn't it strike you as queer that the day Finner is murdered

Humffrey's movements can't be accounted for, and the night Connie Coy gets it—ditto?"

Abe Pearl said, *"What?"*

"You heard me."

His friend was silent.

Then he said, "You're crazy! There might be a dozen explanations——"

"Sure."

"It's just a coincidence——"

"I can't prove it isn't."

"The whole idea is ridiculous. Why . . ." Abe Pearl paused. "You're not serious."

The old man said, "Oh, yes, I am."

Silence again.

"How long has this bee been buzzing around in your bonnet?" the Taugus chief finally demanded.

Inspector Queen did not answer.

"Don't you see you've got nothing to back it up? So Humffrey couldn't be located around the time of either murder. So what? Maybe now that his wife is tucked away in New Haven, he's picked himself up some tasty blonde——"

"Now?" The old man sounded grim. "That could have happened a year ago."

"Dick, you're off your trolley. Alton Humffrey? You have to be human to start chick-chasing. Even if Humffrey had the yen, he wouldn't put himself in such a position. He thinks too damn much of himself and his precious name."

"Be consistent, Abe. One minute you're saying Humffrey might be having an affair with some woman to account for his absences, but when I suggest the woman was Connie Coy and he had the affair with her last year you start telling me he isn't the type. Sure he's the type. Under given circumstances, any man's the type. And especially the Humffreys of this world."

"Humffrey . . ." He could almost see Abe Pearl shaking his head.

"I admit it's mostly hunch. But there isn't much else to go by, Abe. Up to now it's been one stymie after another. First the nephew, Frost, comes up with an airtight alibi for the baby's murder. Then the killer lifts the Humffrey folder from Finner's files and chokes off the obvious lead to the child's mother. When we finally get to the Coy woman by a roundabout route and she's about to come through with the baby's father's name, she stops a bullet between the eyes. I can't wait for the next stymie, Abe. I've got to take the initiative."

"You're heading for big trouble," Chief Pearl said in a mutter. "You can't go after a man like Humffrey with a popgun."

"I don't intend to. I won't move in till I have some man-sized ammunition. And I think I know where I can get some."

"Where?"

"I'll let you know when I get it. Give my love to Becky, will you?"

After he hung up, the old man sank into a chair, scowling.

A long time later he reached for the Manhattan classified directory and began hunting for an address under *Detective Service*.

The gray-skinned man got off the elevator and walked erratically up the hall reading page three of the *Daily News*. He seemed fascinated and slightly sick. He was a big man of about forty in a slim-drape lounge suit and a hat with a Tyrolean feather. The gray skin was drawn angularly over his face bones in flat planes and straight lines. He looked like a cartoon.

He stopped before a pebbled glass door and fumbled in his pants pocket for a keycase without taking his eyes from the newspaper. The door said:

G. W. DETECTIVE AGENCY
Civil—Criminal—Personal
DOMESTIC TROUBLES OUR SPECIALTY
Complete Photographic Service
WALK IN

He unlocked the door and stepped into the ante-room, still reading. The typewriter on the receptionist's desk was in a shroud. There was no window in the room.

His left hand groped near the door, located the light switch, snapped it on. Absorbed in his morning paper, he walked on through, into the inner office, over to the window. He pulled up the blind, sank into the chair behind the desk. As he continued to read he tilted back, nibbling his lip.

"Interesting story?"

The gray-faced man looked up quickly.

Richard Queen was seated in a chair behind the partition wall of the anteroom.

"I said that's an interesting story about that girl's murder last night," he said. "From the way you're reading it, Weirhauser, you agree with me."

The private detective put the newspaper down on his desk carefully.

"Am I supposed to know you, pop?" He had a rough, nasty voice. "Or is this a stickup?"

"Come, come, George, cut the clowning," the old man said mildly. "I thought we could talk before your girl got here, and I didn't feel like waiting in the hall." He rose, put his hat on the chair, and walked over to the desk. "I want some information from you. Who hired you to tail me?"

The investigator looked blank. "Am I supposed to be tailing you?"

"You were pulled off the job Sunday, whether temporarily or permanently I don't know." The Inspector's tone was patient. "I asked you a question."

"See that word *Private*?" Weirhauser said. "Get going."

"You haven't changed a bit, Weirhauser. Still doing a take off on George Raft." The Inspector laughed.

Weirhauser got up. "You going to get out, or do I have to heave you out?"

The old man stared at him. "Don't you realize what you've stepped into? Or are you even stupider than you act?"

The gray was taking on a brick color. Weirhauser set his knuckles on the desk. "Who the hell do you think you're talking to?"

135

Inspector Queen glanced at his watch. "I don't have any time to waste, Weirhauser. Let's have it."

"You talk like you're somebody." The man's tone was jeering, but there was an uncertain note in it.

"You know who I am."

"I know who you were. The trouble with you has-beens is you don't know enough to lay down and roll over. You're not Inspector Queen any more, remember?"

"Hand me that phone."

Weirhauser's color changed back to its normal gray. "What are you going to do?"

"Call Headquarters and show you whether I'm a has-been or not."

"Wait."

"Well?"

The investigator said, "You know I can't give out that kind of information, Inspector." He was trying to sound rueful and put-upon. "Agency work is confidential——"

"You should have stuck to chasing dirty divorce evidence." The old man looked amused. "How do you like being mixed up in a murder? You didn't bargain for that, did you?"

Weirhauser said quickly, "Who's mixed up in a murder? I took a tailing job. I was told to tail you and the woman and to report your movements to my client and I did and that's all."

"You tailed me from hospital to hospital, you tailed me to an apartment house on 88th near West End, you found out I was asking for a girl named Connie Coy and that she was expected back from out of town shortly, and you reported that to your client Sunday evening. This morning, Tuesday, you open your paper and find that a girl named Connie Coy got back from Chicago last night and within the hour was shot to death through her window from a nearby roof. And you say you're not mixed up in it, Weirhauser? You walked in here this morning trying to remember your prayers."

"Look, Inspector," Weirhauser began.

"Suppose we go downtown and tell one of the brass that you, George Weirhauser, holding a license to con-

136

duct private investigations, fingered Connie Coy for a client you refuse to name? How long do you think you'd hold your license? In fact, how long do you think it would be before you began yelping for a bail bondsman?"

"Look," Weirhauser said again, licking his lips. "You're way off base on this thing, Inspector. My client couldn't have had anything to do with this——"

"How do you know he couldn't?"

"Well, he's . . ."

"He's what? All right, maybe he didn't have anything to do with it. Do you know where he was all day yesterday, Weirhauser? Can you alibi him for the time of the girl's murder?"

The private detective shouted, "I didn't go near the guy yesterday! Didn't even talk to him on the phone. He told me Sunday night when I spoke to him that he'd changed his mind, the information I had for him wasn't what he was after at all, he was calling the whole thing off. That's all I know."

The Inspector shook his head. "Try again, Weirhauser."

"What d'ye mean? I tell you that's all I know!"

"You've left one thing out."

"What's that?"

"The name of your client."

Weirhauser got up and went to the window, fingering his lip. When he came back and sat down again his sharp eyes were sly.

"What side of the street you working in this deal . . . Inspector?"

"That," the old man snapped, "is none of your business."

"It just occurred to me." The investigator grinned. "You might be in this up to your eyeballs yourself—you and this dame."

"I am."

"You are?" The man looked surprised.

"Sure," the old man said. "I'm after your client, and I'm going to get him. And the less you know about it,

Weirhauser, the longer you'll sleep in your own bed. I've thrown away enough time on you. Who is he?"

"Okay, okay, but give me a break, will you? Honest to God, if I'd known this was going to wind up in a homicide, I'd have spit on his retainer and run like hell."

"Who is he?" the old man repeated. His eyes were glittering.

"It's understood you'll keep me out of this?"

"Personally, I don't give a damn about you. As far as I'm concerned you're out of it right now. Who is he, Weirhauser?"

Weirhauser got up again and shut the door to the anteroom.

"Well, he's a rich muckamuck, lives on Park Avenue ——" Even now the gray-faced man sounded grudging, as if he were being forced to sell a gilt-edged security far below its market value.

"His name!"

Weirhauser cursed. "Alton K. Humffrey."

"Are you all right, Jessie?"

Jessie said, "I'm fine."

They were in the tall-ceilinged foyer outside the Humffrey apartment on Park Avenue. The wall opposite the elevator was an austere greenish ivory, with plaster panel-work of cupids and wreaths. The elevator had just left them, noiselessly.

"Don't be afraid," Richard Queen said. "This is the one place where he won't try anything. I wouldn't have asked you along if I thought there was any danger."

"I'm not afraid." Jessie smiled faintly. "I'm numb."

"Would you rather sit this out?"

"I'm fine," Jessie said again.

"We've got to move in on him, Jessie. See just how tough a nut he's going to be. So far he's had it all his own way. You see that, don't you?"

"I suppose the trouble is I don't really believe it." Jessie set her lips to keep them from quivering. "I want to look at his face—really look at it. Murder must leave a mark of some kind."

The Inspector blotted the perspiration from his neck and pressed the apartment bell. He had given their names to the flunkey in the lobby with a confidence Jessie could only admire. There had been no unpleasantness. Mr. Humffrey had said on the house phone yes, he would see them. In a few minutes. He would call down when they might be sent up.

It was Friday evening, the second of September, a sizzling forerunner of the Labor Day weekend. The city had been emptying all day, leaving a sort of tautness in the vacuum.

Like me, Jessie thought.

It had been a curious three days since Richard Queen came back from George Weirhauser's office. He had summoned his aging assistants that evening to a council of war. It was surely the strangest conference, Jessie thought, in the unlikeliest place . . . a gathering of old men on a bench in a secluded spot in Central Park. The handsome ex-Lieutenant of Homicide, Johnny Kripps, had been there; the scar-faced Hugh Giffin; ex-Sergeant Al Murphy of the 16th, chunky, brick-skinned, with all his red hair, the youngest of the group; big Wes Polonsky, of the shaking hands; and Polonsky's old partner, Pete Angelo, a slim tough dark man whose face was a crisscross of wrinkles, like a detail map of his seventy years.

They had listened in happy silence as Richard Queen spoke, lonely men being handed straws and grasping them thankfully. And when they had walked off into the night, one by one, each with his assignment, Jessie had remarked, "I feel sorry for him in a way."

"For whom, Jessie?"

"Alton Humffrey."

"Don't waste your sympathy," the old man had muttered. "We've got a long way to go."

"Good evening," the millionaire said.

He had opened the door himself. He stood there sharp and shoulderless in a satin-faced smoking jacket, at disciplined ease, the chill Brahmin with nothing on his wedge of face but remoteness—like a high Army officer in mufti or a Back Bay man of distinction—framed in a rectangle of rich wines and hunt-club greens and leather browns; and Jessie thought, No, it isn't possible.

"You're looking well, Miss Sherwood."

"Thank you."

"I'm not sure I can say the same about you, Mr. Queen. Won't you come in? Sorry the servants aren't here to greet you. Unfortunately, I gave them the evening off."

"Within the last fifteen minutes?" Richard Queen said.

Alton Humffrey shook his head, smiling. "You're an extremely suspicious man."

"Yes," the old man said grimly, "I suppose you could say that."

The apartment was like a strange land, all mysterious woods and coruscating chandeliers, antiques, crystal, oil paintings, old tapestries, glowing rugs—rooms twice as large as any Jessie had ever set foot in, with no cushion crushed, no rug scuffed, no receptacle with a crumb of ashes. The study was like the drawing room, indigestibly rich, with monumental furnishings and impossibly tall walls of books that looked as if they were going to topple over.

"Please sit down, Miss Sherwood," Humffrey said. "May I give you some sherry?"

"No, thanks." The thought was nauseating. "How is Mrs. Humffrey?"

"Not too well, I'm sorry to say. Mr. Queen, whisky?"

"Nothing, thanks."

"Won't you have a seat?"

"No."

"Forbidding," the millionaire said with a slight smile. "Sounds like an inspector of police."

Richard Queen did not change expression. "May I begin?"

"By all means." Humffrey seated himself in the baronial oak chair behind his desk, a massive handcarved piece. "Oh, one thing." His bulbous eyes turned on Jessie, and she saw now that they were cushioned by welts she had not noticed on Nair Island. "I take it, Miss

140

Sherwood, from your being here tonight with Mr. Queen, that you're still pursuing your delusion about poor Michael's death?"

"I still believe he was murdered, yes." Jessie's voice sounded too loud to her ears.

"Well, at least let me thank you for pursuing it so discreetly."

"Are you through?" the old man asked.

"Forgive me, Mr. Queen." The millionaire leaned back attentively. "You were about to say?"

"On the 20th of this month," the Inspector began, "a shyster lawyer named Finner was murdered in his office on East 49th Street."

"Oh, yes."

"Finner, of course, was the man who turned the baby over to you back in June."

"He was?"

"Come, Mr. Humffrey, you're hardly in a position to deny it. Jessie Sherwood went along with you and Mrs. Humffrey to take charge of the child. She saw Finner at that time. So did your chauffeur, Cullum."

"I did not deny it, Mr. Queen," Humffrey smiled. "I was merely making some appropriate sounds."

"On Thursday the 18th, possibly the next day, Finner got in touch with you, told you I was putting pressure on him, and asked you to be present at a meeting in his office with me and Miss Sherwood on Saturday the 20th, at 4 P.M. You agreed to come."

"Now you've moved from the terra firma of fact," Humffrey said, "into the cuckooland of speculation. Of course I can't permit unfounded allegations to pass unchallenged. Pardon me for interrupting, Mr. Queen."

"You deny those allegations?"

"I will not dignify them by a denial. In view of your failure to mention the slightest corroboration, none is necessary. Go on."

"You agreed to be there," Richard Queen continued, unmoved. "But you had a little surprise up your sleeve for Finner, Mr. Humffrey. And, I might add, for us. You went to Finner's office that Saturday afternoon, all right, but not at four o'clock. You got there about an hour and a half early—from the contents of Finner's stomach, according to accounts of the autopsy findings, it must have been right after Finner came up from his lunch. You picked up Finner's letter-knife from his desk and buried it in his heart. Then you rifled his files for the folder marked 'Humffrey' that contained the papers and proofs of the baby's parentage, and out you walked with it. By this time, of course, you've destroyed it."

Jessie was watching Alton Humffrey's face, fascinated. There was no twitch or flicker to indicate that the millionaire was indignant, alarmed, or even more than mildly interested.

"I can only ascribe this extraordinary fantasy to a senile imagination," Humffrey said. "Are you accusing me—in all seriousness—of murdering this man Finner?"

"Yes."

"You realize, of course, that without proof of any sort —an eyewitness, let us say, a fingerprint, something drearily unfantastic like that—you're exposing yourself to a suit for criminal slander, defamation of character, and probably half a dozen other charges my attorneys will think of?"

"I'm relying on your well-known dislike for publicity to restrain them, Mr. Humffrey," the old man said dryly. "May I proceed?"

"My dear man! Is there more?"

"Lots more."

Humffrey waved his long white hand with its curling fingers as if he were bestowing a benediction.

"On the following Monday morning," Richard Queen went on, "you walked into a Times Square detective agency run by a fellow named Weirhauser and hired him to shadow Miss Sherwood and me. Weirhauser reported to you that we were visiting the maternity sections of one metropolitan hospital after another, trying to match up a set of infant footprints with the hospital birth records. This went on for about a week."

"I see," Humffrey said.

"Last Sunday evening, Weirhauser reported to you that we had presumably found what we'd been looking for. Our hospital find had taken us to an apartment house on West 88th Street, where we asked a lot of questions about a tenant named Connie Coy. Connie Coy, Mr. Humffrey."

"You pause significantly. Is the name supposed to mean something to me?" the millionaire asked.

"Weirhauser told you that Connie Coy was out of town filling a singing engagement in a Chicago nightclub, but that she was expected back soon. You then gave Weirhauser a clumsy story about being on the wrong tack and called him off the job."

Suddenly the room turned stifling. Jessie sat very still.

"And for this allegation, Mr. Queen, you're also drawing on your imagination?"

"No," the old man said, smiling for the first time. "For this one, Mr. Humffrey, I have an affidavit sworn to and signed by George Weirhauser. Would you care to see it? I have it right here in my pocket."

"I'm tempted to say no," Humffrey murmured. "But as a man who has played poker with Harvard undergraduates in his day—yes, I think I would care to see it."

Inspector Queen took a folded paper from his pocket and laid it defenselessly on the desk. Jessie almost cried out. But the millionaire merely reached for it, unfolded it, read it through, and politely handed it back.

"Of course, I don't know this man Weirhauser's signature from yours, Mr. Queen," he said, clasping his bony hands behind his head. "But even if this is a legitimate affidavit, I fancy Weirhauser hasn't too sweet a reputation, and if it became a matter of his word against mine——"

"Then you're denying this, too?"

"As among the three of us here," and Humffrey smiled coldly, "I see no harm in admitting that yes, I engaged a detective to follow you and Miss Sherwood last week, simply to see what mischief you were up to. I'd gathered from what Miss Sherwood let drop that you and she were bent on following up her hysterical belief that the baby was murdered; and I felt—in my wife's protection, if not in mine—that I was justified in keeping myself informed. When my man's report indicated that you were chasing some will-o'-the-wisp involving a woman I'd never heard of, I of course lost interest. My only regret is that in hiring Weirhauser I seem to have made a mistake. I detest mistakes, Mr. Queen, particularly my own."

"Then your position is that you never knew Connie Coy, the nightclub singer?"

"Yes, Mr. Queen," the millionaire said gently, "that is my position."

"Then I can't understand your activities the day after you fired Weirhauser. Last Sunday night Weirhauser told you we were asking questions about the Coy girl and that she was expected back soon from Chicago. The next day—this past Monday, Mr. Humffrey—*you spent the entire day and a good deal of the evening at Grand Central Terminal watching the arrival of trains from Chicago.* Why would you have done that if you didn't know Connie Coy and had no interest in her?"

Humffrey was silent. For the first time a slight frown drew his brows toward each other. Then he said, "I think I'm beginning to be bored with this conversation, Mr. Queen. Of course I was not in Grand Central Terminal that day, to watch the Chicago trains or for any other absurd purpose."

"That's funny," the old man retorted. "A red-cap and a clerk at one of the newsstands have identified a Stamford, Connecticut news photo of you as that of a man they saw hanging around the Chicago incoming train gates at Grand Central all day."

The millionaire stared at him.

Richard Queen stared back.

"Now you annoy me, Mr. Queen." Humffrey said icily. "Your so-called identifications don't impress me at all. You must know, from your days as a competent police officer, how unsatisfactory such identifications are. I must really ask you to excuse me."

He rose.

"Just when I was getting to the most interesting part, Mr. Humffrey?"

The old man's grin apparently changed Humffrey's mind. He sat down again.

"Very well," he said. "What else have you dreamed up?"

"The Coy girl got in at Grand Central that evening. She took a taxi uptown, and you followed her to 88th Street."

"And you have a witness to that?"

"No."

"My dear Queen."

"At least not yet, Mr. Humffrey."

Humffrey settled back. "I suppose I should hear this fairy tale out."

"You followed Connie Coy home, you took up a position on a roof overlooking her top-floor apartment, and when you saw me pumping her you aimed at a point midway between her eyes with a gun you were carrying, and you shot her dead.

"Don't interrupt me now," the old man said softly. "Finner was killed because he had the file on the case and knew who the baby's parents were. Connie Coy was killed because, as the mother of the baby, she certainly knew the identity of its father. The only one who benefits by destroying those papers and shutting Finner's and the real mother's mouth, Mr. Humffrey, is the baby's real father.

"You've committed two cold-blooded murders to keep your wife, her relatives, your blue-nosed friends, me, Jessie Sherwood, from finding out that you'd adopted, not a stranger's child, but *a child you yourself fathered in a cheap affair with a nightclub entertainer.*"

Humffrey opened a side drawer of his desk.

Jessie's heart gave a wicked jump.

As for the old man, his hand flashed up to hover over the middle button of his jacket.

But when the millionaire leaned back, Jessie saw that he had merely reached for a box of cigars.

"Do you mind, Miss Sherwood? I rarely smoke—only, in fact, when I'm in danger of losing my temper."

He lit a cigar with a platinum desk lighter and looked at Richard Queen with a mineral brightness. "This has gone beyond simple senility, Mr. Queen. You're a dangerous lunatic. You claim that I not only committed two atrocious murders, but that I did so in order to conceal from the world that I was the blood-father of the unfortunate little boy I adopted. I can't imagine your laying any other heinous crimes at my door, but from the beginning you and Miss Sherwood have insisted Michael was murdered. How does your diseased mind reconcile his alleged murder with my subsequent crimes? Did I murder my own child, too?"

"I think you got the idea when your nephew made that drunken, senseless attempt to break into the baby's nursery the night of July 4th," the Inspector said quietly. "What you couldn't have known, of course, was that Frost would suffer an appendix attack and have to have an emergency operation—an ironbound alibi—for the very night *you* picked. I think you murdered Michael, Mr. Humffrey, yes. I think you selected a night when you knew Miss Sherwood would be off. I think that after your wife fell asleep you deliberately suffocated the baby, and that in the confusion after Miss Sherwood's arrival to find the baby dead you noticed the pillowslip in the crib with its telltale handprint that indicated murder, and disposed of it. And from that moment on, of course, you kept insisting that Jessie Sherwood had been seeing things and that the baby's death was an unfortunate nursery accident. Yes, Mr. Humffrey, that's exactly what I think."

"Making me out a monster with few precedents." Humffrey's nasal tones crackled. "Because only a monster murders his own flesh and blood—eh, Mr. Queen?"

"If he does it believing it *is* his own flesh and blood."

"I beg your pardon?" The millionaire sounded amazed.

"When you found out that Connie Coy was pregnant and arranged through Finner to adopt the baby without her knowledge when it was born, Mr. Humffrey, you did it because you wanted possession of your own child. But suppose after you arranged for the secret purchase of your baby, with a forged birth certificate, with Finner paid off, with Connie Coy not knowing you had the baby and your wife not knowing the baby was yours— suppose after all this, Mr. Humffrey, you suddenly began to suspect you'd been made a fool of? That you'd gone to all that trouble and skulduggery to pass your name on to a baby that wasn't yours at all!"

Humffrey was quite still.

"A woman who'd had an affair with one man might have had affairs with a dozen, you told yourself. Suppose you even checked back and found that the Coy girl had been sleeping around with other men at the same time you were her lover? You being what you are—a proud, arrogant man with an exaggerated sense of family and social position—your love for the child you'd thought was yours might well have turned to hate. And so one night you murdered him."

The cigar had gone out. Humffrey was very pale.

"Get out," he said thickly. "No, wait. Perhaps you'll be good enough to spell out for me just what further incredible flights of your fancy, Mr. Queen, I must protect myself against. According to you, I fathered that child in a sordid affair, I murdered the child, I murdered Finner, I murdered the child's mother. Against these insanities you have abducted just two alleged pieces of evidence—that I hired a private detective to follow you two for a week, which I have explained, and that I was seen in Grand Central Terminal last Monday watching for Chicago trains, which I deny. What else have you?"

"You were in the Nair Island house on the night of the baby's murder."

"I was in the Nair Island house on the night of the baby's accidental death," the millionaire said coolly. "A coroner's jury supports my version of the slight difference in our phraseology. What else?"

"You had the strongest motive of anyone in the world to remove the folder marked 'Humffrey' from Finner's filing cabinet and destroy it."

"I cannot grant even the existence of such a folder," Humffrey smiled. "Can you prove it? What else?"

"You have no alibi for the afternoon of Finner's murder."

"You state an assumption as a fact. But even if your assumption were a fact—neither have ten thousand other men. What else, Mr. Queen?"

"You have no alibi for the evening of Connie Coy's murder."

"I can only repeat my previous comment. Anything else?"

"Well, we're working on you," the old man drawled. "A whole group of us."

"A whole group?" Humffrey pushed his chair back.

"Oh, yes. I've recruited a force of men like myself, Mr. Humffrey, retired police officers who've become very interested in this case. So, you see, it wouldn't do you the least good to kill Miss Sherwood and me, as you tried to do Monday night. Those men know the whole story . . . *and you don't know who they are.* Come, Jessie."

All Jessie could think of was that her back was to him; she could almost hear the blast of doom exploding behind her as she went to the door. But nothing happened. Alton Humffrey simply sat in the baronial chair at his desk, thinking.

"One moment." The millionaire came slowly around the desk toward them.

Richard Queen moved over to block the doorway. Humffrey stopped a few feet away, so close Jessie could smell the after-shave lotion on his gaunt cheeks.

"After reflection, Mr. Queen," he said good-humoredly, "I must conclude that you and your aging cronies have exactly nothing."

"Then you've got exactly nothing to worry about, Mr. Humffrey."

"We're in a sort of stalemate, aren't we? I won't go to the police to make you stop annoying me, because I prefer being annoyed in private rather than in public. You won't go to the police with your fantastic story, because your activities could land you in jail. It looks as if you and I are going to have to grin and bear each other. By the way, that is a gun you're carrying under your left armpit, isn't it?"

"Yes," the old man said, showing his denture for a moment. "And I imagine you have a permit for the gun you decided not to take out of that drawer a few minutes ago."

"Now your imagination is back within bounds, Mr. Queen," the millionaire smiled.

"He pointed a gun at me once, Richard," Jessie said in a piping voice. "The night I came back from New York to find the baby dead. Even after I identified myself he kept pointing it at me. For a minute I thought he was going to shoot me."

"Perhaps I should have." With those eyes turned on her, Jessie felt absurdly like running. Something womanish insinuated itself into Humffrey's voice, taunting and cruel. "I've given you considerable thought, Miss Sherwood. But now I've solved you. You're that most dismal of people, her brother's keeper. Good night."

Late that night Richard Queen snapped to the five silent old men, "It's going to be rough. He's an ice-cold customer, and smart. He's not going to be stampeded into anything stupid. As I said the other night, our best bet is to go backwards. We've got to tie him in with the Coy girl. They must have had a love nest somewhere before he dropped her and she moved to 88th Street. Maybe there's a record of his having paid her rent or hospital bills. We've got to find witnesses who saw them together—in restaurants, nightclubs, hideaways, rooming houses, motels . . ."

He talked until two in the morning to the attentive men. Jessie fell asleep on his shoulder. He did not disturb her.

New York came back from its holiday weekend. Autumn set in suddenly. Children prepared to return to school. Department stores were jammed. Another hurricane threat petered out. A sensational bank robbery in Queens seized the headlines, elbowing out the dwindling followup stories on the Finner and Coy cases.

Alton Humffrey was followed wherever he went. But his comings and goings were exemplary. The homes of friends, the ballet, his attorneys' offices, Wall Street, the Harvard Club. He did no entertaining.

They discussed a wire tap. Johnny Kripps was for it.

"We're in so far, Inspector, we may as well go the whole way."

But Inspector Queen vetoed it.

"He's too smart to say anything incriminating over a phone, Johnny. Besides, whom would he say it to? He's cleaned his slate. There's no business pending on his agenda except keeping an eye on us . . . I wonder why he hasn't gone up to New Haven."

"He's probably keeping in touch with Dr. Duane by phone," Jessie said.

The old man looked troubled.

The reports from Angelo, Murphy, and Giffin were discouraging. If Humffrey had set up a love nest for Connie Coy, they could find no trace of it. Before moving to the West Side apartment the Coy girl had lived in a theatrical hotel in the 40s. The ex-detectives, armed with photographs of Humffrey snapped by Kripps with a concealed candid camera, could turn up no one at the hotel who recognized the millionaire. The trace-back of the girl's New York club dates around August and September of the previous year, when conception must have taken place, was without result.

"She played a lot of dates out of town around that time," Pete Angelo reported. "One of them was a week's engagement in Boston. The Humffreys closed up the Nair Island place right after Labor Day last year and went back to Massachusetts. I better run up to Boston, Inspector."

"All right, Pete. But watch your step. He's a lot better known there than he is here."

"In the hot spots?" Angelo's wrinkles writhed. "If you ask me, this is a case of a guy slipping on his one and only banana peel. They won't know who he is unless they've seen him in their joint. Don't worry, Inspector."

Angelo came back three days later.

"Nothing definite," he reported. "The maitre-dee *thought* he looked familiar, but couldn't place him. He remembered Coy singing there, but he says she kept

150

pretty much to herself. I had to shy off, because he began to get nosy. Said 'another New York detective' had been around asking questions about Coy."

"Routine," the Inspector muttered. "Out of desperation, sounds like. Did the New York cop show this fellow a man's photo, Pete?"

"Nothing but Coy's, and no mention of any particular man. They're still chasing their tails. While I was there," Angelo added, "I checked on the hotel she'd stayed at, and some likely hideaway eateries and motels. But no dice. I get the feeling Boston or around Boston was where they met, but it was a year ago, and it looks pretty hopeless to me."

"He must have seen her in New York early last winter, when she got back to town," ex-Sergeant Murphy said. "But he sure was cagey."

"Cagey," Richard Queen said glumly, "is his middle name."

Kripps and Polonsky shared the shadowing assignment. They kept reporting nothing but tired feet.

On the 14th of the month Jessie announced that she had to go up to Rowayton. Her summer tenants' lease was expiring the next day and she was a little anxious about the condition of her house.

"It isn't much," Jessie said, "but I do have a few nice things and I don't cherish the thought of finding them smashed or made love to."

"I think I'll go with you," the Inspector said suddenly.

"That isn't necessary, Richard. Nothing can happen to me while he's being followed day and night."

"It isn't that, Jessie. I can't understand Humffrey's staying away from the sanitarium so long. You'd think with his wife so ill he'd go up to see her at least once a week. I'm going to tackle Dr. Duane."

"I'll drive you to New Haven."

"I'd rather not risk your being seen there. Not just yet, anyway. Are your tenants vacating tomorrow?"

"In the morning. I've called them."

"Well, we'll drive up to Connecticut around noon, and if you don't mind my borrowing the Dodge, I'll drop

151

you off at your place and go on to New Haven. I shouldn't be gone more than a few hours."

He gave Johnny Kripps, who had the day trick, special instructions. The next morning Kripps called to say that Humffrey had a luncheon appointment in town with an investment banker, and another with some friends for late afternoon at one of his clubs.

Richard Queen found the Duane Sanitarium without difficulty. It was a colossal white Colonial building, with sky-reaching pillars, on a rise of hill overlooking acres of barbered gardens and lawns. But it was entirely surrounded by a high iron-spiked brick wall, and there was a guardhouse at the iron entrance.

The guard was grim-faced. "Sorry, sir, no one gets in without an appointment or pass. You'll have to write or phone."

He flashed his gold shield. "You tell your Dr. Duane that a police inspector from New York wants to see him —and not next week, but right now."

Ten minutes later an attendant was ushering him through a vast flower-spotted reception room and up a flight of marble stairs to the director's private office.

Dr. Duane was waiting for him beside his secretary's desk. He was a tall impressive man with a carnation in his lapel.

"Come in, come in," he said testily, indicating the open door of his office. "Miss Roberts, I'm not to be disturbed." He followed the old man in and shut the door. "And you are Inspector——?"

"Queen." He looked around. The office was like an M-G-M set, with massive blond furniture, potted plants, and tropical fish tanks inset in the walls. "I know you're a busy man, so I'll get right to the point. I want to see Mrs. Sarah Humffrey."

Dr. Duane frowned. He seated himself at his immaculate desk and straightened a pile of medical charts.

"Impossible, I'm afraid."

The old man's brows went up. "How come, Doctor?"

"She's in no condition to see anyone. Besides, Mr. Humffrey's instructions were specific."

152

"Not to allow his wife to speak to a police officer?" Inspector Queen asked dryly.

"I didn't say that, Inspector. The circumstances under which Mrs. Humffrey came to us, as I take it you know, make Mr. Humffrey's wishes quite understandable. She has seen no once since being admitted here except our staff and her husband."

"How is she?"

"Better. The prognosis now is considerably more optimistic. However, any emotional upset . . ."

The man was nervous. He kept fidgeting with his bow tie, the papers, the telephone cord.

"Incidentally, just what's wrong with her?"

"Now, Inspector Queen, you can't expect me to tell you that. If Mr. Humffrey wishes to discuss his wife's illness, that's his affair. As her physician, I can't."

Queen took out a small black notebook and leafed through it. Duane watched him alertly.

"Now, Doctor, there's that business of your phone call on the afternoon of Saturday, August 20th, to the New York office of a lawyer named Finner——"

Dr. Duane stiffened as if his chair were wired. "*My* call?" he cried. "Why do you say that?"

"Because you made it."

"You people are hounding me! I told those detectives long ago I knew nothing about a phone call to such a person."

"Oh, some of the boys were up here on that?" the Inspector murmured. "When was this, Dr. Duane?"

"The last week in August. It seems that in investigating the murder of this man—Finner, was it?—the New York police claimed to have found a telephone company record of a toll call from this New Haven number to the man's office . . . Didn't you know they'd been here?" he asked, breaking off suspiciously.

"Of course. I also know, Doctor, that you did make that call."

"Prove it," Dr. Duane snapped. "You people prove it! I told your men at the time that it was a mistake. We have never had a patient named Finner here, or a patient directly connected with a person of that name. I

153

showed them our records to prove that. It's always possible some member of my staff put in such a call, but they have all denied it, and the only explanation I can offer is the one I gave—that someone here did call a New York number but got this fellow Finner's number by mistake . . ."

"In a way it's a break," Richard Queen said thoughtfully to Jessie when he got back to her cottage in Rowayton. "His lie about the phone call to Finner's office the afternoon of the murder stopped New York cold. Their one lead to Humffrey in this case was choked off at the source."

"You haven't said one word about whether you like my house," Jessie said. She was surrounded by mops and pails, and she was furious.

"It's pretty as a picture, Jessie. But about Duane's lying. Privacy means money to Duane. His whole high-toned establishment is based on it. He can't afford to have his name kicked around in a murder case. He's not protecting Humffrey, he's protecting himself." He scowled into his coffee cup.

"Those *people!*"

"What people?"

"My tenants! The condition they left my beautiful little matchbox in! Pigs, that's what they must be. Look at this filth, Richard!"

"I think I'll run over and see Abe Pearl while I'm in the neighborhood," he said philosophically.

"Would you? That will give me a chance to clean at least *some* of this mess."

He grinned. "Never knew a woman who could look at a dirty house and think of anything else. All right, Jessie, I'll get out of here."

Abe Pearl almost tore his arm out of the socket.

"What's happening, for God's sake?" When the old man brought him up to date, he shook his head. "That Humffrey dame might just as well be rotting in solitary somewhere. Do you suppose she's gone clean off her rocker, Dick, and that's why they won't let anyone see her?"

"No," Richard Queen said slowly. "No, Abe, I don't

think so. What happened up there today only confirms a suspicion I've had."

"What's that?"

"I think Humffrey's main reason for putting his wife out of circulation in a place where he can be sure she can't be got at—and himself staying away, now that he's being tailed day and night—is to keep us from her."

"I don't get it," Chief Pearl said.

"He's put her where nobody can talk to her. He'd like us to forget she ever existed. Abe, *Humffrey is scared to death of something his wife might tell us.*"

"About him?" The big man was puzzled.

"About him and the baby's death. It's got to be about little Mike's murder—she probably hasn't even been told about the other two. And if it's something Alton Humffrey doesn't want us to know, then it's something we've got to find out. The problem is, how to get to Sarah Humffrey . . ."

Jessie wanted to stay over, claiming that it would take a week to clean her house properly. But he hurried her back to the city.

They found Hugh Giffin picking disconsolately at his scar, and Al Murphy staring at the backs of his red-furred hands.

"Hospital," Giffin said. "Nothing, Inspector. The trail goes back to Finner, and Finner only. Even Finner didn't pay the bills directly. Connie Coy paid them with the cash Finner provided. Humffrey kept a million miles away from it."

"Murph," the Inspector said. "Any luck with the cabs?"

"Nope," the ex-sergeant said gloomily. "I must have tackled every hackie stationed around Grand Central. Just didn't hit it, that's all. Either this Humffrey hopped a cruising cab when he followed the girl home that night, or else he used a private car."

The old man shook his head. "He'd have felt safer taking a public carrier, Murph. Actually, all he had to do when he saw her climb into a cab with her luggage at Grand Central was take another cab, maybe on Madi-

son or Lexington, and be driven to the general neighborhood of the apartment, then walk over. After the shooting he probably just walked away—another pedestrian
out for some air."

Murphy looked unhappy.

"It's all right," Inspector Queen shrugged. "We'll just
have to keep digging."

He clapped the two men on the shoulder and sent
them home.

The following night, when Johnny Kripps came up
with his day's report on Humffrey, the old man said,
"I'm calling you off the tail, Johnny. Pete Angelo can
take over."

"You firing me, Inspector?" the bespectacled ex-
Homicide man asked, not altogether humorously.

"At the salary you're getting?" He grinned, not humorously either. "Johnny, have you been spotted by any
of the working details?"

"I don't think so."

"We'll have to start cutting corners. We're getting nowhere. Here's what I want you to do—I'd do it myself,
but you're the logical man for the job. Drop in at Homicide and see some of the boys. A friendly visit to your
old pals, you understand."

"Steer the talk around to the Coy and Finner cases?"

"Especially the Coy case. Find out what they've got.
Don't overdo it, Johnny—I don't want to have to bail
you out of 125 White Street!"

Kripps reported the next afternoon. "They've drawn a
skunk egg, Inspector. All they had on the Finner case
was that New Haven toll call, and Duane's pooped them
on that. The fact that he's an M.D. running a private
sanitarium gave them the bright idea at first that he was
mixed up with Finner in the baby racket, but the more
they've investigated Duane the cleaner he washes. Finner's case files they've exhausted without a lead."

"And Coy?" Richard Queen asked grimly.

"Believe it or not, they haven't been able to come up
with a single witness who saw a damn thing the night
she got it. By the way, they think too that the killer
hopped three or four roofs before he hit for ground lev-

el. Just walked down, and out, and away, probably on West End Avenue."

The Inspector tormented his mustache.

"All they've got in the Coy case is the bullet they've taken from her head and the ones from the plaster." Kripps shrugged. "Three slugs from the same gun. .38 Special ammo."

"Pete dug out the gun permit information on Humffrey today," the old man muttered. "One of the revolvers he owns is—or was—a Colt Cobra, which would fit with the ammo. But the gun is gone, Johnny. That we can be sure of. He probably dropped it in the Hudson the same night he shot Connie."

"Quite a guy," Kripps said unadmiringly.

"How do you know?" Jessie said.

"That he's quite a guy, Miss Sherwood?"

"That he's disposed of the gun?"

They looked at her.

"But Jessie," Richard Queen protested, "possession of the weapon that fired the bullet that killed Connie Coy would be enough by itself to warrant a murder indictment. Humffrey wouldn't be so foolish as to hold on to it. A ballistics comparison test, if we or the police got our hands on it, would mean curtains for him."

"Clever people are often so clever they're stupid," Jessie said. "He might be holding on to the gun out of plain cussedness, just because he figures you think he wouldn't. He strikes me as that type of man."

Ex-Inspector Queen and ex-Lieutenant Kripps examined each other.

"What do you think, Johnny?"

"What have we got to lose?"

"Plenty if we get caught at it."

"Let's not be."

"It might throw a scare in him, too," the old man chuckled. "Maybe even turn up something. I should have thought of it myself! Let's talk to Murph and Giffin and the others and see how they feel about it."

"Feel about what?" Jessie asked. "What are you talking about, Richard?"

He grinned at her. "There's only one way to take the

157

bull, Jessie, and that's by the horns. We're going to raid Humffrey's apartment."

The opportunity came two nights later. Cullum drove Alton Humffrey out to Oyster Bay to visit friends. The women on the staff had been given the night off.

The raiding party gained entrance to the Park Avenue building by way of an adjoining roof and a boarded-up penthouse. They got into the Humffrey apartment through the service door.

"No ripping, tearing or smashing," Richard Queen ordered. "But give it a real going-over."

They found nothing—no gun, no love letters, no receipted bills that tied in with Connie Coy, no correspondence with Finner . . . not a scrap of evidence to link Alton Humffrey with the murdered girl, or the murdered lawyer, or for that matter with the murdered baby.

The phone rang at three in the morning.

"Mr. Queen?" said a familiar nasal voice.

"Yes." He was wide-awake instantly.

"I'm disappointed in you."

"Are you, now."

"Did you really think you'd find anything in my apartment that could possibly nourish your fantasies?"

"For the record, Mr. Humffrey," Richard Queen said, "I don't know what you're talking about."

"Yes. Well." Humffrey sounded nasty but amused. "When you get over your attack of amnesia, you might take stock. Having me followed, ransacking my apartment, investigating my past—none of it will get you anywhere. You're in a pitiful condition, Mr. Queen. Have you considered consulting a palmist?"

His phone clicked gently in the old man's ear.

There was nothing in the next day's newspapers about a robbery attempt on Park Avenue.

The Inspector called another conference.

"Humffrey's right," he said grimly. "I'm calling you all off."

"What?" Jessie cried.

"The tail, too?" Wes Polonsky said.

158

"The tail, too, Wes."

The five old men stared at the sixth incredulously.

"We'll get nowhere attacking Humffrey's strength," he went on without excitement. "All we've done is waste time, money, and shoe leather. He's covered his tracks from way back where Finner and Coy were concerned, and he has nothing to do now but sit tight. What we've got to do is attack his weakness."

"Does he have one?" Jessie asked bitterly.

"Yes. It's mixed up with what happened on the night of August 4th on Nair Island. It doesn't matter which murder we pin on Humffrey, remember. He can only take the long sleep once."

"Sarah Humffrey? You keep coming back to her, Richard."

He nodded. "I should have stuck to her from the beginning. I'm convinced Mrs. Humffrey knows something about the baby's murder that Humffrey is dead scared she'll spill." He looked down at Jessie. "We've got to worm that information out of her. And that means an inside job."

"In other words," Jessie said, "me."

He took her hand clumsily. "I wouldn't ask you to do it if I could see a better way, Jessie. Do you think you could get into the Duane Sanitarium as a nurse?"

5.

AND THEN . . .
JUSTICE

"WHERE is this woman?" Richard Queen snarled. "She's half an hour late now."

"She'll be here," Jessie said soothingly. "My, you don't sound like an engaged man at all. More like a husband."

He colored. "How about another cocktail?"

"I'd *love* another cocktail."

He signaled the waitress hastily.

Jessie felt warm inside. It was not entirely the Pink Lady. Pretending to be engaged for Elizabeth Currie's benefit had been his idea. He had insisted on coming along, and they had to have a reason for his presence.

"Dr. Duane saw you that night on Nair Island, when he came to take Mrs. Humffrey to the sanitarium," he had said stubbornly. "I'd rather sit in on this."

"But he hardly glanced at me," Jessie had said. "Doctors never look at a nurse's face unless she's young and pretty."

"Then he took a good look!"

Not that Dr. Duane was going to be present. It was an exploratory lunch in a Stamford restaurant with Jessie's friend Elizabeth Currie, who had been on the nursing staff of the Duane Sanitarium for years. Approaching the problem of getting inside the sanitarium—and eventually inside Sarah Humffrey's room—through Elizabeth Currie had been Jessie's idea. Still, Richard had insisted. ("I want to feel this out, Jessie. I may still change my mind. After all, once you got in there you'd be cut off from me . . .")

Elizabeth Currie turned out to be a tall Scotswoman with iron hair, steel jaws, and bone eyes.

"So this is *the* man, Jessie. Let me look at you . . . Well! He's a little older looking than I expected, but then . . . I think it's marvelous, two people of your age finding each other after all hope had fled, haha! However did you do it, Jessie?"

"It was love at first sight," Jessie said lightly. "Wasn't it . . . darling?"

"Smack between the eyes," Richard Queen mumbled. "Cocktail, Miss Currie?"

"I'll say! Double Manhattan."

"Double Manhattan," he said to the waitress. "Maybe we'd better order the food now . . ."

An hour later he nudged Jessie under cover of the tablecloth, desperately.

"Well, no, Elizabeth," Jessie said, nudging him back. "As a matter of fact, our plans are a little vague. Richard's firm is sending him abroad for a few months, and we probably won't be . . . married till he gets back."

"What a hor'ble idea," the nurse said. "Why don't you get married now, you fool, and go with him?"

"We uh—we can't afford it," the Inspector said. "So Jessie's looking around for something to do to while away the time——"

"I can't face going back to private cases, Elizabeth. I wish I could find a staff job somewhere."

"You're crazy," Elizabeth Currie said.

"Elizabeth, I just thought! Do you suppose there's an opening at the Duane Sanitarium?"

"There's always an opening at the Duane Sanitarium. Staff turnover is something terrific. But I still think you're crazy. Jessie."

161

"Could you find out? First thing tomorrow? I'd be ever so grateful."

"I'll talk to Dr. Duane myself." Jessie's friend giggled. "I'm tight, do you know? Don't worry, I'll fix it for you, but you're absolutely balmy."

"Maybe Elizabeth has something on this," Richard Queen said. "What sort of place is it, Miss Currie? I wouldn't want Jessie getting into something——"

"That's just what she'd be doing," the nurse said confidentially. "Oh, it's a lovely place and all that—like a lovely prison, that is. Those patients. Phoo."

"Pretty sick people?"

"Pretty sick my eye. Bunch of hypochondriacs, most of 'em. Drive a nurse to drink. Which reminds me. Could I have another Manhattan, you nice man?"

"Better not, Elizabeth," Jessie said. "Talking about patients. You get some pretty important people up there, don't you?"

"Filthy rich people. Could I——?"

"Isn't the Duane Sanitarium where they took that wealthy society woman—what was her name? You know, Elizabeth—that woman from around here somewhere, tragic case of the baby that suffocated in its crib. Last month."

"Huh," the nurse said. "Mrs. Humffrey."

"Mrs. Humffrey!" Jessie said. "She's the one." She thought, If Elizabeth remembers the newspaper stories, I'm sunk. She glanced at her confederate doubtfully, but he nodded for her to go ahead. "She had a nervous breakdown or something, didn't she?"

"Absolutely no control over herself," Elizabeth Currie nodded contemptuously. " 'Bereavement shock,' they called it. All right, it was a ter'ble experience, but my God. She had everybody running around in circles."

"Had?" Richard Queen said. " 'Had,' Miss Currie?"

"Huh?" the nurse said owlishly.

"Doesn't she still have everybody running around in circles?"

"No, indeedy, you nice man."

"Why not?" Jessie didn't dare glance at him this time.

162

"Elizabeth, you talk as if she isn't at the Duane Sanitarium any more."

"She isn't. Big private limousine with two husky nurses in it took her away last Friday morning. And was Dr. Duane glad to see the last of *her*."

"I wonder where they took her."

"Nobody knows. Big hush-hush. Who cares? Richard —I *may* call you Richard, mayn't I?—just *one* more teeny Manhattan? He's real nice, Jessie . . ."

It was late afternoon before they got rid of Elizabeth Currie, blearily bewildered at Jessie's sudden decision not to apply for a nursing job at the Duane Sanitarium after all.

He drove in a fury. "Last Friday morning! And I was up there Thursday asking about her. Duane must have phoned Humffrey, or Humffrey called and Duane mentioned my visit, and bango! the next morning Humffrey hauls her out of there."

"But Richard, he was being followed."

"He didn't go himself. Didn't you hear, Jessie?" He honked savagely at a slowpoke driver. "Arranged the switch to a new hideout by phone, and drew us off while the transfer was made by the new people, who could be anybody, anywhere—maybe Arizona, for all we know. He's smart, Jessie. Smart and quick on his pins."

Jessie shivered. "What do we do now?"

"Who knows? It might take us months to locate her. If ever."

He stared ahead.

A few miles later Jessie touched his arm. "Richard."

"Yes?"

"Why don't we give up?"

"No!" he said.

"But it seems so hopeless."

To Jessie's surprise, he smiled. "Maybe not, Jessie."

"What do you mean?"

"It's his round, all right. But we've just learned something about Mr. Alton K. Humffrey."

"We have?" Jessie sounded dubious.

"This business of snatching his wife out from under

163

our noses confirms my belief that the murder of that baby is his weak spot. It's not theory any more. We've learned something else, too. The way to get at Humffrey is to force his hand. If we can surprise him, get him off balance . . ."

"You've thought of something!"

He nodded. "If it works, it could finish this off at one stroke."

"What is it, Richard?"

"Let me think it through."

For some reason, Jessie felt no elation. The title of an old Robert Benchley book, *After 1903, What?*, crossed her mind. *After Alton Humffrey, What?* She slumped down and closed her eyes . . .

She opened them to see the airy span of the George Washington Bridge moving by on her right.

"I fell asleep," Jessie murmured.

"And looked like a young chicken," he said in a peculiar way.

Jessie grimaced and sat up. "I'd make pretty tough chewing, I'm afraid."

"Jessie."

"Yes, Richard."

"Wasn't it a funny feeling? Back there in Stamford, I mean?" He said it with a laugh.

"You mean whan Elizabeth said Sarah Humffrey had been spirited away? I thought I'd die."

"No, I mean you and me." He was very red. "Pretending to be engaged."

Jessie stared straight ahead at the traffic. "I didn't see anything funny about it," she said coldly. "I thought it was nice."

"Well . . ."

Yes? Jessie thought. Yes?

But when he spoke again, it was to explain the plan he had worked out.

"It's that one over there, Jessie," Richard Queen said.

It was Wednesday evening, the 28th of September.

Jessie turned the coupé into the Pearl driveway and switched off her ignition. It was a spready old white clapboard house covered with wisteria and honeysuckle vines on a peaceful side street in Taugus. Great maples shaded the lawns, and on the old-fashioned open porch there were two rockers and a slide-swing.

He got out of the car, handling a large square flat package as if it contained eggs.

But Jessie was looking at the house. "What a lovely place for two people to live out their lives together."

"It's too big for two people, Abe says."

"I'll bet that's not what Mrs. Pearl says."

"You'd win," he chuckled. "Becky's children were born in this house, and to her that makes it holy. When Abe bought the beach shack, he had to fight to get her to go out there during the summer months. She isn't really happy till they close it up in September and come back here."

"She's lucky."

"So is Abe." He added. "In more ways than one."

Jessie sighed and got out. They went up on the porch, Richard Queen carrying the package carefully.

The door opened before he could ring the bell. "Richard, Jessie." Beck Pearl embraced them enthusiastically. "Let me look at you two! Abe, they're positively blooming. Did you ever see such a change in two people?"

"Well, get out of the way and let them come in," Abe Pearl grumbled. "I don't know why you wouldn't let me go to the door till they came up on the porch——"

His wife's glance withered him. "Let me have your things, Jessie. I can't imagine why Abe didn't insist on your coming for dinner. He's so stupid about some things!"

She carted Jessie off, and Abe Pearl took his friend into the living room.

"I thought you'd never get here. What held you up, Dick?"

"Daylight." The Inspector laid his package gently on the mahogany refectory table. "Mind if I pull the blinds?"

"You're acting damn mysterious. What's up?" The Taugus chief kept eying the package.

"Let's wait for the women." He drew all the shades

165

down to the sills. Then he went back to the table and stood there.

The women came in chattering. But when Beck Pearl saw the old man's face she stopped talking and sat down in a cornor. Jessie took a chair near her and folded her hands in her lap.

"Abe," Inspector Queen said, "what would you say if I told you we've finally got the goods on Alton Humffrey?"

The Taugus policeman looked from him to the package.

"In that thing?"

"Yes."

"So it's back in my lap." The big man came slowly to the table. "Let's have a look."

The Inspector undid the twine and removed the heavy wrappings with loving care. Then he stepped back.

Abe Pearl said, "My God, Dick."

The package contained two sheets of thick plate glass. Between them, spread flat but showing wrinkle marks, as if it had been found crumpled but had been smoothed out, lay a lace-edged pillowslip. The slip was of some dainty fabric; the lace was exquisite. By contrast the dirty imprint of a man's hand, a trifle blurry but unmistakable, was an offense. The print lay just off-center, the impression of a right hand from which the tip of the little finger was missing to the first joint.

"Where did you find this?" Abe Pearl demanded.

"You like it, Abe?"

"Like it!" The chief bent over the glass, scrutinizing the pillowslip eagerly. "That missing fingertip alone—! Wait till Merrick sees this."

"You owe Jessie an apology, Abe, don't you?" Richard Queen said, smiling.

"I guess I do; Miss Sherwood! I can't wait to see that iceberg's face when he gets a squint at this," Abe Pearl chortled. "But Dick, you haven't told me where you got it."

The old man said quietly, "We made it."

The big man's jaw dropped.

"It's a forgery, Abe. And judging by your reaction, a

166

successful one. That's what I wanted to find out. If it's fooled you, it'll fool Humffrey."

"A forgery . . ."

"We've been working on this for a week. Jessie went around from store to store in New York till she found a pillowcase exactly like the one that disappeared. What's this lace called again, Jessie?"

"Honiton. The case itself is batiste." Jessie glanced at the big policeman. "So of course, Mr. Pearl, I'll let you take your apology back."

He made an impatient gesture and turned away. But he turned back at once. "Tell me more, Dick."

"One of the boys, Pete Angelo, went up to Boston. We figured because of Humffrey's missing fingertip he'd likely have his gloves made to order, and we were right. Pete located his glovemaker, and got hold of a pair of gloves the old fellow'd made for Humffrey that Humffrey didn't like. Then we enlisted Willy Kuntzman, who used to be one of the best men in the Bureau of Tech Services—" the old man grinned—"retired, of course —and Willy went to work on the right glove. He came up with a cast of Humffrey's right hand in that plastic, or whatever it is, that looks and feels like flesh. Then, with Jessie describing the handprint she'd seen on the original pillowcase, Willy doctored the duplicate, and this is the result."

"Isn't this taking a hell of a chance?"

Richard Queen returned his friend's look calmly. "I'm willing to take it, Abe. I was hoping you'd be, too."

"You want me to pull this on Humffrey."

"The preliminary work, yes."

The big man was silent.

"Of course, Abe, it's not absolutely necessary. I can do the whole thing. But it would have more of an effect if you set it up. The crime was committed in your jurisdiction. You're the logical man to have found this."

"Where?"

"You don't tell him where. It won't even occur to him to ask. The sight of this ought to throw him for a loop. If he should ask, toss it to me. I'll be in on the kill."

"Listen, Dick, you've got a rock in this," the police

167

chief said slowly. "All right, Humffrey left his right handprint on a pillowcase just like this, and disposed of it that night before we got there. How? It must have been burned up, we said. Or it was cut to pieces and flushed down a toilet. Humffrey knows how he disposed of it, doesn't he? If he burned it, how could we produce it? If he cut it up, how come it's whole again?" Abe Pearl shook his head. "It won't work. He'll know in a flash we're trying to pull one."

"I don't think so, Abe." The Inspector seemed unperturbed. "I didn't agree with you and Merrick when you discussed it that night, although I didn't want to put my two cents in with Merrick there. It's highly unlikely that Humffrey'd have burned the pillowslip. It was a hot night in August. He'd hardly have risked making a fire that might have been seen or smelled by somebody in the house—Jessie here, a servant, Dr. Wicks, even his wife—and remembered later just because it was a hot night in August.

"As for cutting it to pieces, he didn't have to, Abe. The material is so fine you can take this thing and crumple it into a small ball. He could have flushed it down a drain in one piece. A man who's just taken the life of an infant and expects the police any minute—no matter what substitute for blood is flowing through his veins—isn't going to go in for anything fancy. That only happens in my son's books. Humffrey had only one thought in mind, to get rid of the pillowcase in the quickest and easiest way.

"Sure, Abe, I don't deny the risk. But the way I see it, the odds are way over on our side." He shrugged. "Of course, if you'd rather not have anything to do with it——"

"Don't be a horse's patoot, Dick. It's not that." Abe Pearl began to pull on his fleshy lower lip.

The old man waited.

"It is that, Abe." It was Beck Pearl's soft voice. "You're thinking of me."

"Now Becky," her husband shouted, "don't start in on me!"

168

"Or maybe I'm flattering myself. Maybe it's yourself you're thinking of. Your job."

"Becky——" he thundered.

"The trouble is, dear, you're going soft in Taugus. It's a nice fat easy job, and you've gotten nice and fat and easy along with it."

"Becky, will you stay out of this? Damn it all——!"

"How would you feel if that little boy had been Donny? Or darling little Lawrence?"

"You would throw my grandchildren up to me!" The big man hurled himself into the armchair with a crash that made the room shake. "All *right,* Dick! What's your plan?"

The next morning two police cars shot across the Nair Island causeway, drove into the Humffrey grounds, and eight Taugus detectives and uniformed men, headed by Chief Pearl, jumped out.

Stallings, the caretaker-gardener, was on his knees in one of the flower beds, planting bulbs.

"Something wrong again, Chief?"

"Nothing that concerns you, Stallings," Chief Pearl said gruffly. "Get on with your work. Borcher, you and Tinny take the house. You other men, fan out on the grounds—you know what we're after. One of you go down to the beach and keep an eye on that dredger, in case they make the strike."

"One minute," Stallings said uneasily, as the officers began to scatter. "I'm responsible, Chief. What are you up to?"

"This is a search party," the chief barked. "Out of my way."

"But Mr. Pearl, I got my instructions from Mr. Humffrey. He specially said I was to keep cops and reporters out."

"He did, did he? Ever hear of a search warrant, my friend?"

"A warrant?" Stallings blinked.

Chief Pearl waved an official-looking document before the old fellow's nose and immediately put it back in his pocket and turned away. "All right, men."

He went into the Humffrey house on the heels of his two detectives.

Stallings waited.

When all the officers had disappeared, he stole up the driveway to the service entrance, slipped inside, shut the door quietly, and went to the telephone extension in the butler's pantry. He gave the Taugus operator the Humffrey apartment number in New York City.

"The Humffrey residence," Mrs. Lenihan's Irish voice answered.

"Lenihan," Stallings muttered. "Is his nibs there?"

"Who is this?"

"Stallings. Got to talk to Mr. Humffrey. Shake a leg."

"You old fool, what are you up to now?" the housekeeper sniffed. "Drunk again, like as not. Mr. Humffrey isn't here."

"Where is he?"

"I don't know. All he said was for Henry to have the limousine ready. They drove off early this morning." Mrs. Lenihan lowered her voice. "Something doing?"

"Plenty. Cops all over the place. Chief Pearl with a search warrant. Don't you have *no* idea where they went?"

"Mercy," Mrs. Lenihan said faintly. "I don't, Stallings. What are they looking for?"

"How should I know?" Stallings sounded disgusted. "Well, I done my duty."

He hung up and returned to his bulbs.

In Alton Humffrey's upstairs study, Abe Pearl replaced the study extension on its base softly.

At a few minutes past two that afternoon Stallings phoned Mrs. Lenihan again. This time he sounded agitated.

"Isn't Mr. Humffrey back yet, Lenihan?"

"Not yet," the housekeeper said. "What's the latest?"

"They just left."

"That's good."

"Maybe not so good," Stallings said slowly. "Maybe not so good, my fine Mrs. Lenihan."

"Now what? You and the voice of doom! What did they do? What did they say?"

"Nothing. Wouldn't tell me nothing. But Chief Pearl cracked me on the back, and do you know what he says to me?"

"What?"

" 'Stallings,' he says, 'I got the funniest feeling you're going to be looking for a new job,' he says."

"He didn't!" the housekeeper gasped.

"That's what he says to me, Lenihan, word for word."

"What do you suppose it *means*?"

"I don't know," the caretaker muttered. "But I don't like it . . . You better make good and damn sure Mr. Humffrey calls me the minute he gets in!"

Abe Pearl began phoning the Humffrey apartment from his office in Taugus police headquarters at a little past 3 P.M. He called again at 3:30, and again at 4:00.

When he phoned at 4:15 Mrs. Lenihan answered in a voice shrill with tension. "No, he *isn't* here yet, Chief Pearl. I told you I'd tell Mr. Humffrey the minute he comes in. Mercy!"

"Make sure you do, Mrs. Lenihan," Chief Pearl growled. He hung up and said, "Well, that's it. Let's hope it works."

"It'll work, Abe," Richard Queen said confidently.

It was almost 6 P.M. when Abe Pearl put his hand over the mouthpiece and said, "Here he is!"

Richard Queen hurried into the anteroom. The police operator handed him the earphones and he slipped them on and waved a go-ahead through the open doorway.

Abe Pearl removed his hand and said grimly, "Okay, Phil. Put Humffrey on."

Alton Humffrey's voice rasped in the earpiece. "Chief Pearl!"

The chief said coldly, "So you finally got my messages, Mr. Humffrey."

"I've only just got in. May I ask what in the name of common sense has been going on today? My housekeeper is in tears, Stallings keeps babbling some nonsense about a police raid on my Nair Island property——"

"Oh, you've talked to Stallings."

"Certainly I've talked to Stallings! He's been calling all day, too. Is he out of his mind, Chief, or are you?"

"I'd rather not discuss it over the phone."

"Really? By what right do you invade my privacy, ransack my house, trample my flowers, put dredgers to work off my beach? By what right, Chief Pearl?" The millionaire's twang vibrated with anger.

"By the right of any police officer who's got the jurisdiction to search for evidence in a murder case."

"*Murder* case? You mean the baby? Good heavens, are you people singing that tune again? Don't you remember, Mr. Pearl? That case is closed. You closed it yourself."

"An unsolved murder case is never closed."

"It wasn't an unsolved murder case! It was an accident."

"It was a murder case, Mr. Humffrey," Abe Pearl said. "And now we've got the evidence to prove it."

There was a pause.

Then the millionaire said in an altogether different way, "Evidence, you say? What evidence?"

"I'd appreciate it if you came out to police headquarters in Taugus right away, Mr. Humffrey. Tonight."

"Tonight? I'm not going anywhere, any time, until I have more information! What evidence?"

The chief glanced over into the anteroom. Richard Queen nodded.

"Well, you might say," Abe Pearl said into the phone, "you might say it's something we should never have stopped looking for in the first place."

There was another pause.

"I see," Humffrey said. "You wouldn't be referring, by any chance, to that pillowslip the Sherwood woman —that nurse—kept babbling about?"

The police chief glanced over at Richard Queen again. The old man hesitated this time. But then, grimly, he repeated the nod.

"That's right," Abe Pearl said.

"You've found it?" The bitterness in Humffrey's voice was startling.

"I can't say any more over the phone. Will you come out here so we can have a talk about this, Mr. Humffrey? Voluntarily? Or——?" He deliberately left Humffrey dangling.

The wire was quiet.

"Very well," the millionaire said slowly. "I'll be out in an hour."

The instant the connection was broken, Richard Queen snatched the earphones from his head and ran into Abe Pearl's office.

"Convinced now?" he cried. "You heard the way he asked if you'd found it! He'd never have said it that way if he knew the pillowslip was gone beyond recall. He *accepted* the possibility that the slip could be produced! Look, let's get that tape recorder hooked up. Better be sure you plant the bug where he won't spot it . . . I tell you, Abe, we've got him!"

"Chief Pearl," Alton Humffrey said.

"Who wants him?" The desk man kept writing.

"Alton K. Humffrey."

The officer looked up.

"Humffrey?" he said in a hard voice. He rose. "Have a seat."

"I'll stand," Humffrey said.

"That's up to you." The uniformed man disappeared in a hall beyond the water cooler.

The millionaire looked around the room. He was very pale. Several patrolmen and two detectives were lounging in silence, staring at him. Humffrey's pallor deepened. He looked away, fingering his collar.

The burly figure of Chief Pearl appeared from the hall.

"I made good time, you see, Chief," Alton Humffrey said. He sounded nervously friendly.

The chief said, "Reynolds, better fill in at the desk. Harris has to take stenographic notes. No calls of any kind. I don't care if there's a riot."

"Yes, sir." One of the patrolmen went behind the desk and sat down.

173

"This way, Mr. Humffrey." Abe Pearl stepped back.

Alton Humffrey moved toward him slowly. The millionaire seemed puzzled as well as nervous now.

The two detectives got up and sauntered across the room after him. Humffrey glanced over his shoulder at them, looked ahead quickly.

"That door at the end of the hall," Chief Pearl said.

Humffrey walked up the hall, the chief close on his heels. The two detectives followed.

At the door Humffrey hesitated.

"Go in and have a seat, Mr. Humffrey. I'll be there in a minute."

Abe Pearl turned his back and began to whisper to his two detectives.

Humffrey stepped into the chief's office uncertainly. The man who had been on desk duty in the outer room was at one of the windows operating a pencil sharpener. On a chair beside the chief's big swivel chair lay a stenographic notebook. The officer glanced at Humffrey, went to the smaller chair, picked up the notebook, flipped it open, and sat down, waiting.

There was only one other chair in the office. It was straightbacked and uncomfortable-looking. The millionaire hesitated again. Then he sank into it.

Chief Pearl came in alone. He went around his desk and seated himself. Humffrey stole a glance at the door. The shadows of the two detectives were silhouetted on the frosted glass.

"This is all very formidable, Mr. Pearl," Humffrey said with a smile. "Anyone would think you were preparing to arrest me."

The swivel chair squealed as the Taugus chief leaned back, scowling.

"Perhaps I should have brought my attorney," Humffrey went on in a jocular way.

"There's nothing your attorney can do for you tonight," Chief Pearl said. "Tonight you're going to be shown something, and I expect you to make a statement. After that you can call ten attorneys for all I care."

"Shown something?" the millionaire said. "That would be the pillowslip, Mr. Pearl?"

The big man got up and went over to the door of the anteroom. He opened it and said, "All right, Dick."

Humffrey half-rose.

Richard Queen came in with the glass-protected pillowslip. It was wrapped in brown paper.

"Queen," Humffrey said. He was staring from the old man to the paper-covered object.

"You, too, Miss Sherwood," Abe Pearl grunted.

Jessie walked in.

The millionaire got to his feet.

"I might have known," Humffrey said slowly. "I might have known."

"It's your show, Dick. Take over." The chief glanced at the uniformed man with the notebook. "Start taking notes, Harris."

The sharpened pencil poised.

"If you don't mind, Abe, I'll set this down on your desk." The Inspector laid the package on the desk. He loosened the wrappings, but did not remove them. Humffrey's eyes were on the brown paper. The old man straightened up and faced the millionaire. "This is quite an exhibit, Mr. Humffrey. No wonder you didn't want us to find it."

Humffrey was all gathered in now, almost crouching. He could not seem to tear his glance from the brown paper.

"It's a whole case by itself," Richard Queen went on. "It not only knocks that inquest jury's verdict of accidental death into the next county, it proves that Michael Stiles Humffrey was deliberately murdered, as Miss Sherwood insisted from the beginning. But it does even more than that, Mr. Humffrey. It not only proves the baby was murdered, it shows who murdered him."

He whirled and whipped the paper off the glass.

"Miss Sherwood," he said swiftly, "for the record I want you to identify this pillowslip. Is this the pillowslip you saw lying over Michael Stiles Humffrey's face and torso on the night of August 4th, when you found the baby dead of suffocation?"

Jessie stepped up to the desk.

"It is," she said in a stiff voice, and stepped back.

Humffrey quivered. His pallor was yellowish now. He moved toward Abe Pearl's desk in a jerky way, slowly, and stared down at the pillowslip under the glass.

"You never thought we'd find it, did you?" Inspector Queen said softly. "There's the dirty handprint—the dirty print of a right hand, just as Miss Sherwood said. But it's not just the dirty print of a right hand, Mr. Humffrey, as you can see. It's the dirty print of a right hand that has the tip of the little finger missing to the first joint!"

Abe Pearl reached over suddenly and seized the millionaire's right hand in his big paw. He uncurled the little finger as if it were a child's, exposing its deformity.

"You murdering louse," Abe Pearl said. "A man who'd kill a two-month old baby, a kid he'd given his own name to, for God's sake! . . . You won't bull or buy your way out of this one, Humffrey. You're through. With this pillowslip as evidence, you haven't got a chance. The best thing you can do is sit down in that chair and start talking. I want a full confession, and I want it now."

He flung the hand from him contemptuously and pointed to the straightbacked chair. Then he turned away.

"Congratulations, Chief, on a superb performance."

Abe Pearl swung about. Alton Humffrey was smiling. There was nothing uncertain in his smile. It was a smile without humor, angry and cruel.

"What did you say?" Abe Pearl said.

"I should have warned you about Queen, Mr. Pearl. Apparently his lunacy is contagious." He began to stroll about the police chief's office, glancing here and there with fastidious distaste, as if he were slumming. He ignored Richard Queen and Jessie Sherwood utterly. "Beautifully staged, I'll grant you that. The meaningless raid on my property. The repetitious phone calls. The menacing summons. The policemen sitting about, waiting to pounce on the big bad wolf and cart him off to the pound. And finally—" the millionaire's glance shriveled Richard Queen and Jessie Sherwood, shattered the glass-protected pillowslip—"finally, these two mountebanks, and the production of this work of art. Who manufacured it, Chief, you or Queen? I suppose it was you, Queen, and your West 87th Street Irregulars. It has the metropolitan touch. Unfortunately, you slipped. The moment I glanced at this I knew it was a fake. But you couldn't have known that, could you? And so it's all gone to waste. All this loving labor, the stage designing, the suspense, the superb acting, the extras in the wings . . ."

Alton K. Humffrey suddenly strode over to the hall door and yanked it open.

The two detectives looked around, startled.

Humffrey laughed.

"Do we haul him in now, Chief?" one of the detectives asked.

"Oh, get out of my way, you fool," Alton Humffrey snapped; and he walked out.

"I don't understand it," Inspector Queen said. "I don't, I don't."

Abe Pearl said nothing. Patrolman Harris was gone; the three were alone in the office.

"I never should have involved you in this, Abe. Or you, Jessie."

"Please, Richard."

"Up to a certain point he was our fish," the old man muttered to the pillowslip on the desk. "He was hooked. Right through the gills. Then he takes one look at the slip and he knows it's a frameup. What did we do wrong? Could it be the pillowslip itself, Jessie? The wrong material, wrong lace, wrong size or something?"

"It can't have been that, Richard. This is an exact duplicate of the one that disappeared. I'd seen the slip many times, told Mrs. Humffrey how lovely I thought it was."

"Then it's what we did with it. The position of the print?"

"To the best of my recollection, it was just about where I told Mr. Kuntzman to put it."

"Maybe it's what we *didn't* do with it," he said suddenly. "After all, Jessie, you did see it in a dim light for

177

only a couple of seconds. Suppose there was some other mark on it, a mark you missed? Maybe a dirt streak, a smudge, a tear. Something you just didn't notice."

"I suppose that's it," Jessie said lifelessly. "You see how misguided you were to put any confidence in me. Look what I've got you into."

"Let's not talk about who got whom into what." Richard Queen grimaced. "Here's Abe, ready to strangle me——"

"You didn't hold any gun to my head, Dick," Abe Pearl said heavily. "I'm just trying to figure out what gives now. Think he's going to make an issue of this?"

"Not a chance."

"He could make it pretty hot for us."

"He can't afford to, Abe. The last thing Humffrey wants is to stir up a full-scale investigation." The Inspector looked up. "You know, this isn't a total loss. It's confirmed two important points. One, that he substituted the clean pillowslip that night for the dirty one, otherwise he wouldn't have spotted the discrepancy. Two, that he didn't destroy the dirty slip—he was all ready to believe we'd found it. We're not licked yet!"

Jessie stared at him. "Richard, you sound as if you're going on with this."

"Going on with it?" He seemed puzzled. "Of course I'm going on with it, Jessie. How can I stop now? We've got him on the run."

Jessie began to laugh. Something in her laugh alarmed him, and he stepped quickly to her side. But she stopped laughing as suddenly as she had started. "I'm sorry, Richard. It just struck me funny."

"I don't see anything funny about it," he growled.

"I am sorry." She touched his arm.

"Aren't you going on with it, Jessie?" he asked grimly.

Her hand dropped to her side.

"Richard, I'm so tired . . . I don't know."

Their return to the city was a strain on both of them. He seemed depressed, resentful, frustrated—a combination of things that Jessie with her throbbing head did not

178

attempt to analyze. When he dropped her off at 71st Street, promising to park her car in the garage, he drove off without another word.

Jessie floundered all night. For once aspirin did not help, and tension made her skin itch and prickle unmercifully. Toward morning she took a seconal and fell into a heavy sleep. She was awakened by various bumps and crashes to find the clock hands standing at five minutes to noon and Gloria Sardella dumping various bags and packages on the living room floor.

Holy Mother! Jessie thought. It's the 30th!

She decided then and there.

"I'm going home, Richard," Jessie said over the phone.

"So you've made up your mind." And he was silent.

Jessie thought, Is it possible this is the way it's going to end?

"I've sort of had my mind made up for me," she said, trying to sound chatty. "I'd forgotten all about Gloria's saying when she left that she'd be back on the 30th. I guess I've lost track of time, along with everything else. Are you there, Richard?"

"I'm here," he said.

"I felt like such a ninny when she walked into the apartment this morning. The least I might have done was meet the boat! Of course, Gloria was awfully sweet —said I was welcome to stay as long as I wanted——"

"Why don't you?" He was having some trouble clearing his throat.

"It wouldn't be fair to Gloria. You know how small her apartment is. Besides, what's the point? The whole thing's been a mistake, Richard." Jessie stopped, but he didn't say anything. "Last night in Taugus was the straw that broke the lady camel's back, I guess. I'd better go home and back to being a nurse again."

"Jessie."

"Yes, Richard."

"Do we have to talk over the phone? I mean—unless you'd rather not see me any more——"

"Richard, what a silly thing to say."

"Then can I drive you up to Rowayton?" he asked eagerly.

"If you'd like to," Jessie murmured.

He drove so slowly that irate cars honked and swooshed around them all the way up to Connecticut.

For a while he talked about the case.

"I went over some of the boys' reports, from when they were tailing Humffrey. Couldn't sleep last night, anyway. I noticed something that hadn't meant anything at the time.

"That Friday morning when Humffrey'd had his wife removed from the Duane Sanitarium, the report said that his chauffeur left town early, alone, driving the big limousine. Remember Elizabeth Currie saying that Mrs. Humffrey was taken away in a big private limousine? My hunch is that Humffrey sent Cullum up to New Haven while he stayed in town to draw us off. Cullum must have picked up the two nurses on the way, and then gone up to the sanitarium. At least, it's a possibility. I'm going to work on that right away—today."

"Richard, you should have told me. I'd never have let you waste all this time driving me home."

"It can wait till I get back to the city," he said quickly.

"What are you going to do, pump Henry Cullum?"

"Yes. If I can find out through him where Sarah Humffrey is . . ."

But for the most part they were silent.

In Rowayton he carried her bags into the cottage, fixed the leaky kitchen faucet, admired her zinnias, accepted her offer of coffee; but it was all done on a note of withdrawal, and Jessie's head began to ache again.

I won't help him, she told herself fiercely. I won't!

He refused to let her drive him to the Darien station. He phoned for a cab instead.

Then, at the last moment, with the taxi waiting outside, he said suddenly, "Jessie, I can't go without—without——"

"Yes?"

"Without, well, saying thank you . . ."

180

"Thank *me?*" You're overdoing it, old girl, she thought in despair. How do women manage these things? "What on earth for, Richard?"

He toed her living-room rug. "For just about the two most wonderful months of my life."

"Well," Jessie said. "I thank *you,* Mr. Queen. It hasn't been exactly dull for me, either." *And there's a brilliant remark.*

"I don't mean this Humffrey thing." He cleared his throat twice, the second time irritably. "You've come to mean—well, a lot to me, Jessie."

"I have, Richard?" *Oh, dear* . . .

"An awful lot." He scowled at the rug. "I know I have no right . . ."

"Oh, Richard."

"I mean, a man of my age——"

"Are we back to *that* again?" Jessie cried.

"And you so youthful, so pretty . . ."

My goodness, Jessie thought. Now if my stomach doesn't start making blurpy bilge-pump sounds, the way it always does when I'm fussed . . . *And there it goes!*

"Yes, Richard?" Jessie said loudly.

The taxi man took that moment to start blasting away on his horn. Richard Queen flushed a profound scarlet, grabbed her hand, shook it as if it were a fighting fish, mumbled, "I'll call you some time, Jessie," and ran.

Jessie sat down on her floor and wept.

He'll never call, Jessie assured herself. Why should he? I got him into it, and now I've run out on him. He won't come back.

She swallowed the two aspirins dry, as a punishment, and resumed putting her clothes away.

Murdered babies.

My righteous indignation.

The truth is, Jessie Sherwood, she told herself pitilessly as she banged hangers about in the closet, you're a hopeless old maid\ You're a hopeless old maid filled with hopeless guilt feelings, and don't blame it on menopause, either. You've got plenty to feel guilty about, old girl. Not just running out on him. Not just acting like an irresponsible neurotic, throwing yourself at him, leading

181

the poor man on till he began to feel young again, and then making it as hard for him as you could.

It's that pillowslip.

When Jessie thought about the pillowslip, something inside cringed and curled up. She tried not to think of it, but the more she tried the faster it bounced back. She had been so positive the doctored slip was just like the one she had seen. But it hadn't been. One look, and Humffrey had known it was a forgery. How could he have known? What hadn't she noticed, or forgotten? Maybe if she could remember it now . . . That would be helping. That would be making it up to Richard!

So Jessie shut her eyes tight and thought and thought, right there in the closet, seeing the nursery again, seeing herself stooping over the crib in the nightlight, the pillow almost completely covering the motionless little body . . . the pillowcase . . . the pillowcase . . .

But she could not add anything to the pillowcase. It remained in her mind's eye as she thought she had seen it that night.

She dropped the dress to the floor and went over to the chintz-backed maple chair near the window, where she could look out at her postage-stamp back garden. The morning-glories were still in bloom, and the petunias; the berries on the dogwood tree were big and shiny and red, and disappearing fast down the gullets of the birds; and Jessie thought, I will do it for him. I *will*.

So she sat there and thought, desperately.

How *had* that monster disposed of the pillowslip? He hadn't burned it, he hadn't cut it to pieces . . . He had been under pressure, the pressure of his own guilt, the pressure of his wife's hysterics, the pressure of Dr. Wicks's presence, the pressure of the police-on-the-way . . . Pressure. Pressure makes people do things quickly, without much thought. Richard had remarked himself Wednesday night that Humffrey had had only one thought in mind, "to get rid of the pillowcase in the quickest and easiest way."

Suppose I'd been the one, Jessie thought with a shudder.

Suppose I've smothered the baby and the baby's body

has been found by that nosy nurse and the house is in confusion and Dr. Wicks is there and the police are coming and suddenly, like a dash of seawater, I notice the pillow with my dirty handprint on the slip. It mustn't be found . . . they'll know it was murder . . . get rid of the slip quick, quick . . . is that someone coming? whose voice is that? I mustn't be found in here . . . I'm in the nursery—I've got to get rid of it—got to hide it—where? where?

The laundry chute!

Now wait, Jessie said to her racing pulse, wait, wait, that came too easy. . . .

Easy? But that's just it. The easiest way! One step to the door of the chute, one flip of the wrist, one shove, another flip of the wrist . . . and the pillowslip is gone. Gone down into the basement, into the laundry-sized canvas hamper under the chute opening . . . gone to mingle with the rest of the household's soiled laundry. The easiest, the quickest way to get rid of it.

At least temporarily.

Later—later I'll get hold of it, destroy it. As soon as I can. As soon as I can get down into the basement plausibly, safely . . .

And suppose just then the police arrived. And you couldn't, you simply couldn't call attention to yourself by disappearing. Not with a hysterical wife needing attention, policemen's questions to be answered, the dead little body in the crib . . . not with the awful guilt clamoring to be guarded . . . and the servants downstairs whispering over their coffee, in the path of anyone wanting to get to the basement unseen. And always and constantly the need to hear every whisper, to observe every change of expression, every coming, every going, to make sure you were still unsuspected . . .

Jessie frowned. It sounded fine—except for one thing. The police had searched the house thoroughly. "The laundry basement, the hampers . . ." Chief Pearl had ordered. And they hadn't found the pillowslip. So maybe . . .

So maybe they overlooked it.

That's what must have happened! Jessie thought exultantly. They didn't find the slip somehow and Alton Humffrey must have died a thousand deaths while they were looking and was reborn a thousand times when they failed to find it, and kept waiting, waiting for them to leave so he could sneak down into the basement and rummage through the canvas hamper and retrieve the fateful piece of batiste. But dawn came, and daylight, and still Abe Pearl's men were on the premises searching, and still he was afraid to risk being seen going to the basement.

And then, of course, Sadie Smith came, Sadie Smith from Norwalk, driving up in her 1938 Olds that made such a clatter early Tuesday and Friday mornings . . .

Sadie Smith to do the wash.

Jessie burrowed deeper in the maple chair, surprised to find herself shaking.

For of course after that Alton Humffrey thought he was safe. That day passed, a week, a month, and the pillowslip vanished into the limbo of forgotten things. Sadie Smith had washed the pillowslip along with the other hand laundry, not noticing, or ignoring, the dirty handprint; and that was the end of that.

The end of it.

Jessie sighed.

So much for "helping" Richard.

But wait!

Surely Sadie could not have been deaf and blind to what was going on in the house that Friday. Surely Mrs. Lenihan, or Mrs. Charbedeau, or one of the maids, must have told Sadie about the pillowslip the policemen were turning the house and grounds upside down for. Even if the police had missed it in the hamper, *wouldn't Sadie have been on the lookout for it?*

Yes!

Then why hadn't she found it?

It was still light when Jessie parked before the neat two-story brick housing development in Norwalk. She found Sadie Smith changing into a clean housedress. Mrs. Smith was a stout, very dark woman wtih brawny forearms and good-humored, shrewd black eyes.

"Miss Sherwood," she exclaimed. "Well, of all people! Come in! I just got home from work——"

"Oh, dear, maybe I ought to come back some other time, Mrs. Smith. It was thoughtless of me to pop in just before dinner, and without even phoning beforehand."

"We never eat till eight, nine o'clock. My husband don't get home till them. You go on into the parlor and set, Miss Sherwood. I'll fix us some tea."

"Thank you. But why don't we have it here in your kitchen? It's such a charming kitchen, and I get so little chance to be in my own . . ."

Mrs. Smith said quietly, as she put the kettle on the range, "It's about the Humffreys, Miss Sherwood, ain't it?"

"Yes," Jessie admitted.

"I knew it." The dark woman seated herself at the other end of the table. "You don't have to tell me you're still all bothered about how that little child died. It's a terrible thing, Miss Sherwood, but he's dead, and nothing can bring him back. Why don't you just forget the Humffreys? They ain't your kind of people."

"I'd very much like to, but there are reasons why I can't. Do you mind if I call you Sadie?"

"Not you I don't," Mrs. Smith said grimly.

"Do you remember that Friday you came to do the wash, Sadie? The morning after little Michael was found dead?"

"I surely do."

"Did you run across one of those batiste pillowslips with the delicate lace that day—a slip that was very dirty? In fact, that had the print of a man's dirty hand on it?"

Sadie Smith cocked an eye at her. "That's what the detectives kept asking me that day."

"Oh, they did? Did anyone else ask you about it? I mean . . . people of the household?"

"Mrs. Lenihan mentioned it to me first thing I set foot in the house. Told me about the child, and said the policemen were turning the house inside out looking for a dirty pillowslip like that. I told her I'd keep an eye out for it, and I did."

"Anyone mention the pillowslip to you besides Mrs. Lenihan and the detectives?"

"No."

"I take it you never found it."

"That's right. Picked that wash over a dozen times, but it just wasn't there. There's the kittle!" The stout woman jumped up and began bustling about.

"Were there *any* pillowslips in the wash that day?" Jessie persisted.

"Nary one."

"Not one?" Jessie frowned. "That's queer."

"I thought so, too. You take sugar and cream, Miss Sherwood?"

"Neither, thanks," Jessie said absently. "No pillowslips at all . . ."

"Well, you're going to taste some of these sweet buns I just got from the bakery, or I'll take it real unfriendly of you. But about those pillow slips. First thing I thought was that snippety upstairs maid of theirs had stuffed too big a bundle into one of the laundry chutes. She'd done it a couple times, and the laundry'd got stuck, and we had to go fishing for it in the chute with a plumber's snake they have in the basement."

A stopped-up chute!

"Do you suppose that's what could have happened to the pillowslip they were looking for, Sadie?" Jessie asked excitedly. "A chute already stopped up, and the slip just didn't go all the way down?"

Mrs. Smith shook her head. "Wasn't no stopped-up chute. I took some clothespins and dropped one down each chute that morning to see if they was clear, and they was. Then I remembered. Friday mornings was the upstairs maid's day to strip the beds and change linen, and the way things was in the house that morning she just didn't get to do it. You eat one of those buns, Miss Sherwood."

"Delicious," Jessie said, munching. "You checked *all* the chutes, Sadie? The one in the nursery, too?"

"Well, not the nursery one, no. First place, they wouldn't let me in there. Second place, never was any stopping-up trouble in the nursery chute, 'cause *you* always slid the wash down from that room."

Could that be it? Jessie thought hungrily.

But she had been the only one who used the nursery chute. She always stripped and remade the baby's crib herself. And she had always been automatically careful to throw one piece down the chute at a time, even though the sheets were only crib size.

Jessie sipped her tea hopelessly.

"—though there was that trouble with the nursery chute when they was installing it," the laundress was saying. "I'd forgot about that. Maybe 'cause nothing ever happened."

"What?" Jessie looked up. "What did you say, Sadie?"

"When they was installing it. Before you came to work there, Miss Sherwood. Wasn't no nursery or room off it—the one you slept in—till just before Mr. and Mrs. Humffrey adopted the baby. That all used to be an upstairs sitting room. They had it made over into two rooms for the baby and a nurse, and that was when they installed the chute in the nursery. Hadn't been one there before."

"But you said something about some trouble with the nursery chute during installation——"

"And it only just come to mind," Mrs. Smith nodded. "Mr. Humffrey was fit to be hogtied. Seems after the chute was put in and all, and the man was testing it, throwing things down it, he found out there was a defect in it—it had a little piece of metal or something sticking out some place down the chute—and every once in a while something would catch on it. The man poked some kind of tool down in and felt around till he found the snag, and sort of sawed away at it. I guess he smoothed it down, 'cause you never had nothing stick in that chute, Miss Sherwood, did you?"

"No, Jessie thought, I never did.

But suppose that was just luck!

Suppose the night Alton Humffrey dropped the damning pillowslip down that chute . . . *suppose that time it caught on what was left of the snag?*

So Sadie Smith hadn't found the slip, and Alton Humffrey thought Sadie Smith *had* found it and washed it out, and all the time it was stuck in the nursery chute . . . *and it was still there.*

Jessie hung up, collected her coins, and sat in the telephone booth nibbling her nails. Richard's phone in New York didn't answer, so he must be out after Henry Cullum. Taugus police headquarters said that Chief Pearl had left for the night, and there had been no answer at the Pearls' house—they must have gone visiting, or out to dinner and a movie.

Jessie sat there, frustrated.

I've *got* to know, she thought. And not tomorrow, but tonight.

Suddenly she thought, I can do it myself.

She accepted the thought instantly, and without attempting to think through the difficulties. If I think about it, she told herself, I won't do it. So I won't think about it.

She left the drugstore, got into her coupé, and set out for Taugus.

The electrified ship's lantern over the gatehouse looked lost against the black bulk of Nair Island.

Jessie drove across the causeway slowly. Did they maintain guards after the season? If they did, she was sunk. The closer she got to the gatehouse the more foolhardy the project became.

A burly figure in a uniform stepped out of the gatehouse and held up his hand.

And the gate was *down.*

So much for private enterprise, Jessie thought.

"Hey," a familiar voice said. "It's Miss Sherwood."

Charlie Peterson!

"Why, Mr. Peterson," Jessie said warmly. "What are you doing here? I thought you'd quit. At least you said you were going to."

"Well, you know how it is," the big guard said. "It ain't such a bad job, especially after the summer."

"And when policemen aren't driving you crazy," Jessie smiled. What can I say to him? she thought.

"That's a fact." The guard planted his elbow on the edge of her window. "How you been, Miss Sherwood?"

"Just fine. And you?" *I'll have to think of a plausible excuse. But what?*

"No complaints. Say, I never expected to see you again." Peterson looked at her in the oddest way, and Jessie thought, Here it comes. "What brings you to the Island?"

Jessie wet her lips. "Well . . ."

He pushed his big face close to hers, exhaling an aroma of bourbon. "It wouldn't be me, now, would it?"

Jessie almost laughed aloud. Problem solved!

"Why, Mr. Peterson," she said archly. "And you a family man and all."

He guffawed. "Can't blame a redblooded guy for a little wishful thinking! You going up to the Humffrey house? Nobody's there."

How lucky can you get! Jessie thought exultantly.

"Oh, dear," she said. "Nobody, Mr. Peterson? Where's the caretaker?"

"Stallings had to drive up to Concord, Mass. tonight. Mr. Humffrey phoned him to take some bulbs or something there for transplanting. That's their winter place."

"I don't know what to do," Jessie wailed. "Is Stallings going to be back tonight?"

"Tomorrow night, I guess."

"I suppose I could come back tomorrow, but as long as I'm here . . ." She turned her eyes on him appealingly, hoping the bourbon hadn't worn off. "Do you think anybody'd mind if I went up there for a few minutes? Like a fool I forgot some of my things when I packed, and I've just got to have them."

"Well." Peterson scratched his bulging jaw. You big oaf, Jessie thought, I'll—I'll vamp you if I have to. "Seeing it's you, Miss Sherwood . . ." But then he said, with his hand on the barrier, "Wait a minute."

Now what?

"How you going to get in?"

189

"Oh, I'll manage," Jessie said quickly. How, she had no idea.

"Hold it." Peterson went into the gatehouse. In a moment he was back, flourishing a key. "Stallings always leaves the key with me in case Mr. Humffrey should show up while he's off the Island. Need any help, Miss Sherwood?" he shouted after her gallantly.

"No, thanks," Jessie shouted back, clutching the key.

She felt rather bourbonish herself as she drove up the Nair Island road.

Stallings had left the nightlight burning over the service entrance. Jessie parked in the driveway near it, turned off her ignition and lights, and jumped out.

Her feet crunched loudly on the gravel, and Jessie hesitated, her skin itching. What am I so nervous about? she thought. Nobody can hear me.

Still, she found herself putting her feet down as if she were in a bog.

She unlocked the service door and slipped thankfully into the Humffrey house.

But with her back against the door, thankfulness melted away.

She had never seen such dark darkness.

This is what comes of being an honest woman, she thought. Nobody here, nobody on the Island but Peterson, whose blessing I have, and yet . . . It seemed to her the house was full of furtive noises. As if the wood and plaster were breathing.

Remember Michael, she told herself rigidly. Remember that little dead body. She filled her lungs with air, deliberately, then let the air out.

Immediately the house became a house, the darkness friendly.

Jessie pushed away from the door and stepped confidently forward. Her hand touched the basement door. She opened it, felt for the switch, found it, and snapped it on.

The basement sprang at her.

She ran down the stairs. The steps were cushioned and carpeted and her descent was soundless.

At the bottom she paused to look around.

She knew where the outlet of the nursery chute was. She could see it from where she stood, with the big canvas laundry basket still in place under the vent. She had always done the baby's diapers and undershirts herself, refusing to allow Mrs. Humffrey to employ a diaper service.

"I like to know what my babies' diapers are washed in," she said to Mrs. Humffrey. "I've seen too many raw little bottoms."

Funny the things you thought about when . . . Jesse forced herself to think about the problem at hand.

Sadie Smith had mentioned a "plumber's snake." Jessie had only the vaguest notion of what a plumber's snake might be. She supposed it was some device for getting into clogged pipes and things that might choke up and be hard to clean. Where would such a thing be kept? Then she recalled that one of the basement walls was covered with shelving for the storage of tools, light bulbs, and odds and ends of housewares and hardware. The snake would probably be there. Wasn't it at the far end of the basement, behind the oil burner?

Jessie walked past the set tubs where Mrs. Smith had done the hand washing, past the washing machine and dryer, around the burner . . .

There it was.

She found the snake on the bottom shelf among some wrenches, pipe elbows, and other plumbing accessories. It was unmistakable, a large coil of metal cable with a loopy sort of head on it.

She took the snake over to the vent of the nursery chute, set the canvas basket to one side, inserted the head of the cable in the opening, and pushed. As she unwound the snake, she kept pushing upward. The cable made a raspy, rattly sound going up. She kept wiggling it, shaking it, making it go from side to side.

It went up, up, up. Finally it banged against something far overhead, refused to go further. It had obviously struck the door of the chute in the nursery.

And nothing had come down.

Jessie sat down on the basement floor and laughed.

Exit Jessie Sherwood, Female Sleuth.

The only thing to do was return the snake to the shelf, turn off the light, get into her car, and go back where she belonged.

Still seated on the floor under the vent, Jessie began to coil the cable. It came down, scraping, as she rewound it. The head appeared.

And something crumpled and white appeared with it and dropped into her lap.

The material was batiste. It had a lace edging. Honiton lace.

With trembling fingers Jessie took the pillowslip by two corners and held it up.

The imprint of a dirty right hand showed plainly just off the center of the square.

"Why, I've done it," Jessie said aloud in an amazed voice. "I've found it."

A horribly familiar voice behind her replied, "So you have, Miss Sherwood."

Jessie's head screwed around like a doll's.

Her eyeballs froze.

Alton K. Humffrey was standing at the foot of the basement stairs.

In his right hand there was a gun, and the gun was aimed at her heart.

The eye of the gun came steadily nearer, growing bigger and bigger.

Richard, Jessie thought. *Richard.*

"First, Miss Sherwood," the horrible voice said, "I'll relieve you of this."

She felt the pillowslip jerked out of her hand. From the corner of her paralyzed eye she saw his left hand crumple it, stuff it into his pocket.

The gun receded.

Not far.

"You're frightened, Miss Sherwood. I sympathize. But you have only yourself to blame. Not a particularly consoling last thought, I suppose. Believe me, I dislike this almost as much as you do. But what recourse have you left me?"

Jessie almost said, *None.* But she knew that if she opened her mouth, nothing would come out but a chatter of teeth.

Richard, Richard. You don't even know where I am. Not you, not Chief Pearl, not anybody but Charlie Peterson, and what good is he? Alton Humffrey has seen to that, or he wouldn't be here pointing a gun. You're going to die alone, Jessie, like an idiot, sitting on a basement floor in an empty house on an empty island.

Die.

The voice was saying, without bite or pinch, "You must see that I have no choice. You've found the slip, you've examined it. You're probably incorruptible. In any case, you're too close to that busybody Queen. So I must kill you, Miss Sherwood. I must."

This isn't happening, Jessie thought. It's just—not—happening.

"Not that the prospect pleases. I'm not a compulsive murderer. It's easier to commit murder then one would think, I've found, but it isn't pleasant. Your death is even dangerous to me. Peterson knows you're here. I could shoot you as an intruder, saying that I fired before I realized who you were, but Peterson's told me you were here. By the same token, he also knows I'm here. So I'm forced to take a great risk."

I'm going to wake up any second . . .

"When you disappear, suspicion will naturally fall on me. After I row your body out and sink it in deep water, I shall have to concoct a story. They won't believe the story, of course, no matter how plausible it is. But without a body, with no evidence of a crime, what can they do, after all? I think I'll come out of it all right. This is a soundproof room, Miss Sherwood, and—forgive me—I shall be very careful about removing all traces afterward."

It's silly. He's just trying to scare me. Nobody could talk as calmly as this and mean to take a human life. Nobody.

Richard, Richard.

"I still don't understand what brought you here tonight." The millionaire's voice this time was slightly flavored with petulance. "I certainly had no idea I was going to run into anyone. I came for the very purpose you accomplished, to check the nursery chute. That farce in Chief Pearl's office—before Queen produced the forgery—set me to wondering how they could possibly have found the pillowslip. And that reminded me of the obstruction in the chute when it was installed. How did you learn about that, Miss Sherwood?" Jessie stirred, and he said sharply, "Don't move, please."

"I have to," Jessie heard herself say. "My legs have fallen asleep. My neck."

"I'm sorry," he said, as if he really were. "You may stand up."

Jessie got to her feet. Her knees gave, and she leaned against the wall of the chute.

"In a way it was unfortunate for you that I employ a caretaker," the millionaire droned on. "If not for Stallings's being on the premises, I would have examined the chute last night. As it was, I had to go back to New York and find an excuse to send Stallings away. What did make you come here tonight to look the chute over?"

"Does it matter?" How lightheaded she felt.

Jessie shut her eyes.

"I suppose not."

She heard a click.

Her eyes flew open and she stared wildly. He was stepping back, his arm was coming up, it was extending, the gun was glowing softly blue at the end of it, she could see the stump of his little finger at the base of the grip, the index finger was beginning to whiten . . .

"Don't kill me, Mr. Humffrey, I don't want to die, please don't kill me."

"I must," Alton Humffrey muttered.

"Don't!" Jessie screamed, and she shut her eyes tight. The basement rocked with the explosion.

Why, there's no pain, Jessie thought. Isn't that odd? There's no pain at all. Just the roar of the gun and the smash of glass——

Glass?

She opened her eyes. Alton Humffrey's right hand was a bloody pulp. His gun was on the floor and he was gripping his right wrist with his left hand convulsively. His mouth and nose were curled back in agony. A man's hand, holding a smoking revolver, was just withdrawing from a broken window high in the basement wall and two other men were vaulting down the basement stairs to fling themselves on the wounded millionaire and bring him crashing to the floor.

Then an incredibly dear figure appeared at the head of the stairs and Jessie saw that it was he who had fired the shot through the basement window and he was running down the stairs like a boy with the smoking gun still in his hand and she was in his arms.

"Richard," Jessie said.

Then she fainted.

Jessie found herself staring at a white ceiling. There was something familiar about the light fixture and the molding, and she turned her head and looked around. Of course. Her room. The nursery next door. The baby would be gleeping in a moment and the alarm would go off and she would jump out of bed . . .

Then she remembered.

Jessie sat up.

Mrs. Pearl was sitting in the rocker beside the bed, smiling at her.

"How do you feel, Jessie?"

"All right, I guess." Jessie looked down. Someone— she hoped it had been Beck Pearl—had removed her dress and girdle. "Did you. . . ?"

The little woman nodded. She got up to switch off the nightlight and turn on the overhead lights.

"What time is it?" Her wristwatch was gone, too.

"About 3 A.M. You've had quite a sleep. Dr. Wicks gave you a needle. Don't you remember?"

"I'm trying to, Becky. But how is it you're here?"

"They located Abe and me at a friend's home in Westport. When I heard about your terrible experience, I made Abe bring me along. Richard wanted to take you to a hospital, but Dr. Wicks said it wasn't necessary. You're sure you feel well enough to get out of bed?"

"Yes." Jessie swung her legs to the floor stiffly.

"Where's Richard?"

"He's still here. They all are. They don't want to move Humffrey yet. He lost a lot of blood and they've got him in bed, under guard." Beck Pearl's soft mouth set hard. "It's funny what good care they take of murderers. I'd have let him bleed to death."

"Becky, you mustn't say a thing like that."

"You're a nurse, Jessie," the little woman said quietly. "I'm just a woman who's had babies. And I have grandchildren. He murdered a baby."

Jessie shivered.

"I'd better get dressed," she said.

"Let me help you, dear."

"No, please. You might tell Richard I'm up."

Beck Pearl smiled again and went out.

It's all over, Jessie kept telling herself as she wriggled into the girdle. It's really all over.

He was waiting for her in the hall.

"Richard."

He took her by the arms. "You're sure you ought to be up?"

"You saved my life."

"You're so pale."

"You saved my life, Richard," Jessie said again.

He flushed. "You'd better sit down."

He drew her over to the big settee opposite Alton Humffrey's upstairs study.

How tired he looked. Tired and . . . something else. Disturbed?

"What were you doing here, Jessie? When I looked through that basement window and saw you standing down there facing Humffrey's gun, I couldn't believe my eyes."

"I tried to phone you before I came, but I couldn't get an answer. I couldn't even locate Chief or Mrs. Pearl." Jessie told him what she had found out from Sadie Smith, and how on impulse she had decided to investigate the chute when she was unable to reach him or the Taugus chief of police. "What I don't understand,

Richard, is what *you* were doing here. I thought you were in town chasing Henry Cullum."

"I started to, but I ran into Johnny Kripps and Wes Polonsky." He grinned. "They were watching Humffrey's Park Avenue apartment on their own. That was luck, because Wes had his car. We sat around waiting for Cullum to show, so we could pump him about Mrs. Humffrey's whereabouts, when we saw Humffrey trying to take a sneak. He was alone, and he was acting so queer we decided to tail him. He dodged around to his garage, got his car out, and headed for the West Side Highway. We tailed him all the way to Nair Island, and that was that."

Jessie laid her head on his shoulder. "It's all over, Richard."

"No, it isn't."

His shoulder was rigid. Jessie sat up quickly.

"It isn't?" she said. "It isn't what, Richard?"

"Isn't over." He pressed his fingers to his eyes. "I don't know how much more you can take tonight, Jessie. Can you stand a big shock?"

"Shock." Dear God, what is it now? Jessie thought. "What's happened!"

"We sure picked a lulu when we stuck our noses into this one. I don't know that I've ever run across a case like it."

"Like *what?*"

He got up and took her by the hand.

"I'll show you, Jessie."

Chief Pearl's two detectives, Borcher and Tinny, were in the study. Borcher was reading a copy of Plato's *Republic* with a deep frown. Tinny was napping in a leather armchair.

Both jumped up when Richard Queen opened the door. When he waved, Borcher returned to his puzzled reading and Tinny sank down and closed his eyes again.

"Over here, Jessie."

The dirty pillowslip was spread out on Humffrey's desk. Everything else had been removed.

"I was the one who found it," Jessie said. "I fished it

out of the nursery chute. Then he—he came in and took it away from me."

"Then you've seen it."

"Just a glance."

"Examine it, Jessie."

Jessie bent over the pillowslip. Now that she saw it in strong light, at leisure, it was remarkable how well she had remembered the position of the handprint in supervising the forgery.

She shook her head. "I can't see anything special about this, Richard. Is there something on the back? I never did see the back."

"As a matter of fact, there is." He took hold of the tip of the lace edging at the upper right corner of the slip and turned it back a little. Just below the reverse of the lace Jessie saw a small stain, rusty brown in color. "That's a bloodstain, probably from a scratched finger. However, remember that Humffrey didn't get a look at the back of our forgery. We had it face up on Abe's desk under glass." He flipped the corner back. "You still don't see where we went wrong?"

Jessie stared and stared. "No."

"Take another look at that handprint, Jessie. A real look this time."

And then she saw it, and her mind leaped back to that August night in the nursery and her brief glimpse of the pillow over the baby's face. And for the first time since that moment Jessie Sherwood saw the pillow as she had seen it then.

What she had forgotten until now was that the little finger of the handprint was a whole finger.

There was no missing fingertip.

"That's how Humffrey knew the slip we showed him was a fake," Inspector Queen shrugged. "We showed him a handprint with the tip of the pinkie gone. He knew that the original pillowcase had a handprint showing five full fingers."

"But I don't understand," Jessie cried. "Alton Humffrey's pinkie does have the tip missing. How could his right hand possibly have made this print?"

"It couldn't."

198

"But——"

"It couldn't. Therefore it didn't."

Jessie gaped at him. The silence became so intense that Borcher looked up from his Plato uneasily and Tinny opened one eye.

"But Richard . . ."

"Humffrey didn't murder the baby, Jessie. I guess they knew what they were doing when they retired me." The old man sighed. "I was so sure Humffrey knocked off Finner and the Coy girl that I had to wrap it up in one neat package. One killer. But it wasn't one killer, Jessie. Humffrey murdered Finner and Connie Coy, all right, but someone else murdered the baby."

Jessie squeezed her forehead with both hands, trying to force some order into her thoughts.

"Humffrey never doubted for a minute that the baby was his—I was wrong about that, too. He knew it was his. That was the whole point. And when he spotted the pillowcase that night he knew his baby had been murdered, and he knew who'd murdered it. That's when he got rid of the pillowcase. He was determined to make the death look like an accident. That's what made him say *he* had put the ladder there, when he hadn't touched the ladder. It was the baby's killer who'd put the ladder there, thinking to make the murder look like the nephew's work.

"And when Finner got in touch with Humffrey and told him to meet us in Finner's office, Humffrey realized that unless he shut Finner's mouth the story of Michael's real parentage might come out and lead right back to Michael's death. So he killed Finner and removed all the evidence from the file. And when we got to Connie Coy in spite of everything and she was about to name Humffrey as the real father of Michael, he killed Connie Coy.

"It was all coverup, Jessie. Coverup to keep us from learning the true reason for the baby's murder. To keep the whole nasty story out of the papers. To protect the sacred name of Humffrey."

"Someone else," Jessie said, clinging to the thought. "What someone else, Richard? Who?"

"Jessie," Richard Queen said. "Who had the best reason to hate Alton Humffrey's illegitimate child? Who's the only one in the world Humffrey would have a guilt feeling about, a compulsion to cover up? Whose exposure as an infant-killer would smear as much muck on the Humffrey name as if he himself were tagged for it? Who's the one who kept hysterically insisting—until Humffrey got her out of the way and kept her out of the way—that she'd been 'responsible' for little Mike's death? . . . only we all misunderstood her?"

He shook his head. "There's only one possible candidate for the baby's murder, Jessie. It's Sarah Humffrey's handprint on this pillowcase."

Chief Pearl stuck his big head into the room. "Hi, Jessie. You okay now? Dick, he's fully conscious and ready to make a statement. You'd better come."

Jessie went as far as the doorway of the master bedroom. The room was full of men. Taugus police. The State's Attorney's man, Merrick, tieless again. Dr. Wicks. A lot of state troopers. Wes Polonsky and Johnny Kripps.

And Alton Humffrey.

Humffrey was lying on the great bed, propped on pillows, his right arm swathed in bandages. His skin was not sallow now. It was colorless. The narrow wedge of face was without expression or movement, a face in a coffin. Only the eyes were alive, two prisoners struggling to escape.

Jessie said faintly, "I'll wait with Beck Pearl, Richard," and she stumbled away.

"That," Richard Queen remarked, leaning back in happy surfeit, "was the best darned Sunday dinner I've ever surrounded."

"Delicious, Jessie!" Beck Pearl said, not without a slight mental reservation about the wine in the sauce. "She's really a wonderful cook, Dick. Imagine being a trained nurse and having a talent like this, too!"

"It's just a veal roast," Jessie said deprecatingly, as if she were in the habit of standing over a hot oven every Sunday for hours and hours basting with an experimental sauce of garlic salad dressing, lemon juice, sauterne, bouillon, and Parmesan cheese, and praying that the result would be edible.

"But as I was saying," Abe Pearl said, and he belched.

"Abe!" his wife said.

"Beg pardon," Abe Pearl said.

It was Sunday, October 9th, a brisk and winy day, a day for being alive. Jessie had planned and slaved for this day, when Richard Queen's two friends should sit in her little dining alcove in Rowayton and tell her—and him—what a marvelous cook she was. Only Abe Pearl insisted on talking about what Jessie had hoped and hoped would not be talked about.

"Wonderful," Richard Queen beamed. "Just wonderful, Jessie."

"Thank you," Jessie murmured.

"—she's as cold turkey as any killer I ever heard of," Abe Pearl went on. "Match that big mitt of hers to the handprint on the pillowcase—a perfect fit. Analyze her perspiration—it gives the same lab result as the sweat traces in the slip. Analyze her blood—it's just like the blood in the stain on the back of the slip, which got on there when she scratched her hand on the ladder. Dust on ladder same as dust on slip. And, by God, when they work over the slip and bring out some fingerprints left by the mixed dust and perspiration, they're her prints!" Chief Pearl pressed his paws to his abdomen to discourage another belch. "And yet," he thundered solemnly, "I tell you Sarah Humffrey will never go to the Chair. If she wasn't as nutty as a fruit cake—I mean after they got the baby, when she overheard Humffrey talking to Finner over the phone and realized her saintly husband had palmed off his own bastard on her—if she wasn't as nutty as a fruit cake then, she sure is now. She'll get sent to a bughouse on an insanity verdict, and I don't see how the State can stop it."

"Abe," Beck Pearl said.

"What?"

"Wouldn't you like to walk off your dinner?"

So finally they were alone in Jessie's little garden. Abe Pearl was wandering in Coventry somewhere along the waterfront, and his wife was in Jessie's kitchen bang-ing dishes around to show that she wasn't listening through the kitchen window.

And now that they were alone together, there seemed to be nothing to say. That same peculiar silence dropped between them.

So Jessie picked some dwarf zinnias, and Richard Queen sat in the white basket chair under the dogwood tree watching the sun on her hair.

If he doesn't say something soon I'll shriek, Jessie thought. I can't go on picking zinnias forever.

But he kept saying absolutely nothing.

So then the flowers were tumbling to the ground, and Jessie heard herself crying, "Richard, what in heaven's name is the matter with you?"

"Matter?" he said with a start. "With me, Jessie?"

"Do *I* have to propose to *you?*"

"Prop . . ." The sound came out of his mouth like a bite of hot potato. *"Propose?"*

"Yes!" Jessie wept. "I've waited and waited, and all you ever do is pull a grim face and feel sorry for your-self. I'm a woman, Richard, don't you know that? And you're a man—though you don't seem to know that ei-ther—and we're both lonely, and I think we l-love each other . . ."

He was on his feet, clutching his collar and looking dazed. "You mean . . . you'd *marry* me, Jessie? Mar-ry *me?*"

"What do you think I'm proposing, Richard Queen, a game of Scrabble?"

He took a step toward her.

And stopped, swallowing hard. "But Jessie, I'm an old man——"

"Oh, fish! You're an old fool!"

So he came to her.

A long time later—the sun was going down, and the Pearls had long since vanished—Richard Queen's arm shifted from Jessie Sherwood's shoulders to her waist, and he muttered blissfully, "I wonder what Ellery's going to say."